WEATHERHEAD BOOKS ON ASIA

A PRIVATE LIFE

Literature
David Der-wei Wang, Editor

Ye Zhaoyan, *Nanjing 1937: A Love Story*,
translated by Michael Berry

Makoto Oda, *The Breaking Jewel*,
translated by Donald Keene

Han Shaogong, *A Dictionary of Maqiao*,
translated by Julia Lovell

Takahashi Takako, *Lonely Woman*,
translated by Maryellen Toman Mori

History, Society, and Culture
Carol Gluck, Editor

Michael K. Bourdaghs, *The Dawn That Never Comes:
Sihimazaki Tōson and Japanese Nationalism*

WEATHERHEAD BOOKS ON ASIA   COLUMBIA UNIVERSITY

CHEN RAN   A PRIVATE LIFE

TRANSLATED BY   JOHN HOWARD-GIBBON

COLUMBIA UNIVERSITY PRESS   NEW YORK

This publication has been supported by the Richard W.
Weatherhead Publication Fund of the East Asian Institute,
Columbia University.

Columbia University Press
Publishers Since 1893
New York Chichester, West Sussex
Translation copyright © 2004 Columbia University Press

Library of Congress Cataloging-in-Publication Data
Chen, Ran, 1962–
    [Si ren sheng huo. English]
    A private life / Chen Ran ; translated by John
Howard-Gibbon.
        p.   cm. — (Weatherhead books on Asia)
    ISBN 0-231-13196-8
    1. Chen, Ran, 1962—Translations into English.
I. Howard-Gibbon, John.   II. Title.   III. Series.

PL 2840.J37S5313 2004
895.1'352—dc22

                                        2003062653

Columbia University Press books are printed on perma-
nent and durable acid-free paper.
Printed in the United States of America
c   10   9   8   7   6   5   4   3   2   1

Chen Ran was born in April 1962 in Beijing. As a child she studied music, but when she was eighteen her interest turned to literature. She graduated from Beijing Normal University at the age of twenty-three with a degree in the humanities and taught there in the Chinese literature department for the next four and a half years, when she moved to the Writers' Publishing House, where she has worked as an editor ever since. She has lectured as an exchange scholar in Chinese literature at Melbourne University in Australia, the University of Berlin in Germany, and London, Oxford, and Edinburgh universities in the UK. She is a member of the Chinese Writers' Association, and currently lives in Beijing.

Her published works include the short stories "Paper Scrap," "The Sun Between My Lips," "No Place to Say Good-bye," "Yesterday's Wine," "Talking to Myself," Forbidden Vigil," "Secret Story," "Standing Alone in the Draft," the novel *A Private Life*, and a collection of essays, *Bits and Pieces*. Some of her fiction has been published and reviewed in England, the United States, Germany, Japan, and Korea, as well as in Hong Kong and Taiwan. The film *Yesterday's Wine*, based on her short story of the same name, was chosen for showing at the Fourth World Conference on Women, held in Beijing in 1995.

A four-volume *Collected Works of Chen Ran* was published by the Jiangsu Art and Literature Publishing House in August 1998.

In 2001 the Writers' Publishing House published its six-volume series *The Works of Chen Ran*.

In the 1980s, she won acclaim for her short story "Century Sickness," seen variously as "pure" or "avant-garde" fiction, and became the newest representative of serious female writers in the country at that time. Through the 1990s and beyond, her work has been leaning more and more toward the psychological and philosophical as she explores loneliness, sexual love, and human life.

Throughout her writing career, she has been a kind of disturbance on the perimeter of mainstream Chinese literature, a unique and important female voice. She has won a number of prizes, such as the first Contemporary China Female Creative Writer's Award.

Set against a backdrop of the decades that included the Cultural Revolution and the Tian'anmen Square Incident, *A Private Life*, Chen's only novel to date, is not so much a story about the social change and political turbulence of those times as it is about their effect on the protagonist's inner life as she moves from childhood to early maturity. As a result, it is a genuine and compellingly personal human story, from beneath which unobtrusively emerges a powerful and moving political and feminist statement.

Breaking from her previous work, in which she laid great emphasis on plot development and philosophical speculation, in this novel Chen Ran layers over the narrative line with a great number of seemingly disconnected interior monologues, fragmentary recollections, and reveries that flit back and forth through time and space.

The story flickers forth through a complex, sensual, and threatening setting, exploring from its own angle the below-the-surface, deep, and subtle changes that were taking place in Chinese women's consciousness from the 1970s through to the 1990s. It also reflects the complex social life of that time, creating a broad image of feminine conciousness over these decades. Chen Ran's unique and personal postmodern feminist story has created a different and very challenging image of women within Chinese literature of the 1990s.

The translation is based on the 1996 Writers' Publishing House edition, but includes some changes and additions requested by the author and a few corrections in detail suggested to the author by the translator.

Publication History of A Private Life

March 1996, published by Writers' Publishing House

1998, published by Hong Kong Universal Publishing Co., Ltd.

October 1998, published by Taiwan Maitian Co., Ltd.

ACKNOWLEDGMENTS

I would like to thank the people who have encouraged and helped me along the way to publication of this translation. First, Yu Wentao, who initially suggested that I undertake the translation, and who also introduced me to Chen Ran. I must also thank Chen Ran herself for her patience and for believing in my capabilities. Then Robin Visser for her praise and encouragement and for putting me in touch with Gregory McNamee, who recommended the translation to Columbia University Press. Finally, I must thank Zhang Tianxin in Beijing, who checked the entire manuscript against the Chinese to ensure there were no errors in translation. His suggestions have improved the accuracy of my work, although final responsibility for the quality of the translation must rest entirely upon my own shoulders.

These acknowledgments would not be complete without mention of Professor Wang Yitong, who first roused my interest in Chinese literature and culture in 1958 at the University of British Columbia, and of

Li Shuo and my many other Chinese friends and colleagues who have, over the years, through their words and actions, led me toward an ever deepening appreciation of their culture, and thus to a deeper understanding of my own—and of what a rare and wonderful blessing it is to be able to stand between the two.

John Howard-Gibbon

To avoid crying out, we sing our griefs softly.
To escape darkness, we close our eyes.

As the days and months pass, I am stifled beneath the bits and pieces of time and memory that settle thickly upon my body and penetrate the pulse of my consciousness. As if being devoured by a huge, pitiless rat, time withers away moment by moment and is lost. I can do nothing to stop it. Many have tried armor or flattery to dissuade it; I have built walls and closed windows tightly. I have adopted an attitude of denial. But nothing works. Only death, the tombstone over our graves, can stop it. There is no other way.

Several years ago, my mother used death to stay time's passage. I remember how she died, unable to breathe. Like a barbed steel needle, her final, cold, fearful cry stabbed cruelly into my ears, where it echoes constantly and forever, never to be withdrawn.

Not long before this, when he left my mother, my father destroyed almost entirely the deep feeling I had for him, and drove a rift between our minds. This was his way of denying time. He makes me think of the story about the man who planted a seed and then forgot about it. When he chanced upon it later on, it had become a thickly leaved flowering tree about to burst into blossom. But he had no idea what kind of seed it had grown from, what kind of tree it was, or what kind of flowers would emerge from its buds.

Time is created from the movement of my mind.

Now I live a life of isolation. This is good. I have no need for chatter anymore. I am weary of the confusing clamor of the city that invades every corner of my consciousness like the constant whine of a swirling cloud of invisible flies. People rant on without cease, as if speech were the only possible route, their only sustenance. They try countless stratagems to utilize it, to keep it as their constant companion. I myself have no such faith in this ceaseless clamor, but an individual is helpless. Since it is impossible for me to swat so many flies, all I can do is keep as far away from them as possible.

I live quietly in this old city in the apartment my mother left to me. The hallways are long and dark, but the apartment has windows everywhere.

Living alone has not made me any more uneasy. There was no special warmth when I was living with my parents. Things are fine now. For so many years, time seemed to be rushing by. But it was tired, wanted to slow down. It has stopped in my apartment. It has also stopped in my face. It seems that time is exhausted. It has come to rest in my face and does not move, so that my face looks the same as it did a number of years ago.

But my mind has already entered old age; everything has slowed down.

For example, I no longer argue with people, because I now know that ultimately there is no connection between argument and truth. It is nothing more than a matter of who for the moment holds the advantage; and "advantage" and "disadvantage," or who is winning, who losing, no longer holds any significance for me.

I will never again believe that the earth beneath our feet is a highway. I believe that it is nothing more than a huge, chaotic chessboard, and that the majority of people go where their feet take them. Any who insist on making rational choices should be prepared to accept the loneliness of going against the tide, to stand quiet and uncertain by the roadside looking on, their bodies bent into question marks, like old men who have suffered from rickets.

I love vegetables, and I'm practically a vegetarian, because I'm totally convinced that only a vegetarian diet can keep the spirit distinct from the flesh, and the eyes clear and beautiful.

I am fond of the plants on my balcony—a large rubber tree, a tortoiseshell bamboo, and some perennial flowers. I don't have to go to public parks with all their noise and clamor to enjoy fresh foliage and pure air.

. . . . . .

A few days ago, my doctor friend Qi Luo called. He was very concerned about how I was doing, and suggested that I pay a visit to the hospital. I told him I wasn't interested in seeing anybody, no matter who it might be.

The words that I encounter around me are as insubstantial as the false radiance of moonlight. Believing in conversation gives us a kind of solace, much like believing that a picture of a loaf of bread can fill our stomachs.

Just as my spirit has no need for religious faith, my body has no need for pills.

I told him if I needed him, I would look him up.

He told me that my "agoraphobia" was incurable.

I know that the attribution of names to the fantastic variety of people and things is said to be one of the significant elements of civilization. But a name is nothing more than a name. Take mine, for example—Ni Niuniu. All it is is a string of sounds. I can't see that it makes any difference whether you call me "Ni Niuniu" or "Yi zhi gou"—little Miss Stubborn or little Miss Puppy.

At this moment, I am stretched across my huge, comfy bed. It is my raft upon the vast ocean, my fortress in the middle of a chaotic world. It is my man and my woman.

A licking flame of summer morning sunlight, intermingled with the noises of the street, penetrates a crack in the curtain, and its luminous center does its dance of time upon the tired lids of my reluctant eyes.

I don't like the feel of sunshine. It makes me feel exposed and vulnerable, as if all my organs have been laid bare, and that I must immediately place sentries at every hair follicle to ward off the prying light. But, of course, there are too many suns in this world. The light from every pair of eyes burns more than sunlight, is more dangerous and more aggressive. If this light were to invade my frail being, I would be lost, vanquished, and would die.

Because I know that a life that is crowned with any kind of light will be full of false appearances and lies.

I was born on an unremarkable night in the extraordinary year of 1968. Quietly, I left my mother's uneasy womb to enter a world I feared and was not ready for, where I wailed like a frightened lamb. The light in the room where I was born was fluorescent blue. I have disliked bright light ever since.

The Chinese zodiacal and western astrological texts say that girls born at this time are as firm in their faith as the Spanish nun Theresa Davila.

Today, almost thirty years later, I see that I clearly haven't gotten beyond or been able to avoid that piercing light. Now, lying on this huge bed, I can feel the sunlight dancing back and forth on my eyelids, time turning her pages as she follows.

I used to be an angel, but angels can also become mindless demons. As they say, the road to hell may be paved with dreams of heaven.

All this requires is an age that has gone mad; when nurtured under the fierce light that shrouds them, all living cells are turned into lifeless stone.

I don't want to get up. What for? I don't have to leap out of bed and go to the office to scramble after money anymore, like so many others.

As long as I have enough to wear and eat, I have no desire to chase after money.

An odd-looking ink stain on the pillow catches my eyes as I open them. I stare at it for a long time. Suddenly, it seems as if my soul is floating around the bed examining the body on the bed from different angles. I try desperately to account for the ink blot and pull my dark spirit back into my body. In this rose-colored bedroom, on this bed where I have lived and slept alone for the past year, there has been no fluid other than the blue-black ink of my fountain pen. Under the pillow are a few sheets of paper and my pen. I like to prop myself up in bed and write or draw whatever comes into my head. It doesn't matter whether these fragments are diary entries or letters that will never be sent or that have no address; they are a record of my musings, a product of the confrontation between my inner consciousness and the outside world. They are the breath of my life.

I often feel that I have nothing to do with normality, that all around me there are enemies; that I am no longer myself, but have become someone else; even that I am sexless—neither female nor male. This is exactly like the person in the American film *The Looking Glass*, who stands for ages in front of the bathroom mirror, whose bright surface the steam has covered over with a layer of mist. Though the window is tightly closed, a soft breeze still finds its way into the room, swaying the shower curtain, so that it covers the private parts of the person before the mirror. The person has chosen to stay in the bathroom out of self-love, mind and body having been too long exposed to the filthy world outside.

There are invisible eyes lurking everywhere in the air, malevolently watching this person.

You don't know the person's sex because the person doesn't want you to know.

I often think that I am that person in the mirror. Clearly, it is from my image in the mirror that I recognize myself, a combination of analytical observer and one who is analytically observed, a person whose sexuality has, as the result of a variety of outside factors, been obscured or neglected, a sexless person. Through its intriguing allure, this image has the possibility of developing in any number of ways. As soon as I look at typical phenomena of the external world, they are distorted, altered. It seems that everything is an illusion.

Even though a lot of religious or philosophical works, eastern or western, have taught me that if I want to escape ignorance and gain enlightenment, I must go through this feeling of personal alienation. I worry all the same that someday I may lose control over this separation of mind and body and go mad.

This morning, with the light piercing my eyes like slivers of glass, I focus all my attention on the ink blot on my pillow, probably the result of carelessness when I was doodling on a sheet of paper.

It looks like this:

It looks a lot like a map, a map with a hole in the center. It seems to symbolize a number of characteristics of the human beings who inhabit this sphere—emptiness, estrangement, separation, and longing. The top portion seems to be a pair of goats, a male and female, perennially occupying the opposing poles of sexuality, yearning to couple even as they reject each other; in the center there is a dividing ditch, a fathomless black hole; on the left and right are two strange beasts in mad flight from each other.

. . . A huge heart with its center gradually eaten away by passing time—a window to heaven opened in the middle of barren peaks and uncultivated fields—a thirstily breathing mouth exuberant with life—an open womb awaiting a moist rain—an anxiously gazing eye drained of its last tear—a doomed lung that has been eaten away like a leaf devoured by insects. . . .

I don't want to get up. I want to lose myself in my ink blot fantasies.

For the past year a great part of my life has been spent in quiet introspection, clearly out of step with today's hedonistic "playboy" lifestyle.

The truth is, the unalloyed pursuit of pleasure is just as much a shortcoming as indulgence in hopeless grief.

Day in and day out, I feel an endless emptiness and lacking welling up from under my feet. Like cup upon cup of tasteless tea, the days leave me listless and inactive. I don't know what it is I need. In the course of my not very long life, I have tried everything that I should have tried, and everything I shouldn't.

Perhaps what I need is a lover, a man or a woman, young, old, maybe even just a dog. I no longer have any demands or limitations. It's the same thing as my having to make myself understand the need to forsake perfection, to accept less. Because I know that the pursuit of purity is pure stupidity.

For me, having a lover doesn't necessarily mean sex; sex is just a kind of spice, an extravagance.

Sexuality has never been a problem with me.

My problem is different. I am a fragment in a fragmented age.

This woman is a deep wound,
The sanctuary through which we enter the world.
Our road is the light
That shines from her eyes.
This deep wound is our mother,
The mother each of us gives birth to.

I was eleven then, or perhaps younger. The late afternoon summer weather was as unsettled as my mind. The rain would suddenly start pelting down, choosing me as its target. Afterward, I would see that the sleeves covering my skinny arms had angrily twisted themselves into stubborn wrinkles, and that my pant legs, even more obviously angered, as stiff as spindly sticks, kept an uncivil silence.

So I would say to my arms, "Misses Don't, don't be angry." I called my arms "the Misses Don't," because they most often followed my brain's bidding.

Then I would say to my legs, "Misses Do, let's go home to Mama, then everything will be okay." I called my legs "the Misses Do," because I thought that they most often followed the bidding of my body, paying no attention to my brain.

I would then set off with my Misses Do and Don't, soothing them with sweet talk along the way. Of course, these were private, unspoken conversations.

Sometimes I felt like I was a whole group of people. It was a lot more fun that way. We exchanged ideas all the time, telling one another all our problems. I always had plenty of problems.

But what was really strange that day was when I looked up from the soggy Misses Do and Don't and was surprised to see that none of the people around me was wet. Why was I always the first one to get soaked in the rain? I didn't understand, but I was much more easygoing than my Misses Do and Don't. I didn't get angry.

What's the good of getting angry?

Once, after a thunderstorm, an ethereal rainbow hung suspended across the horizon, and our courtyard, still drenched with rain, was carpeted with the rich green leaves brought down by the wind and rain. In front of our house there was a really huge date tree. I was sure that it was much larger than the courtyard date trees described in my schoolbooks, because its great armlike limbs were the largest I had ever seen. Stretching completely across the courtyard, they rested firmly on the top of the high walls, forming a great, protective crown. Every summer they filled our courtyard with round, crisp, honey-sweet dates as fat as little pigs. Right after the storm, before the rain puddles had disappeared, I went out to collect the big dates that had been blown down. There was a tiny sparrow, head cocked to one side, still dazed, clinging to a fallen limb. I quickly cupped it in my hands and put it in a cage we had, with fresh water and millet.

My mother told me that if I kept it, it would die of frustration, because it had its own life, its own home.

I replied that I loved it very much and that I would feed it.

Mother said it wouldn't eat what I gave it.

I wouldn't listen.

And after a few days my sparrow died, because it refused to eat.

When he saw that I had a bird, one of the neighbor's children brought home a pussycat. Already full grown, it was sleek and fat, and its readiness to accept amazed me. It would eat whatever food it came across, sleep wherever there was a place to curl up, waggle its tail and play up to whoever came along, and attach itself to whoever provided its saucer of milk. As a result, unlike my stubborn, intractable sparrow, it survived. Since that time I have detested monsters like that cat who would do anything just to stay alive. To me they are nothing more than a bunch of depraved opportunists, like many more of different types that I have encountered since I have grown up.

The sparrow incident upset me terribly, and, in my eleventh year, gave me a lesson in life. I always counseled my index finger, "Miss Chopstick, we have to learn how to control our temper or we'll do ourselves in."

I called my index finger "Miss Chopstick" because she helped me eat.

I once heard my mama say that the faster you run in the rain, the faster you get wet. But like other people who pay no heed before they get wet, I continued to act and think as before. On the one hand, I soothed my Misses Do and Don't, while on the other, I tried to figure out just what had happened. Eventually, I convinced myself that it was something to do with my nerves or my blood or some other unobservable inner thing that made me run too fast, so I got soaking wet.

I was walking home alone. I knew that none of my little classmates wanted to or would dare to walk with me. No one wanted anything to do with me, because, in addition to being the youngest member of the class, I was skinny and weak and not very outgoing. An even more important reason was that Mr. Ti, the teacher in charge of our class, had been encouraging them to exclude me. I couldn't understand this and had long resented him for it.

I was very angry and hurt because he always tried to embarrass me and make me look stupid in front of the class. Although I was the youngest member of the class and not a particularly clever girl, on occasion I would stand up to him. When I was nervous, I would mix up my left and right hands, and my right hand would forget how to write. But I was always trying to prove that I wasn't the class dunce.

One time, he asked my mother to come into the office. He wanted her to take me to the hospital to see if I was mentally handicapped. He said I behaved like a mute. He had no idea that my brain was racing incessantly.

How mean of him to say I was "handicapped"!

Although only twenty-eight or twenty-nine at the time, and nearly ten years my mother's junior, Ti was terribly abrupt and impolite with her.

I remember my mother standing humbly in front of him, holding my hand. Outside the office, under the green shade of a huge black date tree, the three of us made a tense little group. I remember that there was a crude concrete Ping-Pong table behind us, its surface pitted from constant use by the children, who had very few recreational facilities at the time. The pockmarks must have made it impossible for players to react quickly enough to return the ball, like the distraction of having someone continually shouting at you.

The three of us standing there facing one another formed anything but a friendly, easy group. He was a heavy-set man. I could see angry, invisible flames licking up in the space between us. I remember clearly that his elbow was on a level with my eyes. I am absolutely certain of this detail, because I was comparing our heights at the time and my eyes never left his muscular arms. Although I didn't actually fly at him and bite him, because I kept restraining myself, that thick arm must have borne the imprint of my tiny teeth, because I willed it so.

It was at that time that I realized that even when I grew up, I would not be as tall or strong as he was, nor would I ever be able to get the best of him. It was through my mother's behavior that I discovered a cruel, incontrovertible fact—he was a male.

My mother's patient reserve almost had me feeling that I should apologize to him. She told him I was still an innocent child, just a bit oversensitive and stubborn, and inordinately shy.

Mr. Ti said that I was a "problem child," that I spoke when I shouldn't and was silent when I should speak.

I thought he was a shameless liar. I wasn't like that at all.

Our school's Office of Instruction had been conducting weekly classroom assessments of the teachers. The first time they checked our class, I was the only student who had nothing to say. The others all said what Mr. Ti had instructed them to say the day before. It was nothing more than an orchestrated eulogy to Mr. Ti. The only one who didn't speak up, I stared down at my desk or looked at the wall. When the class monitor spoke of how Mr. Ti exhausted himself marking our assignments, she actually burst into tears.

My heart was pounding, and I was so upset and ashamed that I couldn't utter a single word.

As soon as the man from the Office of Instruction had left, Teacher Ti jerked me out of my seat and dressed me down, making me feel even worse.

At the next inspection, I mustered up enough courage to be the first to speak.

I said, "At the last inspection I didn't say anything, and Teacher Ti criticized me severely afterward. I know I was in the wrong, so this time I want to make up for my bad behavior. Teacher Ti is a dedicated man. For example, to help with today's inspection he stayed very late last night coaching us in what we should say."

After blurting out this long speech, I jubilantly sat down.

But as soon as the inspector had left, Teacher Ti bellowed, "Ni Niu-niu, stand up!"

Again, he jerked me out of my seat and scolded me, this time even more severely than the last time. I really had no idea what I had done wrong. I swear that I meant only to praise him, even though I really didn't want to.

It wasn't only that I didn't understand what I had done wrong; the way his face changed so abruptly had upset me so badly that all I could do was look at my feet and mumble.

He demanded that I explain myself, but I couldn't bring myself to speak to him. As shy and timid as I was, there was no way that I could reveal to him even a single word of my inner turmoil. There was nothing I could do but stand there rigidly like a mute.

After that, nobody in the class would speak to me, and naturally I felt there was no one I could trust. I can't say exactly why, but I felt that even the daily weather was false, and when I was away from home I was a stray black cloud lost in the clear void. As I walked along, I said to myself that without hypocrisy the world would stop turning.

Every day my only wish was to get back home as soon as possible.

I couldn't depend on my father. That was one thing I was very clear on. He was an arrogant and pushy civil servant who never got very far. For many years (probably from about the time I was born), he had been pushed around and passed over. This intensified his arrogance, rancor, and neurosis. He thought it was beneath him to sit down and talk with a primary school teacher, even though it might have an effect on my future. And Teacher Ti himself was such an arrogant male that I was sure that if you gave them a few minutes together, they would hate each other. Because they were males.

So it was always Mother who went to see Teacher Ti, simply because Father had no interest in my affairs. In fact, I could feel that he had no interest in my mother either, that to him our problems were one and the same. He thought about nothing but himself.

I decided that when I grew up, I would not marry a man like my father, who neglected Mother and me. At that moment, it occurred to me that I should marry the Dean of Instruction. He could rake Teacher Ti over the coals, even box his ears. He wouldn't have to let his shame stew inside, as Mother and I had to do.

But then I thought about the kitchen renovations we were having done at that time. Not only was father no good at that kind of work, he also irritated the workers Mother had hired to help with the job, making it very difficult for her, constantly having to apologize for him. Seeing my mother's difficulties, I vowed that I would marry a man who knew how to build kitchens.

By this time my mind was in a mess. Whom should I choose? The Dean of Instruction or a man who could build kitchens?

The black raindrops still fell with a persistent madness out of a clear evening sky, surrounding me with a harsh and jarring clatter.

Through the rain, I suddenly caught sight of the silent silhouette of my mother leaning forward, stepping lightly on tiptoe, at the entrance to our street—a woman unswayed in her conviction, seeking light under the combined oppressiveness of the real rain and of the black rain that falls in human life. To her, the drenched figure of her daughter in the distance was a small slip of flame threatened by the flood around her—a flame that inspired her to rise to her toes in a dance of body and spirit upon the stage of human life.

*Our most profound self-denial comes when
we say yes to our fathers and yes to our lives.*

When I heard my father shouting, the rain suddenly stopped.

Like a baby's crying, which has no prelude or progression from sobs to outpouring of tears, this rain began unannounced, and it ceased just as abruptly. There was no gradual diminution in its intensity, nor did the dark clouds slowly dissipate. To me it seemed as if the raindrops suddenly decided, in mid-flight, to stop their descent, probably because of my father's ability to fill them with terror.

Frightened, I stopped and pulled on my mother's sleeve. "Mama?"

Looking up at the heavy, now rainless sky and forcibly staying her own tears, she put her arm around my shoulders, and we resumed our steps homeward.

That she didn't want to say anything to me made me realize that she and Father had been quarreling again.

"Mama," I said, trying to clear my throat and suppress the fear and confusion in my heart, so that my words might spool out as smooth and unbroken as a cotton thread. I didn't want to stammer or make any awkward pauses. At last, in one breath, I quoted a passage from Mao Zedong's *Little Red Book*, which we read daily in primary school at that time. "Mama, Chairman Mao says that we should work to nurture unity, not division. . . ."

With that, I fell into stony silence.

At that time I did not understand the sexual implications of the word "nurture" in this phrase.

Very clearly, union between a man and woman requires a special kind of nurturing. Their sexual roles, standpoints, thinking, and behavior are so vastly different that without such nurturing it would be impossible for them to communicate. Thus it is that men and women are by nature friends in "struggle," not friends in "concord." Only by nurturing it can they beget "unity" under one roof, in order to face the confusion in the world outside. Only under the advantage that the unity of a home provides can they reduce the differences of their individual sexuality, lessen the contradictions and conflicts resulting from their individuality, and hold the family together securely to present a consistent face to the world outside.

Of course, unions that have been nurtured can break apart. When it reaches the point where the conflicts between these two individuals of different sex become so severe that they can ignore the good of the family as a whole, then this unit will dissolve.

But these are things that I only slowly began to understand with the passage of time.

Following my little outburst, I bowed my head, focusing my attention on the soggy gray mud that was creeping over my sandals and oozing in and out between my toes as I walked.

By forcing myself to concentrate all my attention on my feet and find pleasure in this decidedly unpleasant circumstance, I managed to free myself from the strange sensation of being unable to verbalize my feelings.

From childhood I have had a unique ability to dispel, shift, or ignore the tragic aspects of things. In any kind of antagonistic situation, I always give precedence to my own feelings. I have a kind of strength that allows me to push on recklessly in dead-end situations. This feeling of not caring about ultimate annihilation is much like the passion of a martyr. When I encounter grief, I automatically try to find a way to change the direction of my feelings. Maybe my focus at that moment on the mud between my toes is a good illustration of this quirk of mine.

Mother said, "Your father doesn't want Nanny to live here anymore."

Nanny was the housekeeper who had been looking after us for many years. She only had one eye; she had lost sight in the other one many years ago when her husband had struck her. In the years she spent with us, she cried many times. Whenever she cried, to avoid getting caught in her grief myself, I would carefully watch her blind eye. I discovered that it never shed tears.

I once asked her why she cried.

She told me because of her grief.

I asked why her bad eye didn't grieve.

She said because it couldn't feel grief anymore.

I asked why it couldn't feel grief.

She said it was because it was already dead, that it had been killed by her husband many, many years ago. It was only after she had left him that she had come to work for us, and endure my father's anger.

I told her that when I grew up I was going to find her husband and make him pay for that eye.

She said to me, "Ni Niuniu, if you marry a good man when you grow up, then you won't suffer."

I replied that when I grew up I would make my husband suffer—a man like Teacher Ti, for instance.

I remember very clearly that Nanny wanted me to find a good husband.

In those days, I had a bad habit of dropping my chopsticks (a problem I haven't totally shaken till this day). Because I had little interest in food, I went through two or three pairs of chopsticks at every meal. At the table, my attention would always wander elsewhere. After a few mouthfuls, I would balance my chopsticks on my rice bowl and pick up a book or something else of interest that I had brought to the table. For a while this would take my attention; then I would return to my food, eat a bit, then put my chopsticks down again to pick up the book or whatever. Back and forth, so it would go—my heart always elsewhere. Balanced as they were on my bowl, it was inevitable that my chopsticks would get knocked onto the floor. And every single time, Nanny would fetch me a clean pair, chattering on in her usual way: "'Grip your chopsticks near the tip, your married home will be a short trip. Hold them far away from the tip, and your parents' home will be a long trip.' But you—always carelessly knocking them on the floor—what kind of behavior is that!"

I didn't know if Nanny's traditional wisdom had any basis in fact. I simply pretended that I didn't hear and continued to knock my chopsticks off the table. But I never did it on purpose.

It was only after I had grown up that I understood how much our home had depended on her. Quietly and without letup, she had worked pulling out the weeds and watering to turn part of our neglected yard into a wonderful garden. Day in and day out, her apron swinging, she tirelessly looked after all the little things that had to be done. She daily filled our table, supporting us with the bounty of her work, so that our family might prosper and survive. She sacrificed herself to our family; she knew all its secrets, all that it stood for. She gave it all her strength.

But in the end, she was unable to save it.

With her departure, the family lost its life breath and gradually disintegrated.

When Father's shouts crashed down upon me like thunderclaps, I instinctively closed my eyes. I was afraid that the noise would leave me half blind like Nanny if it should strike my eyes.

I slowed down, tugging on my mother's sleeve, and whispered apprehensively, "Mama?"

"Nanny is waiting to say good-bye to you," she said, putting her arm around me, urging me homeward.

I dragged my feet, asking, "Why? I don't want Nanny to go."

"Niuniu, do as you're told."

I said, "Why is Papa sending her away?"

Mother didn't answer.

Trying to sort out for myself my father's reasons for making Nanny leave our family, I remembered something else. Before I had tried to keep a sparrow, I had had a little dog. Because he had a very big mouth, unusually soft and beautiful Caucasian-style eyes, and an impeccable milky white patrician coat, Mama and I decided to call him Sophia Loren, even though "she" was a he. Sophia Loren was very smart even as a puppy, and had a terrific sense of humor. He very clearly had his own mind and a keen sense of judgment. But his desire to always have his say and to express his views on everything was the seed of his misfortune.

Often on Sunday mornings when I got up I couldn't find my shoes, because on Saturday night when Mother and I discussed going to the park the next day, we had forgotten to include Sophia Loren. The next morning, bright and early, to let me know how important he was and that he was not about to be neglected, he would hide my shoes and then lie beside my bed, waiting for me to wake up and discover they had disappeared.

I remember that in the mid-'70s when very few Chinese families had television, we had a rather fancy Russian-style radio. Early every morning at precisely seven o'clock, my father would irritably turn it on to catch the news and at the same time would issue his order for all of us to get up. Then Sophia Loren would sit motionless in front of the radio and listen intently to the news, making no bones about expressing his approval or displeasure. After my father, he was the "person" in our family most concerned with politics. Following the news, they always played the same piece of music. For Sophia Loren this was irresistible. When the strains of "The East Is Red" began to fill the room, he gaily sang along, "Woof, woof, woof, woof, woof!"

On one occasion, in late 1975 or early 1976, when a news broadcast of the paper "Counterattack the Trend to Exonerate Rightists," criticizing "the mistaken road of Rightist opportunism," concluded, Sophia Loren, displeased for some inexplicable reason, immediately lifted his leg and peed on the radio. This sort of crude behavior was an entirely new departure for him. We were all astonished, because he hadn't relieved himself in the house since he was a puppy. But it seemed that everyone in the house, my father included, understood his displeasure. My father commented, "Even the dog doesn't like to listen to this stuff." So Sophia Loren wasn't punished for that indiscretion.

But a short time later, at about the time of the Festival of Pure Brightness, he did it again. On the radio, a critic from the *People's Daily* was reading a solemn report concerning the "April 5th Counter-revolutionary Incident." This time Sophia Loren didn't wait until the program was finished. He went straight over and gave the radio another drenching.

Sophia Loren didn't like my parents quarreling. If they hadn't been speaking to each other for a long time, he would take first one, then the other by the sleeve and try to pull them together. Before they went to bed at night, he would drag their pajamas together. When they took to actual quarreling, he would yelp and cry to break their hostility.

On the surface, Sophia Loren gave the appearance of being an impartial mediator, but in fact he knew very clearly the way things stood in our family, and his bias was very clear—he was my mother's faithful ally.

My father was, of course, aware of this all along, but he put up with it, waiting for the right moment. The trouble between my father and Sophia Loren had been brewing for a long time. They were both aware of the silent and intangible power struggle that was going on, though nothing was ever said.

Sophia Loren understood very clearly the value of hiding your light under a bushel and biding your time until you had the advantage; he was definitely not going to pit his strength openly against Father. So the violent struggle stirred and developed beneath a calm surface. I have no idea why Father chose a dog as his adversary in such a serious family confrontation. He was always straightforward in his treatment of Mother, Nanny, and me. With us he played his cards on the table; there was no hidden agenda. His displeasure was clearly written on his face. Of course, whether you were talking about authority, physical dominance

(Father was a very big, rough-and-ready man), or economic power, he was unquestionably number one in our family. But seeing how my father suppressed or restrained his attitude toward Sophia Loren led me, after I had grown up, to see another reason for his dominance: his aggressiveness, his despotic ways, and his power were freely given to him by Mother, Nanny, and me. We handed him the power to oppress us through our gentleness and submissiveness. The more tolerant and obedient we were, the more violent and dictatorial he became.

But Sophia Loren was different. If he appeared to be submissive, this was only because he couldn't talk. His apparent acquiescence had nothing to do with capitulation. He used a silent, passive stance to express his active involvement in the life of the family. Although this kind of beneath-the-surface opposition and testing of each other's strength was difficult to detect, both Father and Sophia Loren knew exactly what was going on. It was only because the right moment had not presented itself that they had not committed themselves to open warfare.

Another point that did not occur to me until after I had grown up was that they were the same sex. Father was an out-and-out redneck male, and Sophia Loren was a male dog. And wherever males congregate (or are in the majority), whether it be in the political arena, the world of finance, the battlefield, or even the garden of love, that is where the stratagems of struggle are the most refined, intense, and cruel.

But in the end, the animosity between my father and Sophia Loren could no longer be contained and erupted in open warfare.

I remember one occasion when my father and mother started quarreling. I didn't know the reason, but it probably concerned another man. My father always made himself sick with his doubts and anxieties, suspecting everyone around him, so that he suffered from extreme nervous tension. This time he was especially angry, violent; there was no reasoning with him. My mother also refused to give in, insisting that all of Father's speculations were groundless, all the exaggerated results of his perverted imagination. Father's anger got the best of him and he struck Mother, knocking her glasses off.

Sophia Loren, who had been observing this battle for a long time but staying out of it, could no longer restrain his anger. He barked at my father, and leaping into the air, he gave him a terrific clout with his left front paw.

At first Father was thunderstruck. Never before had his authority suffered such an indignity. Then he bent down and started groping around for his glasses. After he had straightened up and put them on, Sophia Loren's unfortunate fate was settled—he was banished from our home forever, to join the nameless stray dogs on the streets.

Nanny's banishment from our home had made me think of Sophia Loren. I was certain that her transgression must have been about the same as Sophia Loren's.

When I went into the house, Nanny was using her good eye to cry. She was sitting on the edge of the bed, her lustrous gray-white hair coiled in a simple bun held in a black net at the back of her head. Her traditional black jacket was neatly pressed and buttoned across her chest and down the side. On the bed beside her was a bundle, not very large, loosely tied in a dark blue cotton cloth. Together, they looked very much like a painting.

Father was sitting in the big wicker chair in the study, with his back, as imposing as a mountain peak, toward us, so I could not see what kind of mood he was in. Actually, I had no intention of looking at him, because I instinctively feared that he would be angry and I wouldn't be able to avoid him. I had caught a glimpse of his figure from the corridor.

I went and stood in front of Nanny. She started crying again and put her arms around me, then stopped to say, "Niuniu, you're soaked, get into something dry right away."

She got up and brought a set of clean clothes for me from the closet, and was waiting to dry me off and help me dress. But when I was washing my face my own tears started to flow and I repeatedly refused her help. I washed and washed my face, dragging out the time until I eventually realized as she busied herself around me that she had been waiting until I returned home to help me change my clothes.

When I had finally stemmed my tears and finished washing and getting dressed, Nanny's till then busy hands suddenly drooped like wind-broken branches, not severed completely, just hanging there pointlessly.

Finally she sighed and said, "Well, I guess I'd better be on my way."

But she just stood there, not knowing what to do.

I'm afraid of good-byes. I avoid scenes of shared grief as if they were the plague.

I turned abruptly, taking Nanny's bundle, and went out the door.

I heard Mama and Nanny follow me outside. They were talking, but I couldn't make out what they were saying. Actually, I was afraid to hear them and I didn't want to turn and look at them, because if I did, I knew that I would start to cry again and that once my tears started I would have a hard time stopping them. I didn't want that to happen, because I knew it was of no use and would only make me feel worse.

I tried desperately to think of something; I looked around, hoping to find something else that would capture my attention. But this time it was no use: I could not escape the grief of this separation.

When I got to the courtyard entrance, I stopped and waited for Mama and Nanny to catch up. The sound of their approaching footsteps suddenly became unbearable. I began to tremble with grief. I became angry with myself because I had dearly hoped not to succumb to such overwhelming grief while saying good-bye.

At that point, I discovered a new channel for my feelings—anger. Of course, anger. I was enraged.

Nanny had caught up with me. She and Mama stood close together at the entrance to our courtyard.

The lane was still wet after the rain, and the street drains were gurgling with runoff water. The base of the courtyard wall was strewn with fallen leaves and blossoms where water droplets refracted light, and the air was heavy with the redolent odor of pollen.

Nanny gave her key to Mama, then turned to me and took me in her arms to say something.

Not a leaf stirred. It was as if they too were waiting on her final words.

Choking sobs began to well up from my chest into my throat. Without waiting for her to open her mouth, as if I had something urgent to do at home, I hurriedly and with a strange hostility said, "Nanny, when I grow up and earn some money, I'll bring you back home. I'll make him leave. I'll make him pay!"

Then, without looking back, I fled back to the house.

"Him," of course, was my father.

"Willing to go through a keyhole,
but not through an open door."

The heavy rainfall was followed by a series of dull, damp days. My eyes half closed, I was walking alone on the way to school. The passersby were all bigger than me. I had no heart to lift my eyes to enjoy the scenery along the way, because going to school depressed me so much.

A madman came up to me and started to laugh. His withered body was as thin as a straw swaying in a whistling wind. Staring into my face, he laughed as gaily as if he were on a road leading to some blissful heaven. Maybe he wasn't really a madman, but I thought he was. Would anyone other than a madman start to laugh at some stranger on the street, especially at a little girl of no consequence like me?

He darted past me as cheery as a crackling fire. I stopped and turned, unable to take my eyes off him, and continued to watch until he disappeared behind a wall at the corner of the street.

The schoolyard was enshrouded in a thick fog that curled itself around everything. Today Teacher Ti was going to divide the entire class into extracurricular study groups. I dashed quickly toward our classroom.

He was already there, pacing up and down between the rows of desks. He hadn't rung the bell yet, but all my classmates were sitting in their seats as stiff as pencils. Something must have happened. They were on tenterhooks, awaiting Ti's outburst.

The moment I entered the room, I could hear his whistling bronchial wheeze. This was a kind of signal, an omen that something very serious was about to happen.

Once, near the end of the term when I was in fourth grade, just as Mr. Ti was launching into a denunciation of the despicable behavior of someone caught cheating on an exam, the thin, shrill sound of a whistle broke the solemn silence in the classroom. Mr. Ti barked, "Who blew that whistle?"

Struck with disbelief, we listened intently, until we realized that the whistling was coming from Ti's own throat; then we started giggling, hiding our faces behind our hands.

After a moment, seeming to have discovered the source of the noise himself, Mr. Ti cleared his throat angrily. "So you find it amusing, do you? This cruel memento that China's history has foisted upon me. You couldn't possibly understand."

Over the preceding several years, from the few things that Mr. Ti had revealed to us out of his discontent, I knew that he was one of the educated youth who had graduated from middle school at the time of the Red Guards. In 1966 he was labeled one of the rebels among the children of high-ranking officials who had been ousted from office and was sent to the northeast as a soldier in an army agriculture and construction team. Once there, he stayed for eight years, returning only after his father was rehabilitated in 1974. But his father died suddenly only nine days after his name had been cleared, and from that time the family's fortunes began to slip.

Whenever Ti told us of those times, he was overwhelmed with the injustice of his never having had a chance to realize his potential, and he got so upset that he found it hard to breathe.

Much of what I know of Ti's personal history comes from what he revealed to us in those days, but what I know of his inner self comes out of the strange and confused personal relationship that developed between us, which I came to understand only many years later.

When I entered the classroom that day, I very quietly edged my way to my desk. Once in my seat, I started to look around.

My desk partner told me in a veiled whisper, "Someone has stolen some money."

The student behind me immediately countered, "No, someone's been writing reactionary slogans in the toilet."

My heart started to pound.

Like a caged animal, Teacher Ti angrily yet calculatedly paced up and down between our desks, cold nails flashing from his watchful eyes as they swept across our faces. It seemed as if his eyes could see directly into our minds, past our faces into our innermost secrets. I don't know whether it was my racing heart that affected my appearance or whether those cold nails sweeping our faces had actually pierced my cheeks, but my face felt red with blood as hot as chili peppers.

Please, please, don't blush; you haven't done anything, I said to myself.

"One of you," at last Mr. Ti spoke out, "has been passing around pictures of the human body, pictures that display the private parts of men and women!"

Oh, thank heaven, thank earth! It's not stolen money or reactionary graffiti. But private parts—what are private parts?

The way Mr. Ti said "private parts," the words seemed to be coated with phosphorous, which, touched with the heat of his voice, flared to life like the heads of matches for a moment, to stand out from the rest of his words.

From the tone of his voice, I knew that the private parts must be in a special location, probably "that place." But as soon as this occurred to me, my face, without my bidding at all, flushed crimson.

"Ni Niuniu, stand up!" Mr. Ti was addressing me. "Why are you blushing?"

The accusation in his voice isolated me from the others even more. They distanced themselves from me as is I were some sort of plague, a carrier of some infectious disease.

When classes were over, Mr. Ti took me to his office and left me standing there to stew while he graded papers.

After a while, when everyone else had left the office, he at last stilled his busy red pen.

"Tell me," he said, very gently, obviously wanting to make things easier for me. "Why were you blushing?"

I cleared my throat and thought for a moment.

Because Mr. Ti was making an effort to be gentle, I decided not to be totally uncooperative, but to meet him halfway.

I said, "This has absolutely nothing to do with me. I haven't seen the pictures; I have no idea what's in them."

"They are pictures of private parts. If you didn't know, why did you blush?"

So there they were again—"private parts." And again I got the feeling that these words were burning Mr. Ti's mouth. It was like he had put a hot date just out of the boiling water on his tongue and wanted to swallow it but was afraid it would burn.

I hesitated, then said uncertainly, "Private parts . . . where are they? Really, I've never seen them."

"I find that hard to believe. Then why did you blush?"

I didn't respond.

The room was dead quiet for a moment, and my resentment began to grow again. I turned away from him, determined not to look at or speak to him anymore.

Suddenly he spun me around, as if he were getting angry.

One by one, he waved the pictures in front of me and put them down, as if he were laying down a hand of cards.

"Private parts, surely you must know about them?" He paused a moment. Then, "These are your private parts," he said, touching my breasts, "and this," he said, putting his hand briefly between my thighs.

I jerked away from him, my heart pounding, afraid to utter a word. His eyes fixed on my face, Mr. Ti seemed overcome with an uneasy excitement.

"Truly, Ni Niuniu, I have always been concerned about you. I like you very much. Why are you always so difficult with me?" he said, his voice filled with gentleness and sincerity. For a fleeting moment, I caught in his expression a hint of distress over our impasse.

I said nothing. It seemed like something was wrong, but I couldn't speak because I wasn't sure what it was.

"Niuniu, you're a big girl now, you should know about things like our private parts," he said, again putting his hand on my breasts and between my legs. He seemed unable to pull his hand away, as if it were glued to me.

Suddenly I knew the source of our difficulty. It was his hand—he was touching my body.

My faced flushed hot, every bit as hot as it had been in the classroom that morning.

In a confused state of anger, wanting both to defend myself and to strike out, suddenly I felt an urge to put my hands on the same places on his body and say, "These are your private parts, these are your private parts!"

I took a deep breath, but in the end I did nothing.

What I wanted to say and do happened only in my head. Every action, every word, existed only in my imagination.

"Niuniu . . ." Mr. Ti didn't want to say anything. I could see that. All he was doing was repeating my name, "Niuniu." The expression on his face was imploring and conciliatory.

I turned and ran.

There was no one in the schoolyard. To get from the office at the back of the campus to the front gate, I had to go through a long, narrow passageway with high walls on either side. I tried to be quiet, because I was afraid I would think that the sound of footsteps was from someone following me. I kept thinking about the daring nature of the things that I had imagined doing, my heart filled with revengeful anger and fear.

But as I continued, I felt my anger gradually dissipate. As I hurried along between the two smooth, hard walls that stretched ahead of me,

I felt a kind of frightening and strange satisfaction growing within me. Because the passageway was so narrow, there were not "four directions"; there were only two, "ahead" and "behind." With my arms repeatedly bumping against the closely set walls, I felt like I was moving in a dream. And that strange, frightening feeling of satisfaction came first through the repeated bumping of my arms, not through my eyes.

Suddenly I felt an unaccountable sense of triumph.

But what kind of triumph, I had no idea.

The pair of scissors dominating the dressing table, like a bird perched on the topmost branch of a magnolia, had long been waiting their moment. After deciding what to do and how to do it, they flew into my head and borrowed my hands to complete their work.

At last the rainy weather announced its end by suddenly opening a fissure in the leaden gray clouds through which glinting blades of sunlight angled earthward.

It was early Sunday morning, and even though I hadn't opened my eyes, I knew the sky had cleared.

I luxuriated in my bed with no desire to get up. Mother was ignoring me for the moment, and I simply indulged myself in another of my imaginary dialogues.

Father was reading the paper as he ate his breakfast. He obviously read very quickly. The way he wolfed down his food as he read bore witness to this. An intense man, the way he focused on his work and his impatient nature made it very difficult for him to lead a quiet and relaxed life. His mind worked at lightning speed, leaving most ordinary people behind. His thoughts were always a sentence ahead of his tongue or

29

had even jumped to a different subject, to the point where he was unable to express himself clearly, a fact that often caused him great vexation. He could never queue up to buy anything or to get something done. He would sooner do without than stand in line.

From my father's impatience and agitation I knew that he had to go to a meeting. This was just at the time when there had been a major turn in the course of political events in China. From the few things that my father and mother said about this, I gathered that this had resulted in a turn for the better in my father's situation. But at that time I didn't really understand what went on in the adult world outside our home, nor did I have any interest in it. That world had nothing to do with me. The only thing that concerned me was that improvement in the outside situation had brought no improvement to the atmosphere in our home. I was just as unhappy as I had always been.

Wiping here and tidying there, Mother was busying herself with her household chores.

From my bed, through the open window above me that I saw through half-closed eyes, a rusty reddish intermittent sound of breathing seemed to come from the distant horizon. It was the deep and heavy breath of this city that I live in—Beijing. Its breath filled our house and filled my lungs. Like ashen, filthy time itself, it forever clings closely to the arms of all good people as it leads them silently away.

On his way out the door, briefcase in his hand, Father was saying, "Is sleeping in all Niuniu is good for? Doesn't she know how to talk? She'll end up with some job for the deaf and dumb."

Mother said, "She's still just a child."

Father said, "How old does she have to be before she starts to grow up? It's no good, the way you spoil her and turn her against me."

"It's you yourself who have turned her against you; it's got nothing to do with me. You don't know how to get along with anybody. Even the dog didn't like you," Mother retaliated.

Father slammed the door and left.

I was elated. I could spend the whole day at home alone with Mama. I didn't have to go to school or listen to Father's angry outbursts. Lying in bed, it seemed as if I could see the little black car. It was in the shadows just outside the big wooden door to our courtyard, listening for the sound of Father's footsteps. Then, opening one of its doors, it looked like a huge bird with one wing spread, waiting for my father to disappear into its body before they set out in the 8 o'clock morning light.

. . . Then, unexpectedly, the little car suddenly turned into a police car, its siren bleating, and Father into a felon in dark brown prison garb, his hands and feet tightly fettered. He was trying desperately to free himself, but the police car took him to a place so far away that it would be impossible for him ever to come home again. . . .

I awoke with a start from semisleep, and my muddled dream faded away. Father had already left for his meeting.

I continued my silent movies in my head. This habit not only allowed me to avoid the clamor of crowds but also even let me escape my mother without feeling left alone.

But it is this habit of actively longing to avoid people and submerge myself in my own thinking that has made me like a real carrier of an infectious disease.

I continued my stroll through my thoughts:

. . . Again I saw the long, narrow corridor at my primary school. Bearing traces of the passage of countless tiny feet, like the thought patterns of serious young students, the pavement of bare red brick mottled with a patina of dull silver gray bore testimony to its great age. Smiling through half-closed eyes as if harboring some evil intent, Mr. Ti stood at one end of the passageway. I turned and ran as fast as I could for the other end, but when I turned my head to get a better look at him, in disbelief I saw him suddenly turn into my father, tall and imposing. When I finally got out of the passageway, I saw another me run out. We looked at each other intently, eager to discuss just who it was that we had seen. But although we wanted to talk, we also wanted to avoid each other, and in the end we went our separate ways, refusing to have anything to do with each other.

At that point Mother called me to get up for breakfast.

I wanted to, but my body refused to move.

I turned away from my previous thoughts. I really didn't want to think about that day, about anything to do with men.

Sitting down on the edge of the bed, Mother turned to look at me as she gently massaged my skinny back. From the bed, I could see past Mother leaning over me, under the table in the next room, where Father had just eaten his breakfast, to our rather battered front door.

Listening carefully, I could just make out what seemed to be the faint voice of a woman singing somewhere far away across the ruins of temples and crumbling walls, her words taking a very long time to reach me.

As I recall this, I remember that it was a love song expressing the grief of an abandoned woman. Although the plaintive lyrics were much too soft for an insensitive ear to pick up, they came through to me with vivid clarity:

> . . . Open this door,
> This door I beat with my tears.
> All time has passed away
> And left me here alone.

The lyrics seemed to have come on the crest of a distant swell; they rolled back and forth in the hallway and through the entire house, lingering, swirling, their gentle rhythm clinging to me. They crossed through the courtyard dappled in sunlight, following the scattered shafts of slanting sunlight. At last the flow of reverberating melody came to rest at the front door of our neighbor. It was the Widow Ho who was singing. Her voice was as soft and soothing as a cooling balm on an aching wound.

In rainy weather Widow Ho's voice was especially deep and clear, without any hint of fragility. The humid air encased her clear tones in a sleek shell that gave them a kind of seductive sensuality that was both masculine and feminine in quality—or feminine with masculine undertones.

In the long and heavy years since then, the broken strains of that sensual voice have always had the ability to cut through the confused net of memories surrounding me to fill my ears as clearly and distinctly as if they were real. The rain-laden sounds characteristic of such wet weather (actually, I mean during the brief period of clearing skies that often follows a shower) always take me back to the little disconnected fragments of my past life. They are like hair so unbearably messy and disordered that its tangles cannot be washed or combed free. I am helpless in front of these buried feelings with their endless possible ramifications.

The sound of her singing obscured by the monotonous, senseless drone of the cicadas that summer filled me with an indefinable melancholy that I could not suppress.

I slipped out from under Mother's gentle hands, then stood up on the bed and started pulling on my clothes. Through the window I could see some children playing tag in the dusty and withered grass. I could see the June sunlight extending like a thick miasma across the clear and endless sky.

Mother said, "Hurry up and get ready, we're going to go and see a movie." Touched with excitement, I quickly finished dressing and made my bed.

As soon as I was up, Mother carefully spread out a pair of cream-colored woolen trousers on my bed and started pressing them, moving the iron methodically back and forth. I saw at a glance that they were the trousers Father usually wore to meetings. Amid the rising steam, you could easily see that Mother, not very good at this sort of thing, was tense and overly careful.

All the ironing used to be done by Nanny, so I didn't see it as being that important, but it was very obvious that it became very weighty and difficult work in my mother's hands.

Anyway, I had an inexplicable dislike of seeing my mother do this work.

When she was finished, she took the iron into the kitchen and started washing something in the sink.

By this time I had washed my face and felt much more awake.

I glanced quickly over at my clean and neatly made bed. After a quick and silent examination, my eyes came to rest on the cream-colored woolen trousers. While I was rubbing cream on my face, I noticed that the door to my bedroom was closed as tightly as the lips of someone standing rigid, lost in deep thought. Only the window was open, through which I could hear the sound of running water.

As I was putting the skin cream back in the dresser drawer, my gaze fell upon the cold blue glint of the scissors. I shrank back, as if trying to avoid doing something wrong.

Going over to the window, I stood on tiptoe and leaned out as far as I could, straining to hear the tap running in the kitchen. There was no need for me to actually leave my empty bedroom; I could visualize the unbroken icy stream of water falling like a long thin neck from the single faucet. To me it seemed that unfeeling time, because of the existence of that sound, had the desire to flow unceasingly, and it also gave me a strange feeling of strength.

I turned quickly, picked up the scissors, and went straight to the woolen trousers on the bed. I heard the clipping sound of scissors against wool as I sheared off the legs of the neatly ironed trousers, and felt a cold lightning flash of dangerous joy that left me with a sort of postclimactic numbness.

The delight of my little game had me feeling tense yet satisfied.

Then I bounded out of the house like a frightened rabbit.

This woman is a labyrinth, the outer form of a cave, into
which I have fallen. The confining space around us is filled
with darkness. It is like being buried under bedclothes. We
can only vaguely make out each other's faces. We do not
dare converse openly because of the echoes whispering from
the walls around us. The unfathomable depths beneath our
feet render us incapable of moving either forward or back-
ward, and the nothingness around us is spreading. The
dangers ahead of us force us to stop, to remove our clothes,
abandon our duties, and cling together in the darkness.
We are overwhelmed by the feeling of touching each other.
We are pushed to the precipice at the edge of existence.
    She is older than I, but on the horizon of time she is
the shadow behind me.
    She says that I am her salvation and her future.

Of course, we never got to see that movie.

Mother's scream when she went into my room
sounded like she had discovered a man with his legs
severed, spurting out fountains of hot blood—not just a
pair of ruined trousers.

But she didn't rush to call me into the house and give
me a vicious scolding.

She spent the entire day looking at those "gaping
wounds," desperately trying to think of some way to
close them. But the damage was simply too glaring.
After a whole day of painstaking work, the line where
those once sleek and elegant milky white trousers had
been repaired looked like some kind of black worm that
had moved in and fallen asleep.

In the evening when Father came home they had another huge argument, because of the trousers.

I was hiding in my room like a fugitive criminal, holding my breath, afraid to make a sound.

Mother never ever disciplined me for this. It was as if I had never cut those trousers.

As a matter of fact, even if she had asked me to explain why I did it, I could never have done so. Because the impulse to pick up those scissors was part of a very vague and subtle psychological process. In our house, right from when I was a little girl, scissors were one of the things that I was forbidden to touch; also, the sound of scissors cutting something could generate in me a pleasant and subtle sensation of resolution, like the tingling vibration of an electrical current pulsing through my blood. And on top of these factors, it had something to do with the constraints my father placed upon us. It would have been impossible at that time to explain clearly this confused and illogical mix.

The natural attraction toward forbidden things in an immature young girl whose power of reason is not yet developed, my strongly individualistic nature, and my tendency to push the normal stubbornness in my blood to an extreme conspired to determine the inevitability of this incident.

After I fled the house that day, I walked along the streets flooded with morning sunlight, in a highly agitated frame of mind. After wandering aimlessly for a while, I sat down on a cool stone bench in a little flower garden bordering the road.

Looking across the street at a clump of trembling grass stalks growing out of a crack in the wall, all withered by the hot summer winds, I anxiously pondered what was to come.

As I sat there, my mind began to wander. Suddenly, my inner confusion fell away as I involuntarily remembered the arrival of the spring that had only recently departed. I remembered the clear mornings, the damp mustiness, and the end of the depressing wet weather. The rays of the long-hidden sun pushed down through breaks in the cloud cover, ceaselessly spilling their golden and roseate hues on the Sunday houses, the streets, and the mimosa trees thick with pink blossoms. The air was heavy with the fragrance of ferns and creepers, and exotic birds of every hue bathed in the mauve-tinged morning mists.

Recalling the wild vitality of the spring just past as I looked at the dry summer landscape before me doesn't mean that I am one of those who likes to live in the past or who twists reality to fit their dreams. I have always been able to clearly distinguish between fantasy and reality. The fleeting vision of spring that went through my head was nothing more than a passing moment of nostalgia.

After sitting blankly for a while, I again began to wander aimlessly. For some reason, I had completely forgotten about the problem at home and was thinking about something altogether different.

. . . . . .

After walking a while, I suddenly noticed that the bodies of all the people on the street seemed to have turned into biological specimens. They looked like people, but all you had to do was reach out a hand and push them and they would fall to the ground like leaves off cornstalks. These fallen life forms were lying on the thick, rich earth dappled with golden light, gasping their last broken breaths and stretching unceasingly as they emitted streams of bubblelike yawns from the tops of their heads. Then their heads fell to one side and they turned into broken skeletons with only testicles or breasts, like the ones I had seen in Mr. Ti's office, as huge as winter melons. Aside from that, they retained nothing, absolutely nothing.

Or else I noticed that the people around me gradually crouched down, becoming shorter and shorter, their coloring seemingly getting darker and their originally upright bodies assuming crawling positions as they became completely gray. When I took a closer look, I discovered that these people were not people at all but wolves in human form, and that I, totally unaware of it, had been walking in the midst of a pack of wolves. I was frightened because I had discovered that I could neither exist as an independent individual nor change myself into a female wolf. . . .

For a very long time these two visions continued to return to me as I walked among the crowds on the streets.

Over the years since that time, right up to the present day, I have continued to enjoy wandering the streets alone. To avoid a recurrence of the scenes described above, I force myself to avoid major roads and large crowds and walk on uneven, irregular side streets. It seems that my dislike of smooth, solid main roads has become one of my lifelong idiosyncracies. And I've also found that the only roads I enjoy walking on are those that are free of people and illuminated by the first rays of morning sunlight, or suffused with the waning tints of twilight.

Walking along that Sunday, I suddenly thought of someone. I knew that when my mother couldn't find me, she would go to her. Mama always did. She would be waiting under the date tree in our courtyard, sitting there in the cold, damp mist or evening breeze trying to connect with me through mystical Daoist spells. There would be several empty tin cans in front of her, filled with curses or blessings. The can for me would always be filled with blessings; the one for the people I hated, with curses.

She was always sitting in the courtyard waiting for me when school was out. She was, of course, our neighbor across the way, Widow Ho, with her wonderful, enchanting voice. I made a quick about turn and headed for her house.

Ridden with anxiety, I hesitated at the entrance to her courtyard, glanced back at my own home opposite, then went in.

She was playing her old records, and when I entered the room I noted an almost imperceptible flicker in the deep pools of her eyes. Putting down the record she was holding as if it were a fragile wafer, she lifted the needle from the old-fashioned phonograph and the music stopped abruptly.

The languid, graceful beauty of her features and her bearing was accentuated by the silence that filled the room. The pupils of her long and ample eyes sparkled like black porcelain pots; her serene forehead was smooth and wide; her legs, long as a deer's, were as lustrous as slender bolts of silk spilling from her waist.

She calmly extended her arms to receive me.

As I moved toward her, my agitation amazingly began to subside. From nowhere, a feeling that she understood me seemed to be flooding upward through the soles of my feet.

This young widow, well over ten years my senior, always generated in me this strange feeling of understanding, no matter what it was I had done. Just as her voice did, her presence generated in people a fragile feeling of hope.

Taking my hands firmly in her own, she said with great concern, "Niuniu, what's happened?"

It seemed that after blindly walking the streets for hours, I had at last found a place where I could jettison my "garbage."

I said, "Papa's trousers, I cut the legs off."

She said, "So what? Don't be afraid, don't be afraid." She drew me to her bosom. "Those scissors must have taken your hand. They did it themselves, didn't they."

I said, "Yes, they did—really. I had no intention of cutting Papa's trousers. Before I knew what was going on, the legs were cut off. I didn't do it on purpose."

"There, there, it's all right, it's okay," said Ho, gently patting and caressing my back. Her hands moved with such a wondrous dexterity that I began to feel like a leaf floating in the wind.

Then she got up and brought a clean, damp cloth to wipe my face and my feet. After that she had me lie down on her bed with her jade pillow under my head.

The pillow was made with real jade beads of a creamy green so rich that they almost seemed to exude moisture. The oval-shaped beads, stitched to a maroon flannelette backing, felt as cool as snow. As soon as she put it under my head, I felt their coolness moving along the strands of my hair to penetrate my scalp and melt away my confusion.

Mother once told me that the old emperors used to sleep on jade pillows.

Long before that I had heard Nanny say that Ho's family were descendants of a high Manchu official in the Qing dynasty who was born in the area around the Fragrant Hills. One of her early forebears was the Yinyang Overseer in charge of *fengshui* at the Imperial Board of Astrology at the time of Emperor Qianlong, and was also associated with Cao Xueqin for a time. In the fourteenth year of his reign, Qianlong had a special Flying Tiger crack assault battalion of 3,000 officers and enlisted men established in the Fragrant Hills, in accordance with the territorial divisions of the eight-banner system. Qianlong sent this Yinyang Overseer, accompanied by the deputy commander of the Fragrant Hills defense force, to investigate the *fengshui* characteristics of the area. When the Imperial Astrologer looked eastward from the buildings cresting the hills, he noted a mountain ridge running from east to west covered with verdant green forests and fields of wildflowers, like a phoenix with outspread wings. This, of course, is famous Phoenix Mountain. Instantly delighted, the overseer declared that the ridge to the north would be called Turtle Mountain since it looked like the back of a divine turtle; that a peak in the distance, the turtle's head, would be called Red Head Mountain; and that the small hill immediately before him was the turtle's tail. Since the divine turtle was a kind of dragon, he said, the area possessed the energy of both the phoenix and the dragon and was surely a precious *fengshui* site. He immediately dispatched a report to the emperor and had a map drawn demarcating the area. Then the emperor ordered the eviction of people of Han nationality from the Fragrant Hills.

Following this, Cao Xueqin sought audience with the overseer and told him that although the Fragrant Hills were indeed a precious *fengshui* site, they were lacking in water, one of the five elements, and that since forests could not thrive on mountains without water and birds could not survive without forests, it would be impossible for the phoenix to fly. But since the written characters for "Han," or Chinese people, and for "Man," or Manchu people, both contained the three dots symbolizing water, if they were to allow the Hans to be scattered throughout all the villages in the area on the pattern of one Han for every two Manchus, that would mean a total of nine water dots; since nine symbolized plenty, a sufficiency of water on the Fragrant Hills would be assured, the dragon would be able to coil and the phoenix fly, and good *fengshui* would be certain.

The overseer deeply appreciated Cao's reasoning and agreed that this be carried out, and so informed the emperor. So it is that the Han and Manchu peoples have lived in harmony in the Fragrant Hills, generation after generation, ever since.

Ho's forebears had been very well off. Cultured and refined, they had lived in unusual splendor. Although, generation by generation, through the fickle turns of history, the family had gradually descended into abject poverty, an element of their aristocratic and scholarly demeanor still shone through in her.

Widow Ho graduated from university in her early twenties and was assigned a teaching position in a middle school. Her husband, also a descendant of Manchu aristocracy, possessed a casual elegance and was talented and free-thinking. Skilled in music, chess, calligraphy, and painting, he looked very much like Vasily in the film *Lenin in October*. Fair-skinned, tall, and slim, with a high Russian nose, he cut a dashing figure in his peaked cap. He worked as a music teacher in a cultural center. Although his mundane career had nothing in common with the life of his ancestors, he carried on the indulgent excesses in eating, drinking, womanizing, and gambling that were the trademark of aristocratic sons.

In their early marriage he was thoughtful and loving, and they spent every night billing and cooing in each other's arms as the Voice of America rattled on incomprehensibly on the radio. But it wasn't long before he found a new pleasure, having become infatuated with a Miss Xu, a middle-aged accordion player who had been assigned to the cultural center after her release from a song-and-dance troupe. The two of them sang and played together, small talk turning to sweet talk, until he began spending nights with her, using the excuse that he was performing with the center's propaganda team. Eventually he came down with a mysterious fever and died very suddenly, making his wife a widow before she had time to get pregnant or even reveal his tawdry behavior.

Not long after the death of her husband, she came down with diabetes, and in less than a year she was so weakened that she had to give up her job and live on a disability allowance.

All these things I had picked up from listening to our one-eyed Nanny on those long summer evenings when she would fan me as she whiled away the time chatting with Mother.

In those days I thought that Ho was very aloof, a mysterious and eccentric woman. I felt that she was different from other people, but in what way, I couldn't say. Even though I liked to be with her, I was also a bit afraid of her.

It was only after I had grown up that I understood that loneliness is a kind of power.

I remember that after Ho's husband died, every time Nanny cooked something good, Mother would have me take some over to her. Nanny said that life was hard for her on her own like that.

Ho's husband, however, had made very little impression on me. I only vaguely remember that there used to be a man always coming and going, and that he was so tall he had to duck when he went through the door. If he wasn't chewing something, he would have either a straw from a whisk broom or a toothpick between his teeth, and when he saw my mother he would smile and say hello. I also dimly recall that sometimes, if I happened to be near him, he would take several huge puffs on his cigarette and bend down to blow the smoke slowly into my face, and then chuckle to himself. The smoke was thick, with a strong aroma. Afterward, I heard that he became severely ill with shingles, which later developed into some strange kind of fever. When he died, it was said that his internal organs were covered with herpes blisters.

I remember considerably more of the events that followed. I often watched Ho jab needles into her own body. She explained that they were insulin injections. I remember her always leaning against the door frame, shielding her eyes with her hand to block out the pallid evening sun. She gazed into the distance as if she were waiting for someone to return home. She would stand there for a while, then go back inside, but the sense of loss on her face would persist. Maybe she was tired.

By this time, I was feeling a lot calmer, and lying there on Ho's bed, I became aware of a delicate feminine fragrance that gradually enveloped me. A clear scent of lavender and mint floated on the room's increasing shade. I lifted my head and looked around at the oppressive greenish light reflected from the pale, bare walls. The gloomy atmosphere of the room made the light slanting in through the window particularly noticeable.

In my memory, Widow Ho's place has always had the air of a changing room, with invisible mirrors on all sides. As soon as you enter a room like this, you feel like you are lost in a labyrinth endlessly beckoning you left and right. This room is for women only. Here, without break, one or two women try on clothes and take them off. They do not talk. They use code to communicate. It seems there are male eyes hidden behind the room's invisible mirrors, furtively watching, using their sight to touch the secrets in the women's gestures. The women here deeply fear that others will reveal their secrets, deeply fear the passage of time, deeply fear contact with the world outside. They deeply fear, too, that the world will abandon them when they reach menopause. The light here always leads people to misconceptions; the image of woman is at once genuine and false. Women feel like they are suffocating, like the supply of oxygen is uncertain. They are uneasy. From the distant horizon on all sides, rumors of every sort press in upon them. They have a vague feeling that they are forever in danger.

Most of Ho's furniture was old-fashioned, in yellow rosewood. The traditional depictions of dragons and phoenixes that had been carved into the chairs and tall and short cabinets created an overall feeling of age and decay, without the least hint of freshness.

Ho enjoyed smoking her long, thin-stemmed pipe. Looking for something to do to fill the time after her husband died, she perhaps dug his pipe out from among their old things and started smoking to dispel her emptiness. The pipe stem had a sparkling emerald-green jade mouthpiece. The silent jade flowers on it intrigued me, for it seemed that they had been coaxed into blossom by her constant kisses. She didn't smoke like those old grandpas and grannies you see. Taking tobacco leaves of the finest quality, she would work them carefully between her long, slender fingers to the consistency she wanted. Anyone watching her do it could not possibly think that this was simply a matter of getting the tobacco crushed and into the bowl of the pipe. The leisurely, lingering way she went about it made you feel that her fingertips were savoring the pure fragrance of the tobacco. Only after this would she fill the pipe and light it. After she had inhaled deeply a few times, a pink glow would suffuse her face, as if the smoke were turning into blood and gradually mounting to her cheeks.

Her long, slender arm crooked to support the long-stemmed pipe created a pleasing geometrical figure. When she smoked, her eyes would partly close as a hazy bluish nebula slowly swirled and grew above her face. She seemed to be entangled in some shattered, irrelevant past occurrence, waiting interminably for some sweetheart, or for someone like herself who never came.

I remember that at that time she was twenty-five or twenty-six years old. It was only after many, many years that I realized that for all those years she had been waiting for me to grow up—all the way from the

1960s when I was born. Waiting so long that the distant mountains grew taller, covered with withered vines like white hair; waiting so long that her house was totally covered with ivy that hung down in green curtains from the eaves; waiting until I had become a grown woman capable of independent thought and action like herself. The time separating us was like an intervening mountain or desert, a dividing wall, a dense fog, an inviolable taboo. These cruel obstacles obscured her vision and frustrated her desires.

All these things, of course, I became aware of only many years later.

At that time, I felt that watching her smoke was a kind of pleasure. Several years before that, in my children's books, I had seen pictures of drug addicts smoking opium. Haggard in feature with sallow complexions, those men and women had been reduced to little more than skin and bone. A breath of wind would blow them away like dried leaves. Their open mouths revealed yellowed teeth, and their breath must have been foul. It made me think that muck rather than blood must have flowed through their veins.

But watching Ho smoke was a totally different kind of experience. The delicate scent, her graceful manner, reflected an aristocratic decadence. When she exhaled, the fragrant smoke, like the soft warmth of sunlight breaking through clouds, brushed delicately across my skin, curling upward, its bluish tint set off against the room's pale walls. Still today, that delicate, resinous fragrance remains fixed in the depths of my being.

Holding her pipe, she cuddled up next to me. Whispering some comforting words, she cushioned my head on her breast. Her bosom was soft and cool, and I felt very secure with my head there. With her free hand she began caressing my back, just as I used to pet our little Sophia Loren.

"Aren't you hot?" she asked.

"No," I said.

Then she pulled my short-sleeved shirt out of my trousers, and pushing her hand up inside, she fluttered it gently. My back tickled under the repeated touch of her delicate fingertips, and when I squirmed with laughter, she stopped this and softly caressed my back.

Finishing her pipe, she slid down from the headboard until she was lying beside me, my head still cushioned on her breast. Her eyelids trembled with drowsiness. After a while she began kissing my hair, then lifting my head with her hand, she began kissing my eyes and my cheeks.

Softly she murmured, "Niuniu, your eyes are beautiful, do you know?"

I said, "I didn't know."

She said, "You're going to be very beautiful when you grow up."

I said, "I'm not beautiful like you. Nobody likes me."

"How could anyone not like you? I like you very, very much," she said.

Her words rather amazed me. Aside from my mother, no one in the world had ever said anything like that to me so openly. My heart filled with joy and love.

I said, "Mr. Ti, my father, and many of my classmates don't like me. I know."

"But I like you," she said.

"And I like you, too," I replied.

Closing her eyes, Ho smiled a moment. "What do you like about me?"

"Oh . . . I like to look at you."

"What else?"

"Well, I like to be close to you."

Ho opened her eyes, and putting her arm around my neck, began to kiss me feelingly.

"Do you like me to kiss you?"

"Yes," I said.

Kissing me on the forehead, cheek, and neck, she slid her hand under my shirt again and began softly caressing my back. I understood why Sophia Loren had lain so quietly, with his eyes closed, when I petted him. It is wonderful to have someone caress you.

I pressed myself quietly against her, letting her do whatever she wanted, because I trusted her totally.

We stayed like that for a while, until I saw a tear roll from under a partly closed eyelid, cross her delicate cheek, and slowly re-form on her earlobe.

I said, "What's wrong?"

She didn't answer.

After a while she said, "Niuniu, would you like to kiss me?"

Not knowing what to say, I just stared at that glinting crystal teardrop as it grew, then fell to her jade pillow. It was quiet for a moment. Then I haltingly queried, "Well . . . I . . . kiss where?"

She pulled me to her breast as she began to cry.

I said, "Don't cry. I'll kiss you."

Then I started kissing her here and there on her chest. I said, "I think your chest is a lot like my mother's, not at all like mine."

"Niuniu, when you grow up yours will be the same."

Her breath heavy, she said, "Would you like to kiss them?"

I didn't say anything. I was a little bit afraid. Mr. Ti had gotten very angry over those drawings of private parts. Maybe it was wrong to look at them.

Ho had already opened her blouse and unfastened her brassiere. Her creamy white, translucent breasts tumbled out like a pair of peaches. Cool and as swollen as spring silkworms about to spin their cocoons, they looked like they would burst if you touched them.

"Kiss them, Niuniu."

I took her nipples into my mouth and began to suck them just as I had done when I took my mother's milk as a baby.

After a while, her breathing became agitated. I looked up and saw that her eyes were tightly closed and one of her hands was pressed tremblingly between her legs.

Frightened, I said, "Are you all right?"

Silent, she drew me down to her again.

We continued as before. Every now and then it seemed like she was about to say something, or she moaned in a peculiar way. I left only when Mother called me home for supper.

46 My memory of past events is like a sieve that retains only those things I want to remember—those old-fashioned, melancholy songs that seemed to float from afar through the dusky evenings of the rainy season, and dim images of Ho in the fading light of her room. These things are imprinted in my mind forever.

Time is an artist. I am a stone rubbing: the lineaments of a range of peaks, of the caves of a grotto. Before I came into this world, the picture was already complete. As I slowly proceed along the watercourse of this segment of time, I discover my place in it. I see that the picture itself is a piece of history, a depiction of the life of all women.

Summertime, with its long, long days, is my favorite season. It is not like winter, with the skies darkening so early in the day and the wind wailing outside the windows, filling your mind with all kinds of frightening tales.

Though the summer heat was scorching, it was shady and pleasant in the house. But the main thing was that for the whole summer season I didn't have to wear anything but a cotton top and a short skirt. My arms (the Misses Don't) and my legs (the Misses Do) were bare, so I had lots of chances to talk with them.

I discovered that they grew very quickly in summer, especially over the long summer holidays. When I awakened from my long afternoon nap each day, I could see that my languid, lazy misses Do and Don't, which looked like the long, slithery cold noodles we often ate in summer, had again grown a bit. I didn't like being in the sun because it made me feel dizzy, so whenever I was out, I would try to keep in the shade. As a result, my misses Do and Don't were pale as coral, with a winding tracery of blue veins under their translucent skin that made me think of the rivers marked on the big map of China on the back of our door. Every day after my afternoon nap I would have a long conversation with my misses Don't and Do.

Mother said that when summer came I grew as fast as the nettles in our courtyard.

Thus, with the passage of several summers, I was almost as tall as my mother.

The Wanjiao Primary School I attended had become an integrated ten-year primary and middle school, called the Wanjiao Key School. Entering this middle school, I remained one of Mr. Ti's students.

After the incident with the nude pictures, Mr. Ti remained hostile toward me, finding fault with me and rebuking me at every turn. As I grew taller, Mr. Ti was getting shorter, in my eyes, but his arrogance toward me was becoming more and more pronounced.

I could see that a number of my female classmates who had formed a circle around Mr. Ti were completely infatuated with him. Their eyes glued to him, they sat straight as pencils through his language and literature classes. After class they crowded around him with invented questions. They even imitated the way he tossed his hair, and would use pieces of chalk to mimic the way he flicked his cigarette butts out the window. Because I knew he didn't like me, naturally I kept as far away from him as possible.

It can happen in any class that someone will become the center around whom others gather, usually one of the teachers or one of the student leaders. Students will follow and attempt to ingratiate themselves with such a person for their own security and convenience, so they will not be ignored or rejected. But I don't like this kind of behavior. If I can't say what I want to say, then at the very least, I would rather be isolated and alone.

Once during class break, when a number of the girls were chattering as usual around Mr. Ti, in order to avoid the awkwardness of being marked a stranger or outsider, I bent over my desk, working on an assignment.

I chanced to raise my head to look directly into Mr. Ti's eyes as he stared out over the circle of little chatterboxes who were pinning him in on all sides. His gaze shot through me like an icy, burning jolt of electricity. I immediately looked down, to stare at the misshapen characters in my calligraphy exercise book. With their humped shoulders and drooping heads in their little square frames, they were a mess.

His voice rang out, "Ni Niuniu, you know it's against the rules to do your assignments during class break. Go to my office!"

Out of the corner of my eye I could see his huge, shadowlike frame suddenly towering over my desk.

I didn't dare raise my head to look at him. I knew that my face would flush crimson again if I did, because it already felt like it was on fire. I swallowed hard, trying to suppress the urge to hiccup brought on by the sudden tension.

I had no idea why he always had to shout at me, why he couldn't talk to me calmly and quietly. With my head still down, I looked at my pale, tightly clenched fingers as they methodically smoothed the creases out of a balled-up scrap of paper, then violently tore it to shreds as if it were Ti's hateful skin.

I eventually stayed my busy hands, then followed him reluctantly to his office.

Of course, I missed the next class, as I spent the entire time listening to his scolding. I refused to look at him, defiantly keeping my face turned away from him, while he repeatedly took me by either the shoulder or the arm to make me look at his stern face. When he ran out of things to say for a moment, he would stare at my face or my breasts, his eyes transfixed and blazing with fury, as if I were some sort of monster. I don't know what was different about me that so unsettled him.

He stared at me and also forced me to stare at him. He sat rigidly in a chair in front of the office desk and I stood on his right, near the latticed window. When I cast my eyes down I found that I was looking at the top of his head. I saw that his hair was naturally curly, dark chestnut in color, and pushed into a disheveled mess on the top of his head. Perhaps as a result of his sweating in the hot weather, it was very damp, as if he had just washed it, with a slightly salty smell, and it exuded an irrepressible vitality. A shaft of sunlight slanting in through the window fell upon his head in such a way that this curly mass of hair looked very much like a luxuriant bird's nest in a tropical rain forest.

When he eventually noticed that I was staring at his hair, he got up uneasily. Involuntarily he started running his hands through his hair and nervously shrugging his shoulders, as if the clothes he was wearing were uncomfortable.

From the expression in his eyes, I could tell that my staring at him like this left him bewildered, but, in fact, it was my intention to make him feel that way, in just the same way that his stare bewildered me.

Ti was definitely an unusual man.

Of course, at that time I had no way of knowing that the hostility in an overly proud man often stems from an arrogance of which he himself is unaware. The extent of his vilification of and indignation toward a person can in fact be in direct proportion to his attraction to and love for that person. In the same way, a man's ardor or importuning in the chase frequently stems from a deep-seated hostility, not from love.

There are a great many such contradictory and violent men, who cannot be gotten through to.

Through primary and middle school there was always a deep rift between me and those around me. At that time, our primary school grades and classes had graduated "all in one pot" into middle school. I should have been familiar with every face, but all through school I was like a newcomer. Never able to become part of the group, I had to learn to bear the feelings of rejection by strangers. But the other girls, with their hair done in braids or cut short, joined in the fun without any problems. For them, the school was their playground and their heaven, but not for me.

The pleasure of becoming part of a group is something that seems forever beyond me.

I remember very clearly the wood-grain patterns of the pale brown desks and chairs in the school, the rasping scratch of inferior chalk scraping on the blackboard, and my seat on the left side of the third row of desks from the window; and more than anything else, I remember every single humiliating incident that I endured. But I have very few memories of what went on among the students as a whole or among the little groups they formed.

Only many years later, when I read Maria Kuncewiczowa's *The Stranger*, did I begin to understand that you do not necessarily have to come from a strange place to be a stranger. It is only when you yourself feel like a stranger that you become one. Similarly, when you yourself feel that you are no longer a stranger, you cease to be one. This, of course, is only one way of looking at it. Another way that I look at it is that when you reach the point where you clearly understand everything going on around you, then nothing will be strange to you, and you will no longer feel like a stranger.

Thus, when I was a student, my classmates and I were strangers to one another despite our familiarity.

In fact, this phenomenon of estrangement in familiarity was to accompany me for many years to come.

In the house, in the scorching heat of summer, I usually wore just a long and very loose cotton top that reached past my bottom like a dress, so that much of my body was bare. As a result, I had plenty of opportunity to observe the physical changes I was going through. Stirred by the way Mr. Ti glared at my face and chest, I spent long periods examining myself in the mirror. To my surprise, I discovered that there really were some changes. The first thing I noticed was my breasts, which I felt were suddenly becoming round and full. After watching them for a number of days, I thought it seemed like there were lumps of dough rising in them, making them swell more every day. I also felt a faint pain there that I had never felt before.

This discovery made me feel very strange.

Just at this time Mrs. Ge, the neighbor in front of us, developed breast cancer. Some people said that she had discovered a hard lump when she was washing herself. Others said that her husband had first found it on a wet night when the mugginess and the pervasive sound of the rain wouldn't let him sleep. With nothing else to do, he started gently caressing his wife and eventually felt the irregularity. After that, she was taken to the hospital, given a number of tests, and eventually diagnosed as having cancer.

I heard my mother say that she had already undergone massive surgery, with the doctor cutting out both her breasts as if they were nothing more than persimmons on a tree, as well as most of the associated lymph glands in her armpits. And that in the oppressive summer heat, the intense pain and feeling of suffocation experienced by this woman, with her breasts removed and her bosom, flat as a cutting board, bound in bloody gauze, stemmed from mental as much as from physical pressures.

Mother also said that even though Ge was going through this suffering, she would die fairly soon anyway, because the cancer cells had already spread, though she herself did not know this.

Lying on my little bed in my room that night, I was deeply frightened by the indistinct sounds of Mrs. Ge's moaning coming from the front of the courtyard. The rustling of the trembling leaves, which sounded like it was right beside me, seemed to be responding to her cries. Filled with dread, I put my hand on my chest and started exploring.

And sure enough, I found a hard little lump just under the nipple of one of my newly developing breasts. Moving to the other one, I found a similar little lump. With this, I was overwhelmed with fear.

I tossed and turned all night, unable to sleep, imagining that, like the lady next door, I was about to die.

According to Mother, dying was a total destruction of life. There is no other kind of leaving that carries us as far away; there is no other kind of renunciation that is as final; there is no other kind of forsaking of relatives and friends that is as thoroughgoing. Death is the irreversible termination of life.

Lying on my bed, I felt like I had been forced to don long, brocade burial robes, which try as I might I could not take off. I stared through the window at a night sky that was as clear as a limpid blue pool, while my heart sent blasts of tropical heat and arctic cold racing through my veins. I didn't want to renounce anything; I didn't want to forsake my mother, nor Widow Ho, whom I liked so much. Why would I want to die? Of course, being able to get away from Mr. Ti and my father was the one thing that made death attractive to me. But still, I didn't want to die.

I didn't dare go into my parents' room to wake them, so I lay there alone, a victim of my mind's wild imaginings.

. . . Hearing about death was like listening to some ear-piercing musical instrument, the sound as shrill as glass or as hard as metal. With one click of the latch, the door would be shut, and I would be forsaken by the world around me.

At that moment, my corpse dropped abruptly out of the darkness onto the bed beside me and lay next to me as cold as ice. I rolled away from her and looked at her huge eye sockets in the obscuring darkness, but those despairing eyes refused to look at me. Her lips moved ceaselessly, but she refused to talk to me. She was sneezing repeatedly, but the sound was very strange. Her sneezes sounded like those of our former dog, Sophia Loren.

After a while she got so restless that she got up from the bed and started pacing back and forth in the room, like a shadow moving along a wall. Her intangible image flickered waveringly with no apparent left or right or front or back, seeming to move in a space of infinite dimensions. Whatever she wanted to see, she could see.

After strolling about the room alone for some time, my corpse came up to me. Suddenly she smiled and asked how I was. She said that she didn't like graves, that she liked to wander through cedar forests. For some reason, I wanted to reach out and touch her bosom to see if she was still breathing, but when I did so I discovered that she did not have breasts. I was filled with terror, but at the same time couldn't bring myself to ignore or abandon her. . . .

Only when the sky began to lighten did I finally drop off into a fitful sleep.

In the morning, Mother was astonished when she came in to get me up and saw how pale and distraught I was. She couldn't understand how such a change could take place in just one night.

Putting her hand on my forehead, she asked, "Niuniu, are you sick?"

I said, "Mama, is the lady next door going to die?"

This perplexed Mother even more. She had no idea what had happened.

I said, "Mama, I'm going to die too. I've got cancer too." Then I started to cry, my tears gushing down like a midsummer deluge.

Mother started examining my breasts, and indeed found what seemed to be a hard little lump. I pulled back, saying, "It hurts."

In disbelief, Mother said, "Who ever heard of a child having breast cancer?" But even as she said it she started to look upset.

That morning I didn't go to school as usual, because Mother took me to the hospital.

At that time there were no physiology classes in school, so we were not like today's adolescents who learn about the sexual development and maturity of, and differences between, males and females in their regular sex education classes. Although I was almost the same height as my mother, my awareness and knowledge of sexuality were abysmal. My mother refused to accept that I was growing up and continued to treat me as a child.

In the obstetrics ward at the hospital, most of the women coming and going were expectant mothers with stomachs swollen like drums. One woman about to give birth was stretched out face upward on a high, hard bed. Her bare stomach looked like a huge white drum that had been pumped so full of gas that it was ready to burst. A middle-aged male doctor was pressing here and there all over her stomach as he asked her questions. I was waiting off to one side, terribly afraid that her stomach would split from the pressure of his hand.

When it was my turn, Mother took great pains to explain my condition to him.

He had a very thin face, wide-set eyes, and a very offhand manner. His thin face made his large mouth look huge, which only served to make his disapproval more obvious.

I was too bashful to undo my blouse in front of a strange man, but since he asked me to, I did so. Very casually, but with meticulous thoroughness, he felt my breasts; then he laughed at my mother as if mocking her and said, "There's nothing wrong with her. She's entering puberty."

My mother said, "But she says she has some pain."

A bit impatiently, the doctor said, "You're a woman, surely you've gone through puberty yourself. This is quite normal."

After that, perhaps realizing how he had behaved, he asked in a friendly tone, "How old is she?"

Mother told him.

He replied, "She's noticeably thin for a girl her age. You should make sure she eats more nutritiously."

The examination for my "illness" over, both Mother and I heaved a sigh of relief as we left the antiseptic-laden air of the hospital.

In the little shop at the hospital entrance, in an instant response to the doctor's admonition, Mother bought me a bottle of yogurt and a ham sausage to make sure I ate more nutritiously, as if I would start getting fat the moment I ate them.

I was eating all the way home.

As I walked, images of Widow Ho's pale breasts, like a pair of plump peaches, hovered vaguely in my mind.

Her father let her be born in a "zoo." With her amazing
adaptability she was able to flourish within this "cage"
and learned through experience the pleasures of the
hunter and the hunted. . . . She stands at the paling
with one hand supported on her buttocks and the other
one clamped over her mouth. Her voice is submerged
within her own body.
    She has no history.

When I was fourteen, I finally found among my classmates a companion who enjoyed talking to me. We got
to know each other after Mr. Ti put us together in a
summer vacation study group.

Yi Qiu and I were the only members in our little
group. She had contracted infantile paralysis as a child,
and though one of her legs was normally developed, the
other was skinny as a broomstick and a bit shorter in
length, which made her walk with an exaggerated shuffle, her plump buttocks swinging back and forth, rather
like a supple and nimble-footed orangutan. She was
unusually tall and sturdy, and her rambling gait always
announced her approach before she appeared in the
doorway.

Yi Qiu was three years older than me. When she was
seven, she didn't enter primary school like most chil-

dren her age. Instead, her uncle took her to a small town in the north for medical treatment. There was a folk doctor who was supposed to be able to restore normal movement to the atrophied limbs of his patients by regularly rubbing into them a thick medicinal ointment. But after two years of treatment, Yi Qiu's crippled leg showed no sign of recovery. Eventually her uncle couldn't afford to have the treatments continued, and she returned home.

Although she was only three years older than me, Yi Qiu was already a fully developed, sexually aware young woman. She was amply bosomed, with full breasts that trembled with each step she took. They pushed upward so vigorously under her thin Dacron T-shirt that people around her were afraid that if she should start laughing or breathe heavily, the shirt would burst. In short, there was no way they were to be concealed.

But as fortune kindly had it, Yi Qiu had no desire to conceal her ample breasts. I could tell from the way she behaved that she took pleasure in her own sensuality. It is almost impossible to explain a feeling that I sensed in her—that she, in fact, deliberately took advantage of her sexuality to entice men into illicit and obscure doings. She swayed her hips in a suggestive mince and jutted out her buttocks erotically.

Although Yi Qiu was awkward and clumsy in speech and fat and ungainly, she had a strikingly beautiful face, with the large, gentle eyes of an antelope; long, thick, black eyebrows; and a milky white complexion suffused with a delicate pink glow. Setting off her beautiful oval face, her generous, eager mouth looked as if it were capable of swallowing down everything in this world—the pure and the polluted, the painful and the hideous. Her strong teeth could grind the sweetest song to dust, could crush the cruelest of tragedies to nothing.

It seemed to me that Yi Qiu's face exhibited the nature of her intelligence. At the same time that it exuded a kind of stupidity, it was filled with a contradictory, stubborn brilliance that found its expression through her stupidity.

. . . . . .

I rode my bicycle as if it were a huge bird, alternately along a narrow road lined with trees and between the bare, gray walls of a long corridor. I wasn't the least bit worried about going too fast, because I knew the roads I was rushing down were in my dream; they were not the real roads of an early morning. The beech trees along the narrow road kept me feeling wonderfully cool, refreshed, and content. I noticed that the road looked very familiar. It was long and narrow and sloped consistently to the right. For the moment I couldn't figure out why it felt familiar.

So I kept on going, entering a bare corridor with towering walls rising abruptly on either side. There was not a person to be seen, but the many dull red beams of light staring out from the cracks, like so many watchful eyes that had been set into the walls, filled me with fear. I had a vague feeling that this corridor was also strikingly familiar. It was a bit like the long, narrow passage from Mr. Ti's office to the front gate of our school, but it was somehow different. I was again puzzled because I couldn't account for this feeling of familiarity.

After thinking about this for a long time, I eventually realized that in all these dreams I was riding a bicycle. I thought that when I came to the next street, when I entered the next tree-lined path, the next bare passageway, I would indeed be going down a real road that would take me to Yi Qiu's home in about seventeen minutes so we could start our lessons. . . .

Just at that moment the alarm clock went off.

Opening my eyes, I jumped quickly out of bed and into my clothes, and grabbed something to eat as I dashed off to Yi Qiu's.

In fact, I don't know how to ride a bicycle. I have a negative attitude toward modern, mechanized things.

I was a bit surprised when I entered the courtyard of Yi Qiu's home because it was not at all like ours. In its spacious interior there was a single large structure, its wooden door and window frames in terrible disrepair, its dark red roof tiles askew, and its walls covered with a layer of green mold as a result of the humid wet season. It looked more like an empty workyard with an abandoned warehouse than a place where people actually lived.

On the clothesline, I caught sight of a faded pink dress that belonged to Yi Qiu waving listlessly in the shade, so I knew this was definitely where she lived.

Crossing the dark gray bricks of the courtyard, I brushed past some sunflowers slightly withered by the heat of the scorching sun and stopped before the old house.

Standing there, I called, "Yi Qiu! Yi Qiu!"

A space creaked open in the wall of the old house, and Yi Qiu poked her head out from behind the old wooden door that was weathered almost beyond recognition. She greeted me happily and invited me inside.

When I entered the house, I saw that she was standing solidly and very erect in her bare feet on the uneven concrete floor, combing her hair. She was wearing a very ordinary short skirt with an embroidered hemline and the neckline of her blouse was cut very low. She was plaiting her hair into a long, thick braid, which she then coiled into a bun on the back of her head. Her sensual arms held high above her head in front of the mirror kept moving so that it was impossible for me to see her face in the mirror. From behind I could see that this dated, old-fashioned hairstyle in her hands had a wonderful new freshness and charm.

When I looked around the large old house, I noticed that it contained a separate suite. The door was ajar, and I could see that it was dark inside and apparently had no windows. I could vaguely make out a military cot with some white bedding or clothes piled on it.

The furnishings of the front room were totally dilapidated. There were two identical old-fashioned cabinets so tall that they almost touched the ceiling. In many places across their bottom sections, the finish had peeled away, revealing slivered white wood. It looked like the family once had a cat or a dog that left the scars sharpening its teeth or claws, and the bronze handle rings were mottled with patina.

The concrete floor was swept clean enough, and a wooden chair, a rice pail, a flower stand, and some dirty clothes were scattered here and there around the room. There was not a single picture on the blank, yellowing walls, only some damp mildew stains that looked like blossoming green flowers.

I was surprised to see a battered collection of books that reached halfway to the ceiling in the corner behind me. Nothing there had been cleaned, and the dust lay like a thick blanket over the books. It was obvious that the owner of the house had been a book lover, but I had known for a long time that Yi Qiu had lost her parents very early in life and had been brought up by her uncle. Now, she lived by herself.

I wasn't sure where I should sit, so I turned back to watching Yi Qiu comb her hair in front of the mirror. Looking over her left shoulder, I could see her milk-white reflection in the mirror, her arms raised as if she were running wildly. Though I could not see those eyes that were capable of flashing fire, I was nonetheless aware that the image in the mirror was at the height of its youth and vigor.

After a while, I dragged the single wooden chair, which was very sturdy despite its peeling paint, over to the table. Then I sat down, opened my exercise book, and without much enthusiasm started writing.

When Yi Qiu finished fixing herself up, she swayed over to me on her crippled leg, accompanied by the cool peppermint smell of prickly heat powder. She sat on the bed facing me, the table between us, and then she too opened her exercise book.

The two of us had never really talked to each other during class. Because she was two years older than her classmates, and crippled as well, they all made fun of her, even imitating the strange way she hobbled along. But she never got angry, not even when they made her the brunt of their jokes. She appeared to be even more delighted than they were and couldn't stop laughing.

Though she had opened her exercise book, she hadn't started to do her lessons. Rather, she sat there staring at me.

After a while she said, "Ni Niuniu, how come you never say anything?"

I looked up and laughed bashfully.

I said that I never knew what to say.

Yi Qiu said, "If you lose the use of one leg, then you're a cripple; if you lose the use of both legs, then you become an immortal. You can fly."

I didn't really understand what she was trying to say, so I didn't answer.

"There is a kind of hunger that is the same as time. The longer you suffer it, the more it makes you think," she said.

When I still didn't respond, she continued her conversation with herself. "When we're talking to an ox—a 'niu'—we can't use the language of dogs."

I knew that in class Yi Qiu would often laugh uproariously when there was nothing to laugh at, and would frequently say strange things that didn't seem to make any sense. Because she was crippled and because she was older, nobody took her strange talk seriously or paid much attention to her. And even though I was outside the group, I too, of course, didn't know what it was she was trying to say.

I became aware that she was continuing her one-sided dialogue. "One bird makes music, many birds make noise."

After talking for a long time without any response from me, she got bored and turned to her exercise book.

The room became silent for a time, the only sound the quiet scratching of our pens.

A short while later, unable to bear the isolation, Yi Qiu spoke up again. "Ni Niuniu, to tell the truth, it's wonderful to be like you are. Speech is a tangled mess of leaves; only silence is a tree with a solid heart. Too many leaves impede a tree's growth."

I felt that the things she had to say were truly interesting. How could it be that I hadn't found out earlier how much she liked to talk?

I looked up from my exercise book and smiled at her, saying, "I like listening to you talk."

She laughed joyfully, her breasts shaking in rhythm.

Then lowering her voice she said softly, "Ai, do you know why Teacher Ti put just the two of us together as a study group?"

I thought about it for a while, then said, "No."

She said, "Because you and I have something in common."

I felt surprised. "You and I? Something in common? What?"

Though I really had no idea what Yi Qiu and I might have had in common, I ventured, "The only thing different about us and them is our ages: I'm a year younger than the other students, and you're two years older."

She gave a sigh and said, "We are not accepted by the rest of them. We're not part of the group. We're like two strangers standing on the outside. They ignore us."

At this point, I expressed my disagreement. "But we're not the same," I said. "With me, it's because I don't like them." The implication was that it wasn't because they didn't like me.

My pride was asserting itself.

Yi Qiu said, "Your not liking them is the other face of their not liking you. In the end they're the same thing."

"I don't think they're the same."

But even as I spoke, my conviction was already weakening underneath. In my mind, I went over her words again and again. In the end, I was convinced that she was right and made no more objections.

At that point, I suddenly felt that although Yi Qiu gave the appearance of being a sensual and empty-headed fool, in fact, she was the more intelligent of the two of us.

Only many years later, when I reflected on what it was that Yi Qiu and I shared in common at that time, was I able to see that, in fact, we were fundamentally different in nature.

Yi Qiu had strong survival instincts. She understood that regardless of the individual's reasons for doing so, it was self-destructive for a person to cut all ties with surrounding society, that to do so would lead to the danger of isolation, and that any individual who did so ran the risk of withering away. She knew that she had to make every effort to establish a relationship of mutual interdependence and trust with her classmates if her life was to have a solid and healthy foundation. She truly worked hard to bring this about. But because of her disability, she was rejected by this excessively normal and healthy group. Yi Qiu's isolation from this group, clearly, was not her own doing.

On the other hand, my isolation from it was. My behavior stems from a fear of the world outside the self; or, to put it another way, my disability is a mental one. I have never been willing to adopt an exploratory attitude toward the outside world, which would have created opportunities for me to establish real contacts with my companions within the group. Even today, I still have this kind of fear. I am stubbornly unwilling to recognize this fact: to reduce or abandon my concentration on self and open wide the door to socialization within the larger group would be to open the obvious door to my own survival; but, to look at it another way, would be to open the door to my own extinction.

We didn't complete our assignment for that day. Yi Qiu brought out her pictures of her parents to show me. The old-fashioned black-and-white photographs were ragged around the edges and starting to yellow with age. Yi Qiu told me lots of things about her life. Of course, she had heard these things from her uncle.

Yi Qiu's father had been the headmaster of a primary school. He was a big, tall, good man who cut an imposing figure. He was always extremely painstaking, easygoing, thoughtful, and modest and respectful in dealing with people in his school; but underneath, he was very easily upset by the people around him, was cynical and anxiety-ridden, and had no more courage than a mouse. Her mother, a member of a drama troupe, was spirited, cheerful, and attractive, with an aura of sexuality about her. Although she was not well educated and lacked a proper upbringing, she exuded a surface jauntiness and passion that fueled men's fantasies and turned them on, so in the eyes of the local males she was the number one "star," the woman they would fight over. Yi Qiu's father, after chasing her for eight years, finally won her over with his scholarship and his graciousness. They were married in early 1964 and the following year gave birth to little Yi Qiu, who inherited her mother's good looks and her father's submissiveness.

But the times were against them, and the idyllic scene soon ended. In 1968, when little Yi Qiu was three years old, her anxious father could no longer bear the vicious infighting of the political campaign that was going on in the country at that time. He had been ordered to sleep between two corpses, one of them one of his female teachers who had been beaten to death by the Red Guards, the other, the Dean of Instruction of his school, who had "jumped to his death for fear of facing his crime." He was ordered to not only lie between the two corpses but also continuously stroke them so that he could respond to questioning the next day "with a cleansed mind." The night of mental torment cracked his nerves. At the first hint of dawn the next morning, when the guard had dropped off to sleep for a moment, he fled from the cowshed where he was kept and went home. On that cold January morning, before the sun had risen, his depressed and weak spirit suddenly broke and he sank into a deep manic depression, which set the stage for the final bitter scene of the family's extinction.

When tiny Yi Qiu was dragged from the river by a passerby, she was very close to death. She had been stabbed several times with a pair of scissors, and it was easy to re-create the scene. Taking a pair of scissors with him, her father had carried her in his arms to the river. When she saw the demonic expression that had taken over his face, she beseeched him again and again, "Papa, I'll be a good girl, I won't bother you." After he had stabbed his baby daughter several times, he could still hear her pleading feebly, "Papa, I'll be a good girl," and unable to continue, he dropped her in the river.

The bodies of Yi Qiu's father and mother were found together in a grove of barren, bent-over trees on the outskirts of the city. They were hanging separately from two adjacent trees.

One summer a number of years earlier, Yi Qiu's father had gone to this place with a number of his colleagues for a weekend to escape the heat. At that time, the entire grove was filled with countless pink peach blossoms—a virtual peach garden paradise, like a totally romantic stage set in the midst of the gray city suburbs. In the center of the grove, completely surrounded by peach trees, was a clump of small birches, all canted over at an angle of about 45 degrees. Those slanted birches must have made a deep impression on Yi Qiu's father.

The bodies were discovered early in the morning by a woman doing calisthenics. She said that she was doing waist bends in an area facing and a little bit higher than Yi Qiu's parents' leaning birches. At first she only vaguely noticed what appeared to be a man standing in front of a bare tree, his cap pulled down very low, almost completely covering his face. It puzzled her that anyone would stand there so long without moving on such a cold day. Then she noticed a second person, apparently a woman, with her long hair around her shoulders, standing before another tree close by. She was convinced that it was a pair of lovers meeting secretly. She continued exercising, but her attention had shifted, and she kept an eye on the man and woman. At first, she thought it a little strange that they didn't move, but when they had been rigidly motionless for about twenty minutes, she was sure there must be something amiss. Lovers just wouldn't behave like that. She stopped exercising and started moving closer for a better look, until she could see that they were not standing, they were hanging about a foot above the ground. She gave out a stunned scream. . . .

As I listened to Yi Qiu talking about her life, I did everything I could to suppress my fear and discomfort. We agreed to meet again the next day.

When I was leaving, she pressed close to my ear and whispered that she had a "boyfriend," and enjoined me not to tell anyone else. From the way she said this I could more or less imagine what kind of secrets were involved. I was filled with the kind of admiration for Yi Qiu, with her unique life experience, that a young girl feels for an older girl.

For women, the inner room is referred to in a different way; it has a different name. It is a wound, it seems, that comes along with birth, that others are not allowed to touch, that secrets itself in shadow as deep as the obscure darkness within the womb that quickens the heartbeat of men. Our maturation process involves our gradual acquiescence to and our seeking for and ultimate acceptance of "entry." During the process of seeking, our girlhood ends and we enter womanhood.

One morning shortly after eight, when I arrived at Yi Qiu's place as usual, I had to go to the toilet because I had had a bowl of thin gruel and a glass of milk before I left home.

Yi Qiu was putting on a blouse that was so tight she could hardly do up the buttons. Her plump breasts threatening to tumble out, she used a bare foot to point to the westernmost corner of the big room. "Nnn! There!" she said.

Only then did I notice a white door curtain hanging against the wall, but no doorway.

"Where?" I said.

She waved me over. "I'll show you."

I followed her, her bare feet padding across the rough but clean floor like a pair of big fat bugs.

Lightly lifting the curtain with one hand, she gestured, "Here. Most of the time I don't use the communal toilet. I go here."

I was totally surprised to find that this big square box of a house, in fact, had a "sleeve" attached to it. There was a long, rectangular space behind the curtain, which really did stretch out like the sleeve of a sweater. There was a triangular steel stand that had been painted blue, with a washbasin on it. A pair of underpants, a bra, a pair of stockings, and a handkerchief were hung to dry on a crooked length of wire that ran at an angle from one corner of the ceiling to a screw above the doorway. Like a miniature airplane, a big mosquito with transparent wings was perched securely on the wire, its stomach distended with blood it had probably sucked from Yi Qiu. A simple toilet that looked like a wooden stool stood in the center of the room, its bowl speckled with rust.

Yi Qiu said, "Xi Dawang fixed it up for me. You can't flush it like the ones in apartment buildings, but you can rinse it out with the water from the washbasin. It's connected to the sewer."

"Xi Dawang?" I asked. "Who's Xi Dawang?"

Yi Qiu smiled. "My cousin." She started tidying her hair as if the person she mentioned was about to appear in front of her. "Actually, he's my boyfriend."

I went into the toilet and dropped the curtain. The seat was wet and not very clean, so I sort of squatted rather than sitting right down. When I was finished, I put my toilet paper in a big bag for waste paper beside the toilet. As I stood up, I suddenly caught sight of a blood-soaked wad amid the waste paper in the bag. Its strident red color seized my eyes. It was like a budding flower that had burst into blossom hidden among a heap of white paper. My heart pounded wildly for a moment.

I had seen older women doing this sort of thing in public toilets. They were very open about changing the paper, making no effort to hide what they were doing. It seemed it was something that everyone did; there was no need to be secretive about it. Nonetheless, I would always turn away in embarrassment, unable to watch. But even though I didn't look directly, I could still see them dropping the red wads of paper into the filthy pit. I thought it was very strange, but that was all, because it was something that concerned adults.

When I saw that my companion Yi Qiu also had this problem, I was amazed. Only then did I begin to realize that this was going to happen to me too, and I couldn't help feeling confused.

When I came out of the "bathroom," I pretended nothing had happened and without a word, I opened my exercise book.

After a while, Yi Qiu said she had to go to the toilet, and disappeared into the "sleeve."

Unable to suppress my curiosity, I raised my head from my book and looked at the curtain.

Through a gap at the curled edge of the curtain, I could just make out Yi Qiu sitting on the toilet. She had something in her hand that she was rubbing herself with. I could see that it was red in color. My heart started to pound wildly all over again, so I dropped my head and forced myself to calm down.

Even today, I still believe that Yi Qiu was the catalyst that initiated my passage into womanhood, because when I got out of bed the morning after I had witnessed this, I discovered a small patch of blood, like a living crimson plum blossom, among the printed green flowers on my sheets.

I was fourteen that year.

When Yi Qiu opened the curtain and came out of the "sleeve," I had my head down and was practicing my written characters with grim deliberation. They were square and solid as bricks.

She said, "How strange. You're so thin and frail, but your characters are so sturdy and solid."

I said, "What's strange about that? My mama says that looking at a person's writing is like looking into her heart."

"Heart?" Yi Qiu thought about it, but she couldn't see the connection between written characters and the heart, and said, "Your mama's an intellectual. Intellectuals are a pain, they want to connect everything to the 'heart.'"

"But it makes sense," I answered.

"What sense? I don't think your heart is anywhere near as rigid as your characters." She opened her own exercise book and said, "Look at how round and soft my characters are. According to your mother's theory, I should bawl when I look at a falling leaf. In fact, I never cry. What is there that's worth crying about?"

Because of the weird business with the red wad of paper that had just happened, I was confused and illogical and couldn't explain myself clearly.

I said, "She doesn't mean your heart, she means your temperament; well, not really your temperament, it's. . . . Anyway, Mama's always correcting my characters. She says people who write characters like mine will get more and more stubborn, more unreasonable . . . and . . . and . . ."

Just then someone outside shouted, "Yi Qiu!"

We immediately fell quiet, straining to hear who was there.

"Yi Qiu!" Again a shout. There was definitely someone outside, but I had never met anyone at her house before.

I watched with great curiosity as she went to the door.

A tall male came into the room, with black, flashing almond eyes, a lowering brow, and a narrow forehead. He was sturdy as a gatepost and gave the appearance of having an endless store of vitality.

When he saw that there was a strange girl in the room, he smiled stiffly and seemed a bit too reserved, but he looked very sweet.

Yi Qiu introduced him: "This is Xi Dawang. I told you about him." Then she pointed at me and said to him, "This is my new friend, Ni Niuniu."

He came over to me, holding out a big, raw hand. "Hello," he said. "Yi Qiu has told me about you."

I shyly offered him my hand. His palm was oily and damp with sweat.

He and Yi Qiu sat close to each other on the bed, across the table from me. Yi Qiu and I had put our homework aside, and the three of us were sitting a bit awkwardly around the table as if we were having a chat, but not knowing what to say.

He picked up my exercise book and bumbled out, "Your calligraphy is very beautiful."

In those hands of his, which had probably been carrying bricks for many years, my exercise book looked very thin and fragile. He was turning the pages with great care, one by one, as if it were not an exercise book at all but a collection of expensive silks.

"My calligraphy isn't the least bit beautiful," I said.

Without responding to my comment, he fished some tomatoes from his rather worn military haversack, and wiping them with his hands, said, "Have one, please."

Yi Qiu passed one to me immediately.

All three of us started to eat, and with the tomatoes suddenly easing the tension among us, we started to chat.

From Xi Dawang's conversation I gathered that he had been on regular service in the air force as ground crew in a small northern city, working mostly as a lineman, a ditch digger, and in a factory manufacturing oxygen. Later on, he left the force because he had developed a brain disease.

I asked what kind of disease can affect the brain.

Neither of them answered.

When I finished my tomato, I got up to go to the "sleeve" to wash my hands. I noticed that Xi Dawang was wiping the red juice off his hands on his trouser legs. Yi Qiu was going to go with me to wash her hands, but when I got up she said, "You go first. You go."

As I was washing my hands, I watched them through the gap at the edge of the curtain.

Like bolts of lightning, they were into each other's arms. Xi Dawang madly clasped Yi Qiu to him, with his thick, strong arms enclosing her shoulders, like a prisoner who had not eaten the tender breast of a fat chicken for many years and now suddenly had before him a huge portion. Yi Qiu eagerly pressed herself against him, moving her breasts against his rib cage like plump hands passionately brushing the strings of a harp.

I dragged out my washing as long as I could, then went back to my chair and opened up my exercise book as if I hadn't seen a thing.

By this time, they were sitting separate again.

For a while nobody said anything.

To lighten things up, Xi Dawang started to tell us that one evening at dusk, when he was in the air force, he had sat down for a rest on a mountain slope. Leaning against a large rock, he was idly picking some of the brilliant yellow wild blossoms of the "gold watch" flower when he noticed an owl not very far away from him devouring a marmot it had caught. Putting down the flowers, he hid himself and watched quietly. Unlike other birds, the owl has its eyes on the front, not the sides, of its head, with the feathers around them radiating outward in a circle so that it appears to have a face, though, in fact, this is not so. Eventually the owl saw him; then after they stared at each other for a moment, it disappeared as silently as a shadow. It frightened him deeply to discover that an owl can fly silently, without a whisper of sound.

Xi Dawang said that the next day he fell ill. He firmly believed that his sickness was brought on by his staring into the owl's eyes.

"When you're in the mountains," Xi Dawang said, "you live among unfettered forces, and communicate with the silent stones though they have no way to speak."

When he loosened up and started to talk like this, I discovered that there was indeed something about him that was not quite right.

His eyes were focused straight ahead, but he wasn't looking at anyone. It seemed as if he were holding a very urgent conversation with some little person inside his head. I also saw that his hand was continuously stroking Yi Qiu's waist, and that her waist was a substitute for whatever it was that was in his mind. A definite nervous twitch pulled at the corner of his mouth, as if his fingers were at that moment discovering some as yet unperfected pleasure at Yi Qiu's waist, as if his desire for this unspoken place was nerve ending by nerve ending being ignited—trapping him in the throes of sexual hunger.

Yi Qiu responded to his fingers with an unbroken thread of silvery laughter, a laughter that in fact came from that same distant and secret place, that dim, obscure place from which desire emanates. It was "that place," grinning like an open mouth, that was laughing.

I kept writing in my exercise book but couldn't stop listening to them.

Then Yi Qiu told me that she and Xi Dawang were going to the other room to discuss something personal.

The two of them got up and went into the inner room.

I was left alone in the outer room, separated from them by a wall. I suddenly felt isolated and left out of life. That inner room had an indefinable attraction that so seduced my power of concentration that it was impossible for me to focus on my lesson. But what was going on in there was really beyond the scope of my imagination, because there was little in my own personal feelings or experience that had any connection with it. That area of experience for me was essentially blank. But at this moment it was as if that room were at the center of a powerful magnetic field that had captured me in an unidentifiable tension from which there was no relief.

Finally, I could no longer control my curiosity or my "thirst for knowledge," and I crept silently over to the door of the inner room.

I listened very carefully for a while, but they weren't talking. All I could hear was a faint sound of movement.

The door to the inner room was of traditional design. Vertical and horizontal wooden slats divided the top half of the door into square panes, which were covered with a layer of white window paper that let through a yellowish light. The paper was covered with water stains, and there were many large and small holes poked in it. Because it was darker in the inner room, the holes looked like black eyes watching me.

A little afraid, I put my eye against one of the holes and peered in.

The first thing I saw was a painting on the wall of what appeared to be a broken bathtub, with blood-red water pouring out through a crack. There was no one in the tub, but there was a frightened-looking cat standing beside the gush of red water.

When I looked down I saw a clutter of old furniture scattered about the room, and finally I saw the military camp cot and the two of them tangled together on it, moving regularly like a pair of sleepwalkers, not without some sense of pattern, but rather as if, without conscious effort, they were moving in response to each other. They had taken off all their clothes, and Yi Qiu lay with her arms and legs spread out, her full, round breasts jutting firmly upward. Her eyes partly closed and her head turned toward the door, she looked worn out, like a different person altogether. With Xi Dawang sitting astride her hips as if he were riding a horse, she moaned softly again and again. His sturdy legs were doubled under him, gripping her on both sides, and the muscles of his buttocks were tightly contracted. With both eyes tightly closed and his face turned upward in an attitude of abandon, he strained his entire body jerkily toward the ceiling, while one hand worked feverishly between his thighs and his breathing became increasingly labored. Suddenly a white spurt erupted from his hand, and, like a toppled mountain peak, he collapsed with a great groan on top of Yi Qiu. . . .

Shaking with fear outside that door, I experienced two different feelings: at first, every pore of my skin opened and dilated and I started to breathe heavily. My mouth hung open like the maw of a dead fish, and my entire body seemed to have increased in size, as if I had been smoking opium. The door in front of me also increased in height and breadth, and I pressed even closer to the window. Then I was overcome with a violent nausea and felt a sudden urge to throw up. . . .

It has been said that it is only before and after the occurrence of the real and fleeting phenomena of life that we experience them. The actual events that we think we perceive are only dreamlike fabrications invented by our own bodies.

Only now, more than ten years later, when I recall from among those already faded and dim past events that disturbing scene I covertly witnessed (perhaps only thought I witnessed) from outside the door to Yi Qiu's inner room, do I finally understand that the scene as I perceived it was of my own making, a product of my imagination at that moment.

The creative imagination is the mother of all memories.

My attention to the accurate depiction of the fragmented memories of past events is not motivated by a passion for personal reminiscing, nor am I fanatically nostalgic. The reason my focus persistently returns to the bits and pieces of the past is that they are not dead pages from history; they are living links that connect me to my ever-unfolding present. . . .

*Through the open eyes of the dead, all that we can see is
what has become of their bodies, but their spirits have
not died. When the miasma of death from the netherworld in a twinkling suddenly reclaims their bodies,
these "fragmented" people at last become aware that
their lives were never lived as authentically or as passionately as they thought, and that they never understood this world in the way that they thought they did.*

The wind is the despot of Beijing's North China winters.
At one moment, its fierce, leaping blasts tear and pull at
the black mantle of bare earth; at the next it becomes
gentle under a warming sun, and the earth beneath
one's feet is transformed into an endless river of golden
light. Such extreme weather changes make the people
who live through them moody and temperamental.

Winter is an endless season.

One winter day, the heavily falling snow soon above
my ankles, I spent the entire afternoon building a snowman in our courtyard. For her eyes, I stole two lumps of
coal from under the eaves of Mrs. Ge's house in the
courtyard in front of us—the lady who had breast cancer. From our own kitchen I took some cabbage leaves
for her hair, and I made an army cap for her out of a
piece of cardboard. I made her look like a fearless

woman soldier waving an arm in the empty, barren courtyard. Her blank eyes were open wide, as if she were pursuing some unseen or simply nonexistent enemy.

I chose a name for her—Ni Niuniu, same as myself.

That night after dinner, I was totally tired out.

When I went to my room and started writing in my diary, I couldn't stop yawning. The words in my diary, strung together like my yawns, were all awry and uneven, as illegible as the magic scribblings of a ghost. My head felt heavier and heavier, and all my bones seemed to have been pulled from my body so that I slumped in my chair.

. . . . . .

At that moment my mother's image wavered into view before me. What was odd was that she hadn't called to me as she entered my room like she usually did, but had waited until she was beside me to call me quietly and mysteriously. Even more strange was the anachronistic sequence of actions: she was already beside me when I heard her knock at the door. But the knock was definitely my mother's. She tapped the door with her middle and index fingers, as if she were plucking a lute, not two or three times, but four times, in a very distinctive way. So that knock could not have been anyone else's.

Frightened, I shrank back.

Mother said, "Niuniu, I want you to come with me to the Ges' courtyard. Mrs. Ge has died, but there's nothing to be afraid of."

I said, "Why would I be afraid? Dead people's yards are safer than living people's."

Then I flew next door to see.

The courtyard had become a brightly lit funeral scene. Green bristlegrass, lilies, "never-die" portulaca, and sunflowers vied in the brilliance of their reds and golds, filling the space with such a rioting blaze of color that everything in the yard shimmered with glowing hues. The scene was dominated by a huge black wooden coffin so high that it blotted out half the wall of the house behind it. When I got closer, I saw that it was the propped-open lid that made it look so high.

One of the men in the Ge family was standing stiffly beside it, holding a small book in his hand. He raised his head to look around at the crowd of people, then look into the coffin again, and finally wrote something in the little book, showing absolutely no sign of grief.

When I came up to the coffin and looked in, I saw a female figure buried in a welter of brightly colored brocade. Her head, covered with a piece of white cloth, was resting on a pretty lotus-pink pillow with a floral border. Looking at her, I was very upset, but I wasn't really frightened.

Then I noticed that the body in the coffin appeared to be breathing. Under the white cloth covering her face, just below where the nose would be, there was a mouth-shaped oval indentation that was rising and falling rhythmically. I jumped back, scared out of my wits.

At that point, the lady in the coffin extended a long, emaciated arm and grasped my hand. I was astonished to find that her hand was warm. Then with her other hand she lifted a corner of the white cloth covering her face to reveal an eye, or, to be more precise, half an eye.

She smiled at me and very softly and weakly said, "Don't be afraid."

I said, "You haven't died yet?"

She said, "No, I haven't died yet. I'm conducting an experiment."

"Experiment?"

"I'm not too inclined to believe in people, including my husband. Look at him. All he's doing is making a list of the funeral gifts. He doesn't look the least bit grief-stricken; on the contrary, he actually looks quite happy. No doubt he's happy because he's gained a new chance."

"What kind of chance could your death give him?"

"The chance to choose a new, young bride."

I said, "He doesn't know you haven't died?"

She said, "No, he doesn't know. It's a secret. Only you and I know, and you mustn't tell anyone else. All I wanted was to know, while I was still alive, who was saddened by my death and who was happy, who would truly grieve for me and whose tears were false, and whose silence was truly out of grief."

She paused to take a breath, then continued, "One person's place in another person's heart is revealed by how much of that person's heart consists of tears. All I want to do is measure the amount and quality of the tears people shed over my death."

I heaved a long sigh. "Anyway, I'm glad you're not dead. I'll stay with you. I'm not afraid."

She continued her one-sided conversation. "Everywhere you go in this world there is filth and deception. I can't stop worrying about where my coffin will be buried. Look at this eulogy. It says that during a certain incident in the struggle to cleanse class ranks in a certain year, I took a firm position, identifying what was correct, what incorrect, and that I gave the enemy no quarter, thus revealing my fearless spirit. You probably think that this was meant to praise me. Actually, it slanders me, since that was a particularly ruthless and bloody incident."

"Really? Why would they want to do that?" I asked uncertainly.

"Because everyone has ten mouths, and the only one of them that's sincere is the one that's silent in sleep." The more she talked, the feebler her breathing became. Every word that she spoke floated through the air of the crowded, chaotic courtyard like a thready note from a long-silent ancient lute.

"When you die, I promise I won't slander you," I said.

"Oh well, my real burial place will always be in my own heart," she said.

She smiled at me for a moment, then added, "Don't worry about any of this. When you're my age, everything will be perfectly clear. What do you think of my funeral gown? Isn't it lovely?"

She let go my hand and began removing the colorful material covering her and the fragrant blossoms that filled the coffin so that I could see her funeral gown, and finally she lifted the white cloth from her face.

Only at this point did I see that the body in the coffin was not Mrs. Ge at all. Through the fresh blossoms and pear branches, the woman I saw emerge from under the burial clothes was a different person altogether. The woman I had been staring at all this time was the Widow Ho, who was now gazing wearily heavenward.

When I realized I was looking at Widow Ho, I was at first frightened, but then, stricken with grief, I started to cry, fiercely and silently. Standing alone beside the coffin, I shed my inconsolable tears, but I didn't want anyone in the courtyard to know. It was as if Ho and I cherished a special secret.

. . . . . .

I was awakened by my own sobbing to find that I was lying with my face in my exercise book, its pages wet with my tears.

Just at that point, the wind outside my window began to howl as if it had gone mad, with such intensity that it seemed it would blow itself out. Sitting up straight, I tried to concentrate, but my mind was too confused. I could make no sense of what had just happened. In the end, I was so unsettled that I ran over to see Widow Ho.

There was no moon and it was very dark out, with only the dim light reflected from the snow on the ground. I made a wild dash from our courtyard through the raging blizzard to pound on her door.

When she opened the door, she looked as alert and cautious as a cat, but when she saw that it was me, she gave a sigh of relief and suddenly looked tired and sleepy. She lay down on her bed again, looking rather ill.

"What's wrong, Niuniu?" she asked me in a husky, tired voice, as she was lying down. It was as if the words came only with great effort, not from her lips but from somewhere deep within her body, because her lips did not seem to have moved at all.

"I just came to see if you were okay."

"Thank you, Niuniu, I'm fine."

Standing in the doorway, I was looking at her smooth, milk-white skin. She was wearing a long, white nightgown that was far too big for her thin frame. Lying there on her big, soft, fluffy bed, she looked like a pure white lily, as peaceful as still water, although she had suffered her share of the endless uncertainties of life.

I have always had a special kind of feeling about her. She was my neighbor and I was always able to catch a glimpse of her coming and going. She was a kind of light in my otherwise bland inner life. In her I had found a warm and close friend, a special kind of woman who could take the place of my mother. When she was near me, even if we were silent, a fragrant warm feeling of security and gentleness enclosed me. This feeling was a kind of intangible glow that bathed or illumined my skin. And unlike the energy of remote control devices that can be blocked by intervening objects, it was of such strength that nothing could stay it.

I think it is principally bonds like this that can develop between people that distinguish us from stones.

When I saw that there was nothing wrong, and how lovely she looked lying there on her bed, I went back home reassured and was soon asleep.

Early the next morning, I knew that I was sick when I awoke with the cold shivers and a terrible headache. I was definitely running a fever. Although my entire body was hot and my pajamas were soaked through with sweat, I felt like an open refrigerator spilling out its icy air.

Lying on my bed, I made an effort to call my mother, but my voice sounded like a bunch of fluttering feathers and my ears started to ring. I called a number of times, but for some reason the entire house remained silent, and there was no sign of my mother. I didn't have the strength to call anymore, so all I could do was wait.

It was only after I stopped calling that I heard a commotion in the courtyard outside. A confused scuffling of feet seemed to come from the courtyard facing ours. I was able to make out a few words, like "died" and "police."

Just then, my mother strode into my room in great agitation, saying, "Niuniu, Mrs. Ge has been murdered. Whatever you do, don't leave the house."

When she came close and saw that I was burning with a fever as fierce as glowing coals and curled up in a ball shivering uncontrollably, she cried out, "Oh my god!"

My father was busy with meetings in another province and hadn't been home for many days. This morning, my mother, alone and suddenly faced with crises both at home and at the neighbor's, couldn't avoid feeling flustered.

She made me open my mouth, and in the light from the window she checked my throat. "Look at that," she said, "your throat is swollen almost shut!"

She nattered on about a grown-up girl like me making a snowman as if I were still a child, while she was looking in the closet for our thickest padded cotton coat to bundle me up in. She was convinced that my fever was the result of my spending too much time playing in the snow.

I rode to the hospital on the back of Mother's bicycle. As we passed by the Ges' courtyard, I saw many people milling around their door with strange expressions on their faces, their chatter spilling out on the snow. Like a layer of deep shadow, this atmosphere wiped away the lifeless emptiness of winter in the courtyard. The police were also there, like so many green trees on little wheels. With little to say and showing no signs of being the least bit touched, they shunted about the snow-covered courtyard telling people to move, to stand back. From the irritation on their faces, I could see that they detested disorder. They were trying to provide a framework of stability for the disquieted crowd, to bring some order to the chaotic courtyard.

From childhood I have always suffered from a kind of unaccountable inner chaos, as if the cells within my body could exist only under a frightening state of total anarchy. So I have always instinctively stayed clear of the kind of order represented by the police. Now, when I saw that the police had arrived, my entire body suddenly became tense.

I heard some of the neighbors secretively discussing how Mr. Ge had fled without leaving a trace after strangling his wife with his belt.

These frightening details stabbed into my brain to explode like great rolls of thunder. I felt dizzy and had to gasp for breath. My fear turned the short path through their front courtyard that I was so familiar with into a black and endless corridor.

It seemed that the air was filled with the smell of rotting flesh, and the withered and bare wisteria in their courtyard suddenly reminded me of my dream.

I began to shake uncontrollably.

When we got home after my injection and picking up my medicine, Mother had to leave for work immediately, so she asked the Widow Ho to come over and look after me.

Looking out the window from my bed, I could see that it was a heavily overcast day. Last night's raging storm had blown itself into a gentle breeze that stirred the bare branches of the date tree so that their shadows flickered against the rice-paper panes in my window. My fever had begun to drop and I felt much better. The hospital procedures in the morning had taken almost two hours, and I was exhausted. Lying on my bed looking out my open window at the low-hanging winter clouds, now shot with the orange glow of the sun, now leaden gray, I fell asleep thinking about the frightening affair with the Ge family in the neighboring courtyard, and didn't wake up until Widow Ho called me at noon.

Feeling my forehead first, then pressing her own against mine to double-check my temperature, she said, "Much better, but you still have a little fever. Sit up and have something to eat. I've made you some shredded mustard root and egg-drop soup with black pepper and sesame oil. Have some while it's hot. It'll make you sweat and drive your fever out."

I said, "I'm not hungry. You eat it."

She said, "Niuniu, be a good girl. Sit up."

As she spoke, she pulled back my quilt and bent over to help me up. Resisting her, I said, "I feel sick, I'm sore all over. I don't want to eat."

By this time, I was almost as tall as she was, and because she had suffered from diabetes for many years and could eat no more than two and a half ounces of grain a day, she was thin and not very strong. If I just lay there not wanting to get up, she couldn't possibly move me.

I said, "You eat. I'll watch you."

"Ai!" she sighed. "I'm not going to eat by myself."

She sat down on the edge of my bed and tucked my quilt in around me again, saying, "You're like a candle. After burning with fever for just one night, you're almost melted away."

Like a sleepy cat sitting on the edge of my quilt, she twisted around so that she could look at me. The whites of her eyes were the limpid pale blue of lake water, and an anxious loneliness lurked in her dark pupils. The loveliness of her eyes was like a virus that made me drug dependent. It was as if some hidden desire flowing in her blood was projected through her eyes.

I pulled up my knees so she could make herself comfy leaning against my legs. Though my legs were soft and weak, the moment she touched them they felt as powerful as wound-up springs, and I rooted them firmly in the bedding so that she could lean against me.

"Well then, I'll just sit here so we can have a chat." She shifted around to get more comfortable, and leaning against my legs, she wrapped an arm around my knees.

I said, "It must hurt when you give yourself injections."

She said, "No. All you have to do is pretend it's nothing and relax. Then you hardly feel a thing. The more tense you are, the more it hurts."

I said, "The nurse who gave me my injection this morning must have been angry at someone, and she took it out on me. You would have thought she was giving an elephant an injection." I pulled my panties down below my hips. It was all hard where she had stuck in the needle and was already turning blue. "Look."

She winced when she saw it, and said, "Don't go to the hospital for the rest of your shots. I'll do them for you. You won't feel a thing."

I said, "You know how to inject penicillin too?"

"They're all the same." While she was talking, she pressed the swelling with her fingers, rubbing it very lightly.

Her fingers were very cool and limber as snakes, as if they had no bones. I could see her long, curved neck above me and the gentle swell of her breasts inside her sweater as she leaned over, pressing her thin body against me. Her body curved in an arc that was as fluid as a beautiful melody. Her face was a bit too pale, but the skin of her entire body bespoke a tender readiness to rush to me at a moment's notice, to watch over me, to protect me, and to drive away any pain or misfortune that threatened me.

All of this made me feel totally at ease, especially her touching me, allowing my senses to run along vague and unexpected paths. I thought of that time many years ago when she wanted me to lie next to her and kiss her breasts, which glistened like the polished jade stones on her pillow, and of the doleful tears that slowly gathered to roll across her cheek and fall. Then, for some reason, an image of the two naked bodies entwined on the military cot in Yi Qiu's inner room flashed briefly through my mind.

Switching my attention, I looked at the door to my room, and I noticed that the December light slanting in through the window was much brighter than it had been in the morning. I could see the dust motes floating in the light.

Purposely switching my train of thought, I asked, "Did Mrs. Ge really die?"

Ho replied, "Yes. Just after six in the morning a man from their courtyard who works an early shift noticed that their front door was wide open. He called a couple of times but there was no reply, so he stuck his head in the door. He thought something must be amiss when he discovered that the bed was unmade and there was nobody home. He stood outside a while, uncertain what to do. He suspected there might have been a burglary, and he was afraid to go into the house. So he called some other people, and the longer they shuffled around outside, the more convinced they became that something was wrong. Mrs. Ge was bedridden. How could it be that her bed was empty? If she had gone to the hospital, surely they would have locked the door? So everyone was certain that something untoward had happened."

"Weren't any of the women home?"

"After a while, some people ventured inside for a look. Only after a thorough search did they discover her, tied up and pushed face down under the bed with a towel jammed in her mouth. Frightened, they rushed from the house and called the police."

"Was she really dead?"

"The police came right away, and they didn't take her away until eleven. She was dead."

"Was it her husband who killed her?"

"It's hard to say what things were like in that family. They spent half their lives quarreling. Stuck together under one roof, these two perfectly normal people gradually became enemies. The bed was about the only place they acted in harmony. Their neighbors all said that they used to spend their life in the bedroom making love at the same time they were making war, but that after Mrs. Ge became ill, the only stage where they had ever acted together in harmony ceased to exist. At last this war without winners is over. It takes more than one cold day to make three feet of ice." Ho sighed and continued, "Although marriage can sometimes be an inexhaustible source of life, it can sometimes also be an inexhaustible source of bitterness. It can be creative, but it can also be destructive."

I thought of my own parents and my mood immediately darkened. "My mama and papa don't fight, but . . ."

"Their kind of 'cold war' can burn just as badly. Have you heard of Spinoza's leaves?" said Ho.

I had long known that Ho liked books. I was very excited the first time I saw those two long, black boxes filled with foreign books under her big bed. Once, probably during the summer holiday at the end of my first year in middle school, when I told her I would like to look at her books, she chose two novels from one of the boxes. I remember their titles: one was *The Adventures of Robinson Crusoe*, the other, *The Gadfly*. She told me I could read all of them if I wanted to. But after that, because I was busy with tests and assignments, I didn't borrow any more books from her. I knew, however, that she had read the lot of them.

"Spinoza?" I shook my head indicating I hadn't.

"No two leaves are exactly alike. Just look at the families in our courtyard."

After a moment, I said, "Why must we always get married? Men are too undependable."

Ho said, "Too true."

Then she fell silent, probably thinking about her own life.

After a long silence, she spoke again. "Sometimes marriage seems like some kind of hoax. Only the walls, the windows, and the furniture are real, can be counted on. Human beings are the least dependable of all creatures. The blossoms of marriage are plastic ones. They look like the real thing, and they may never fade and die, but they are nonetheless false."

I said, "I don't want you to look for a new husband. Please. My mama has my papa, but the only thing he's good for is causing trouble." Then I lowered my voice and continued, "A few days ago I found an old book about men and women in my father's bookcase. The book said that women were a rampant noxious weed, that they were dangerous and crude predatory beasts. It must have been written by a man. I'm sure that my papa has read many books of that sort. But, in fact, I think it is the men who behave that way."

Ho started to laugh, saying, "But Niuniu, you melonhead, if it wasn't for your father, you wouldn't be here."

"But you, you don't have any children. And I'm not going to have any when I grow up," I said.

"But what about when I'm old?" she asked.

"I'll take care of you. I'll always be good to you. Really."

Ho looked at me quickly, her eyes shining. She put her arms around me, quilt and all, and hugged me fiercely, then she bent down and kissed my face. "Just like I'm taking care of you now?"

I nodded.

"But will you be able to carry me on your back?"

"When I'm better I'll try. I'm sure I can. You're so thin."

This seemed to please her, and she bent down and hugged me tightly again, without uttering a word.

Even though they were outside the quilt, I could feel her thin arms as she slid them around my waist and hugged me as desperately as if she were holding her own future. I heard her breath quicken slightly as she repeated softly, "Niuniu, Niuniu." Through her sobs and her unsteady voice I could feel the complex tangle of feelings of injustice, grief, loneliness, and hope that she was caught in.

In my mind, Ho always had a very powerful aura of the tragic heroine about her. This stemmed in part from her delicate, natural loveliness, and in part from a very strong self-destructive urge that had always burned within her, an air of decadence and ennui that came to her through her regal Manchu blood. These qualities, which she passed on to me, so much younger than herself, made me feel a special tenderness and devotion toward her.

At this point, she sat up beside me, apparently a bit surprised to see that her dress with its tiny blue flower petals was spotted with tears. Then she raised her eyes and asked, "Are you hungry? I'll heat up some lunch for you."

I said, "No, thanks."

She stood up, then felt my forehead again to check my temperature. Her cool, gentle fingers were as soothing as a fresh facecloth.

I poked one arm out from under the quilt to pick a piece of thread off the shoulder of her dress, then I took hold of her hand on my forehead, wanting her to stay beside me.

As soon as I touched her hand, she forgot about going to heat up lunch. Slowly and hesitantly she sat down again. I lay on the bed unable to move. It seemed as if the beautiful petals on her dress were drifting down, covering me with a pure blue fragrance.

After hesitating a moment, she said, "Niuniu, would you like me to rub your back?"

I was lying face up on the bed, unable to move or to say anything.

"Mmm?" she queried again.

I lay there stiffly, like a corpse, without the strength to respond in any way.

She pulled back the quilt, and, grasping my shoulder, she eased me over onto my stomach. Then she put her two cool hands up under my pajama top and began to gently rub my back. Her fingers were like a wonderful kind of cool fire on my skin. It was as if I had jumped from a very high place and the free fall generated in me an indescribably beautiful sensation of dizziness.

At that moment, tired and relaxed after my fever had dropped, I wanted Ho to stay with me forever, I wanted desperately to die in this state of bliss. I knew that she too didn't want this moment to end, because she was bent over, pressing herself as close to me as she possibly could.

I was terribly afraid that I wouldn't be able to cling to this beautiful moment for very long, afraid that the next instant it would fall away forever. I couldn't think of a way to keep it from ending, so I pretended I was sleeping and abandoned myself to the touch of Ho's cool, gentle hands on my skin.

In this way, I found myself trapped between two contradictory states: a pleasurable feeling of ease and a tense feeling of panic. The wonderful feeling came naturally from some kind of vague adolescent desire growing within me. But under my tranquil guise of sleep, panic slowly began to overwhelm me, because I couldn't think of a way to make it look like I was really waking up.

This was very similar to the panic I felt on another occasion when I had "calmly" lied to Mr. Ti. On that day, he was standing on the dais, about to ask some of the students to stand up and read their written assignments out loud. His gaze swept back and forth across the classroom like a searchlight, ready to seize upon any information that our eyes might reveal. I was much more frightened than usual, because I had not finished my assignment. So all the while, I was furtively inventing a story. If he were to ask me to read aloud, I would say that I had forgotten my composition book at home. If he told me to go back home and get it, I would say that Mother had my key. But if he stubbornly insisted on phoning Mother after class, then. . . . It was at this point that panic really struck me. I was afraid that my trembling with fear as I sat there rigidly at my desk would attract his attention.

My tension on that occasion was very much like the tension I felt at this time, lying there on the bed feigning sleep.

But on that occasion, the look of equanimity that I was able to keep on my face saved me. Mr. Ti didn't see through my false calm, and he didn't call upon me to read my essay to the class. It turned out to be just as easy as getting a good grade from him for one of my spirited essays. The final bell that day was like the all-clear siren after an air raid. I flew out of the classroom, and the air and the sunlight outside were filled with a fragrance and joy as they had never been before.

Although Ho's hands touched only my back as I was lying there on my bed, they were the source of everything that I was feeling. I don't know why at that moment I chose to waste so much time recalling that insignificant incident in composition class, even though it had turned out very well.

My eyes closed and my mind empty, breathing in only the touch of Ho's fingertips on my skin, I slowly became aware of moving toward some very deep or distant and still indistinct idea that was entwined somehow with the anxious happiness of that moment, that seemed to enclose it. I made a great effort to focus my thinking, wanting to give some kind of order to these obscure and disconnected thoughts, to find out just what this intangible feeling signified.

Gradually, the feeling began to clarify: it was my indefinable longing and desire for Ho. It seemed as though at that moment she was not beside me at all, that she was somewhere far, far away.

People who are introspective and in the habit of sitting in quiet reflection, and for whom reading the newspapers is not enough, often look back to philosophize on the wonderful, floating, shadowy reflections of the events of their childhood that were steps along the path of their growth.

I am like this, because I know that there is nothing like regularly looking back on your past to help you understand the enigmas of human existence and the material and spiritual changes that are going on in the world we live in today. I have never been able to live a life limited to childhood, nor to one family, nor to a single courtyard, nor even to one country. But every human being's understanding of themselves and of the world can only be reached by crossing the bridge to their past experience and thought.

For me, this is the underlying implication of the sentence, "If you lose touch with childhood, you will never enter heaven."

Compared to my primary school years, my years in middle school were a time of momentous changes in China. I lived through and witnessed the closing years of the 1970s and the restoration of the university entrance examination system in the early 1980s, which pitted middle school graduates ruthlessly against one another as they converged like swarms of wasps on the universities. The close relationships between students of earlier years were gone, although, on the positive side, the entire student body joining together to isolate a particular student became a thing of the past. Getting higher grades than other students was tantamount to threatening their chances to attend university and their future as well. The ideals of collectivism were slowly but surely being swallowed up by a vigorous and untried individualism. In this vicious struggle, grades were everything. In school you were taught answers, not methods, and the answers were fixed. Individual ideas and imagination were of no importance or significance whatsoever.

In primary school, I lived my life outside the pale of the then current group happiness of collectivism that overrode the value of the individual, but although I was lonely, in the background, there was still a kind of indirect, shadowy illusion of belonging. But from the time I entered middle school, especially as the university entrance examinations drew near, I felt that I had become enmeshed in another extreme—the then current net of individualism, which lacked completely the warmth of the old collectivism. Companions were brought together in a single classroom, but were as cold and indifferent to one another as strangers. The shattering of old feelings of group identity plunged me into a genuine psychological isolation and sense of meaninglessness, where I felt the fear of being alienated from my companions and trapped within myself.

When I think back on it today, the collectivism of our youth, which ignored the individual, was in fact the hotbed that nurtured our present inhumanly arrogant individualism. Any phenomenon that is carried to an extreme will gradually lead to the emergence of its opposite.

I remember the morning of the last day of the winter holiday of the year that I graduated from upper middle school. Snowflakes as big as goose feathers were falling everywhere, as if the sky itself were coming down. I awoke to the soft swish of the falling snow, snugly nestled in my quilt, with no desire to get up.

I stuck one arm out from under the quilt to turn the clock on the night table so I could see what time it was. It wasn't eight o'clock yet. We had to go to school that day at ten o'clock to register.

When I saw that it was still early, I snuggled back down into my bed to indulge myself in my fantasies.

I noticed that the arm I stuck out had changed. Because of my heavy workload and the pressure of exams, I had been neglecting my private conversations with the misses Do and Don't for a long time. My arms and legs, once thin as sticks, had become plump and sleek without my noticing it. I began feeling myself all over, and discovered that my body had indeed been undergoing great changes. I was amazed by how unobservant I had been. How could I not have noticed this when I was bathing? My former familiarity with my body seemed truly a thing of the past.

My breasts, now round and soft, were like two peaches stuffed into the top of my pajamas. My groin had suddenly become broad and flat like a field that seemed big enough to grow lush and fragrant wheat. My buttocks now boldly asserted themselves, full, round, and heavy, curving out from my waist so that I couldn't lie flat on the bed anymore, and my thighs were long, firm, and lithe, like a pair of exclamation marks.

Under my quilt, I kept feeling my Misses Do and Don't. I felt very clearly that since I was becoming an adult I didn't want to spend so much time conversing with them. My inner discourses had already quietly developed in new directions, for example, with my neighbor the Widow Ho and with my only friend among my schoolmates, Yi Qiu— but especially with Ho. When I was alone, I often thought about when she was young and about how things had been between her and her husband, and if they had been happy together. She was almost the only light, the only support in my life. After a tasteless and depressing day, she would help me shuck off the pressure and the indefinable sense of emptiness that school engendered and let me enjoy for a moment the warmth of her conversation. We didn't have to be together for these conversations, nor did there have to be an actual exchange of words. We could meet in my mind.

Curled up there contentedly under my quilt, like a young heifer quietly chewing her cud, I savored my imaginary dialogues. It was as if I were building a house out of words, words chosen with meticulous care.

Then I became aware of the voices of my father and mother talking in the room next to mine. It sounded like they were "discussing" some problem. The reason I use the word "discuss" is that their tone was obviously neither sharp nor urgent enough for it to be an argument. It seemed more like they were casually discussing which brand of household appliance to buy. But I knew that my father never, either seriously or casually, exchanged views with my mother on the petty affairs of the household. When I cocked my head to listen more closely, I realized that Mother was talking about "divorce," and I could sense that she spoke of it freely and easily, as if she had been preparing for it for a very long time—although her voice had become less mellow, a bit hard-edged, with the seriousness of the subject.

Feeling very depressed and gloomy, I was on the edge of tears, but I hated letting myself sink into helpless despair, so I immediately shifted my focus of attention. I got up and dressed, sneaked into the kitchen for something to eat, then left for school with my winter holiday exercise book to report for registration.

A light breeze whispered unhindered through the gray debris and past the doors at the top of stone steps along the almost deserted street. Like a great white coat, the snow had covered the city's crumbling walls and its withered yellow patches of grass. A four-wheeled horse-drawn wagon passed in front of me, the horses' hooves as quiet as a cat, the only sound the scarcely heard groan of the heavy wheels as they turned, as if the wagon too were shrouded in an invisible net as it slowly and silently progressed. A wan light glinted on the branches of the trees and danced and flickered on the coarse brown wooden palings at the road's edge.

I like to go for a stroll when it is snowing. You cannot see the sky or the horizon, and your mind can freely wander along any path it chooses. The pristine white snow squeaks under your feet like fluttering sparrows. The sound makes you feel as if you are walking among the living, and when you look back at your footprints, you know that you are alive. When you feel this way, you are in touch with the spirit of all things. The heavy despair that I'd felt before leaving home was dispelled by the grandeur of heaven and earth, and the griefs and worries in my life seemed small and insignificant.

After walking in the snow for a while, I was able to push my parents' discussion of divorce that morning out of my mind for the time being, and I also managed to suppress my grief.

When I got to the main gate, I saw that our school grounds were deserted, a layer of milk-white snow covering the courtyard, the paths, and the walkways. Because it was overcast, the lights were on in all the offices. I entered Mr. Ti's office to find him smiling at me. It seemed as if he had been purposely keeping an eye out for me, waiting for my arrival.

And indeed, as I entered the office, he said, "I've been watching you through the window—every step of the way. You look like you stepped out of a fairy tale, you're so beautiful." As he spoke, he lifted his tall frame from his chair to greet me, as if I were a formal guest, not just one of his students.

His deep-set eyes revealed an uneasy urgency, as if he were suppressing all the things he had been longing to say over the entire winter holiday, and these things, clamoring for expression, were creating a tremendous pressure in his breast.

Just then, a number of my classmates arrived, including Yi Qiu, who came panting in, swinging her one bad leg.

Like everyone else, I handed in my exercise book, registered, and had my student card stamped.

When we were done and I was just about to leave with Yi Qiu, Mr. Ti suddenly said, "Ni Niuniu, don't go yet. There's still something I want to see you about."

Feeling uneasy, I asked, "What?"

He hesitated a moment, then said, "Why don't you go and sweep up the snow in front of our classroom first, then we can talk."

As he spoke, he was collecting the exercise books from the students who had come late.

I thought it was unfair that I had to stay and sweep snow while all the other students could go home, but I nonetheless obeyed his order, taking Yi Qiu along with me.

I let her wait on the classroom steps under the eaves while I started sweeping.

As I was sweeping, I looked up at the flurries of snow still drifting softly down. Without letup, the soft, fluffy down was busily covering everything. In no time at all my hair and shoulders were covered with a layer of white.

When I straightened up and turned to look back at the area I had just swept, the black pavement had already been covered with a fresh layer of white. I stood there hopelessly for a moment, then went back and started all over again.

I would sweep a bit, then look back, only to see that the place I had just swept had again been covered in snow.

I swept and I swept until I was overcome with hopeless exhaustion, feeling that I had been condemned to nothing more or less than an endless test or an unending labor detail. The test or the work would go on forever, all part of a plot or trap devised by Mr. Ti. I suddenly thought of all his rudeness, cunning, oppression, and unfairness. Not only did he hold back on my grades and criticize my morals, he also controlled my speech, my thinking, and even my feelings. All this was grossly unfair! How could I put up with this sort of humiliation? Why did I always submit to him, let him push me around as if I were a stupid melonhead?

At that moment I suddenly saw my endless sweeping of the snow as a symbol of my future life, my fate.

And only then did the despair and emptiness that I felt in the morning when I overheard that discussion of divorce come back to crush me.

At that time, naturally, I had not yet read the myth of Sisyphus. It was only after I entered university that I came to know this old western legend of how the gods punished Sisyphus by making him roll a huge stone to the top of a mountain, then letting it roll down again, only to have him push it back up again. He was forced to do this over and over, without cease. Exhausting himself at this futile and hopeless task was his life. But Sisyphus found a significance in this lonely, absurd, and hopeless existence. He discovered that something deeply moving and wonderful emerged from his struggle with the stone. In pitting his strength against it, he created a new energy with all the beauty of the dance. He was so intoxicated with this new joy that his old misery fell away forever. When the huge stone ceased to be a weight on his heart, the gods no longer rolled it back down the mountain.

Mankind possesses intelligence.

This kind of intelligent attitude toward fate was something I would only later come to understand.

Standing in the snow outside the classroom, I was completely swallowed up by the endless disaster that I had created with my excessive imagination.

Suddenly, I started to cry.

Yi Qiu looked up from where she was sitting under the eaves, watching me curiously.

I cried and cried as all my old resentments and my present hatred poured out.

It was already noon when, harboring in my breast all the hatred that I felt toward the men that Ti and my father stood for, I left Yi Qiu and burst into Ti's office to confront him.

Puzzled and concerned when he saw that I had been crying, he asked, "Ni Niuniu, what's wrong?"

As he spoke, he brushed the snow from my hair, my chest, and my back, with a blurred, dreamy look in his eyes.

Without uttering a sound, I glared at him, my eyes like sharp fangs that could slash his hypocritical face to ribbons.

Seemingly oblivious to the daggers flashing in my eyes, he continued to brush my shoulders as he asked me with great concern, "Whatever has happened?"

I jerked his huge hand free from my shoulder and shouted at him, "I've come to tell you something!"

"What is it?" he asked uncertainly.

I fixed my gaze angrily on his face, "I came here to tell you . . . those are your private parts! There! There!"

I "returned the compliment," jabbing him where he had earlier touched me. And I did this with all my strength!

He looked astonished and perplexed.

Only after I had gotten control of my inner tension and excitement did I realize that I was still standing in front of Mr. Ti and that I hadn't moved a hair. My hands were still rigidly by my sides. I hadn't even raised them, let alone touched him. They hung there as stiff and lifeless as stones.

The scene I described above had taken place only in my imagination.

I realized then that there were two opposing people in my head trying to control me at the same time, leaving me in a state of confusion. I stood woodenly in front of him, unable to do a thing.

When I realized that I had not hurt him, I was filled with grief and indignation. I despised myself. I was totally ineffectual, incapable of striking back.

I spun around and ran out of the office.

When I left the school, I didn't go straight home. I wandered the streets aimlessly, oblivious of the crowds passing by and the shop windows with all their expensive goods, completely caught up in my own spiritless, confused thoughts.

I wandered the streets the entire afternoon, until the soft streetlights came on, pushing the evening shadows behind the rooftops along the streets. The glittering neon lights of the great buildings and the entertainment spots splashed the scene with iridescent color.

I have always treated the streets and alleyways as a kind of second home. When you feel lost, with no place to go, they are your hotel. When the people close to you are far away and you feel lonely and helpless, they are your friends. Even when the weather was icy cold, my love for them did not diminish. And as I wandered the streets, I conversed with the voices in my heart.

My home, not so very far away, was awaiting my return, but for the first time in my life I felt totally alone.

It is said that the sounds we hear are an illusion, that there is no absolute connection between the objects that produce sounds and the objects that receive them. Without our minds, without illusionary desire, all the ears in this world would be silent voids.

In reality it is our own skin that cries out, and the sounds we make sink into our own bodies and fade away within us.

In all my years as a student, most of the serious events took place during my final summer holiday at the end of middle school, the most intense two months of my entire school life.

In July that summer it had rained without letup, and the endless, unbroken string of examinations, like the interminable rain, had tried my patience to the limit. By forcing myself to fight to the bitter end, I was able to muddle through the exams successfully and win a place in one of Beijing's liberal arts universities.

I remember that when the tests for each subject were finished, I took the course texts, which I knew from cover to cover, tore them up, dropped them in an examination hall toilet, and flushed them down with my feces so I would never have to carry them home again.

By the time the exams were finished, I was as thin as a beggar, without an ounce of extra fat on my body.

Another thing that was still going on at this time was my parents' covert and "civilized" divorce agreement. In this major event in the history of the family, my father displayed an unusual male gallantry, like a war hero of the first order leaving the field of battle (except that this was a special battlefield where there were no winners or losers). Early one morning when it was raining torrents, he pulled on his trousers, put on his glasses, picked up his briefcase, and departed—a stirring spectacle.

Ultimately, his final departure forced me to stand up among the ruins on this civilized battlefield and take on the role of a mature woman.

I don't want to go through the story of the destruction of my family, because it is unimportant. What is important is that the belief in marriage of every person who scrambled out of the ruins had been totally destroyed. My mother and I had both become cynical about that institution, which the majority of people consider wonderously beautiful.

In China in the early '80s, it was really very difficult to find anyone who wished, as I did, that her own parents would get out of their unfortunate marriage, but I never felt awkward or guilty about feeling this way. On the contrary, I always believed that I was the staunchest supporter and advocate of their "liberation movement." At the same time, I never blamed any of my personal distrust or negative feelings toward any aspects of society, such as its outworn ways of thinking, on the mess at home.

I have never thought that the family alone could generate in an individual such powerful negative feelings.

Not long after my father left, an official order came down for the demolition of the houses on our block, and we were given two apartments in a new high-rise residential complex in the western sector of the city.

To our good fortune, it was fated that Ho would move into the same building, two floors directly below my own apartment.

Mr. Ge from the courtyard in front of us had disappeared without a trace after the murder of his wife, and his daughter's family had moved into the house. So she too was moved into our building.

On the day that Mother, Widow Ho, and I went to look at our new quarters, the building, which had just been completed, towered gray and empty on the construction site. As there had not been time to plant trees and grass, the surrounding land was barren on all sides. Like a man caught naked in broad daylight, the building seemed displeased and unwilling to be seen, and we had to look for a long time before we found the path to the main entrance.

The elevator wasn't working yet, so we started up the narrow but gently inclined stairway. After climbing around and around, Mother and I finally found ourselves standing at the end of a hallway on the eleventh floor before the door to a three-room apartment.

It was a depressing door, gray and huge. As we stood there catching our breath, I noticed that the weak, unsteady light came from a ventilation hole covered with a steel grid, which served as a sort of skylight in a corner above the door on the left. Through a crack in the door I could hear a strange, faint noise, perhaps from air in the water or heating pipes, that sounded like unbroken sneezing from some tormented netherworld. I put my ear against the door, straining to hear more clearly, but the noise had faded away.

This was to be my mother's apartment, my own being down the corridor. At the very outset, a kind of cold, ominous premonition had twisted its way out through the crack in my mother's door and crawled up onto my face. In some vague way, through that gray steel door that made me step back as soon as I looked at it, I felt I had touched upon something associated with death. This totally groundless premonition made me reluctant to open the door for my mother, as if doing so would open the door to some disaster.

And in fact, not too many years later this turned out to be true.

It was a dreadfully hot and long summer. Like unleavened loaves of steamed bread that never seem to be done, no matter how long you leave them in the steamer, the days dragged by interminably. I opened all the windows in my apartment, but it was very noisy outside because on the opposite side of the street not too far from our building, another high-rise apartment building was under construction. From my window, where I could see the scaffolding that was being erected in the construction area, the building modules seemed more like toys than actual parts of the building. I stood by my window thinking that it wouldn't be long before that building too would be jammed full of people, all separated by walls into their own square spaces, all living their not very real lives.

I turned around and examined my own place. The light blue of the lower part of the walls looked back at me serenely. The front room, the kitchen, the bathroom, and the bedroom—all told me that this was a home where I could pass the days peacefully. The hubbub of the crowded living of earlier years was a thing of the past. The furniture and the walls would no longer be troubled by the tension and confusion caused by the endless traffic of people.

I had always dreamed of having a place of my own, because it is a prerequisite for the pursuit of a life of reflection.

In her apartment down the corridor from mine, my mother was trying to recover from the invisible "wound" left by her almost twenty years of marriage; and I could communicate with Widow Ho, resting on her big, soft, warm bed in the apartment two floors below mine, by knocking on the water pipes. And more important than this, my special silent conversations with her were not impeded by the concrete slabs separating the building's floors. With my mother and my dearest friend so close to me, I was calmer and more at ease than I had ever been before.

Late one evening an unexpected guest suddenly arrived at the door of my new apartment.

I assumed that it was Ho coming to see me, so when the bell rang, stuffing my feet in my slippers and slipping into a cotton T-shirt that reached to my thighs, I went to open the door.

When I opened it, I was caught completely off guard.

Tall and handsome and dressed to the nines, Mr. Ti was standing there holding a bouquet of fresh flowers. His flashing eyes betrayed a kind of confusion, but he had a stiff smile fixed firmly on his face.

For the two months prior to the university entrance exams the students studied at home and no longer attended classes, so I had not seen him for three months.

Ti's sudden appearance left me confused, especially the unexpected bouquet of flowers. I had no idea what I should do. A cold chill ran through me to my very fingertips, which felt like icicles.

For many years, Ti and I had apparently been caught in some kind of subtle entanglement or relationship, but it had always been like a balloon pushed beneath the water's surface, lurking there where I wasn't quite conscious of its existence. Perhaps it was our uncertainty and blindness that had exasperated him to the point where he was at times rude and contemptuous toward me, and at other times affectedly solicitous and understanding.

This abrasive, confrontational, even antagonistic relationship had gone on this way for many years.

My feminine intuition had made me dimly aware that these years of confrontation and antagonism perhaps stemmed from some latent, unspoken danger that had always had a secret existence between us, even though I couldn't clearly identify it. So I instinctively avoided him, keeping him at a distance.

When I opened the door and suddenly saw him again, after we had already parted, it felt like the huge door that had been closed between us had been reopened, catching me completely by surprise.

Standing there at the door, I was nonplussed for a moment; then I moved aside and invited him in, while I very self-consciously pulled down on my big T-shirt.

Ti said, "I've come to congratulate you."

I was terribly embarrassed, my face flushed hot, and for a while I could think of nothing to say.

Finally, when he was already in the living room, with a great effort I managed to say, "Sit down."

He again said, "I've come to congratulate you!" and the stiff smile on his face seemed to relax a bit.

Awkwardly and a little coldly, I said, "For what?"

"For all that you've managed," he said.

After he sat down on the sofa, since I still hadn't gone over to take the flowers from him, he very casually put them down on the tea table in front of him. I sat down in the chair facing him.

He rattled on about whatever he could think of, not at all like the urbane teacher at the front of the classroom. I responded somehow or other, not really thinking about what I was saying.

I felt very uneasy sitting there, because my thighs were almost completely exposed.

Eventually I drummed up enough courage to stand up and say, "I'm going to put on something more suitable."

"It's not necessary, Niuniu. I like you the way you are." He paused a moment, then went on, "Your legs are slim and shapely. They're extremely beautiful." As he spoke, he stood up as if he were going to stop me, as if he were afraid I was going to leave to change my clothes.

I hesitated a moment, then went to the bedroom.

When I had taken off my T-shirt and before I had time to get my dress from its hanger, the bedroom door groaned as it was pushed open.

With a hopeless look on his face, Ti stood at the door, breathing hard, with tears welling up in his eyes and streaming down his face. His tall, strong frame looked like a crumbling stone monument that was about to collapse in ruins.

I was so stunned I didn't know what to do or say.

He walked unsteadily toward me, and without uttering a word he wrapped his arms tightly around me.

Locked firmly in his arms, I whispered desperately, "Don't do this, don't do this," as I twisted angrily in an attempt to get away. But his arms were like fetters, and the more I struggled, the tighter they became.

His body, as hot as a stove, was all over mine. He cried out softly, "Niuniu, Niuniu, I beg you, stay in my arms." Because he was so tense, the sound of his voice had changed.

"No. I don't like you." And again I tried to get away from him.

"I have always, always loved you, Niuniu. I swear it." His lips were trembling so much that he could hardly speak.

"You're lying!" I answered angrily. "I've always hated you." I was gasping for breath from my struggle to get away.

Ti's tears were spotting my shoulder like rain. Unable to speak, he clasped me even tighter in his arms, pumping his groin hard against mine, as if he were suffering muscle spasms.

Staring at him with hostile intensity, all I could see was that his usually arrogant face was as pale as a girl's, and that a seemingly uncontrollable and dangerous grief and longing shot from his eyes and from every pore on his body. It was as if this apparently sturdy, handsome male had crumpled into a great heap of garbage around my shoulders.

This made me recall the scene on the army cot in the inner room at Yi Qiu's and the sudden spurt of lightning from between Xi Dawang's legs.

I began to feel a bit frightened.

His rapid and heavy breathing gave an indication of how long he had been tormented with desire. There seemed to be a deep hurt lurking beneath his expression of sexual passion.

Gripping me tightly by the shoulders, he murmured brokenly, "Niuniu, you're a very seductive girl. Do you know that? Everything about you, your body, your face, has a special attraction. You're like a garden filled with exotic flowers and grasses that allows me no exit, that tortures me. Why can't you see how I . . ."

My shoulders hurt in his grip. Tears were streaming down his face and he was sobbing uncontrollably.

This was the first time I had ever received praise from a male. And what stunned me was that it came from a male whom I had detested for many years.

Only after living through many different experiences did I discover that women (including myself at that time) are highly susceptible to praise. Such praise is an ingenious weapon that can make women lose their sense of judgment and their sense of place, reducing them to mindless little girls, to the point where they are nothing more than female animals who subserviently do what they are told, becoming praise's willing prisoners and slaves, the spoils of battle. It is only the most mature of women who can remain cool and rational in the face of this invincible weapon.

That day Ti's sobbing frightened and disgusted me, but at the same time I felt an obscure kind of pity for him. His intense grief, in fact, placed a restraint on my own feelings, suppressing my resistance to his pleas.

Twisting this way and that way around the bedroom, with me trying to get away from him, we looked like a pair of combatants in a mixed-sex wrestling match.

I was gradually losing strength in my struggle to get away.

His tears of despair fell without cease on my face, and I could feel their coolness penetrating into my body, where wondrously it was transformed into a feeling of languor, which in turn passed outward through my skin, to be drawn in by the intense heat of his body.

Eventually, I stopped resisting him.

All the time I was touching him, I kept seeing animated images of Yi Qiu and Xi Dawang's entwined bodies, which further stimulated my imagination and my senses. I felt a delicate shuddering spreading outward through my body to my skin, leaving me feeling faint.

So I closed my eyes.

Then in the darkness behind my eyelids I dimly saw that the image of Yi Qiu and Xi Dawang entwined together had suddenly changed. The stage properties and the set were still the same. It was still the inner room of Yi Qiu's house, and the same old army cot was still there in the semidarkness. But it was not their bodies twined together on it. Hand in hand, Yi Qiu and Xi Dawang had risen from the bed, and, smiling slyly, Xi Dawang was saying, "It's your turn on stage. What a beautiful thing it is!" Yi Qiu turned to me and said, "Don't be afraid. You have to step onto this stage sooner or later anyway." Then the two bodies on the cot turned into Ti and me.

When this cartoon image in my mind changed, something even stranger happened. As if I had been hypnotized, my body suddenly possessed a demonic strength. The terrible fatigue that I felt as a result of the struggle to free myself was suddenly transformed into a new and opposing strength, and I pressed myself rigidly against Ti. . . .

In the twilight of that summer evening in August, as the light in the room slowly faded, the passionately hot body of Mr. Ti, a mature male, was grinding against the almost naked body of his female student, his chest pressed helplessly against her breasts. It seemed that an agonizing pain was mounting in his lower groin. The warmth of his hot breath washed past her cheek, over her neck, down her spine, and into her loins, where she started to feel a tingling sensation.

He held her tightly by the waist so that they were pressed as close together as possible. She felt what seemed to be something like a hand increasing in size in the front of his trousers. This "third hand" was vigorously and wildly probing, as if trying to find a way to reach within her body. The student was straining her upper body away from him as much as possible, trying to leave a little space between them. But he inclined his head toward her to press the tip of his tongue in her ear and into the hollow of her neck. Then he buried his face between her breasts and began kissing and sucking their nipples and marble-white skin. Her eyes slowly closed as she lay there, unable to resist.

Then she felt him thrusting violently as something hot seeped through his trousers, soaking her groin. . . .

It was twilight outside, and the last warmth of the day flowed languidly into the room through the open window. Ti and I, soaked with perspiration, could both hear our hearts beating as fast as the second hand of my watch.

When I extracted myself from his embrace, I saw that the crotch of his trousers was all wet, and that my stomach too was all sticky. It was disgusting.

I was angry and at the same time embarrassed by my own behavior.

I said to Ti, "Please go. I want to have a bath."

His face was filled with shame, guilt, and loving tenderness, all at the same time. Looking rather awkward, he said, "Niuniu, Niuniu, I'm not a playboy who chases after women for the fun of it. I'll be good to you, I'll take care of you."

I said, "Please go. I want to have a bath."

"Why don't we go out for dinner?" he suggested.

I said, "No. I'm having dinner with my mother. Some other time, perhaps. I have to think about it."

"Niuniu, please don't think badly of me. I've always yearned for you, hoping that someday maybe you and I . . ."

"Nonsense." The moment he started to talk this way, my anger flared and, heedless of everything, I confronted him. "You have always made life difficult for me, always criticizing me, making me feel embarrassed!"

"But I never wanted to be like that. I have no idea why I treated you like that. Niuniu, I swear it. I need you, I want you, I love you."

I persisted, "You have to go now. My mother will be calling me for dinner in a little while."

Ti heaved a sigh and said resignedly, "All right, Niuniu. I'll come to see you again tomorrow."

"I don't want you to come again," I answered in haste.

"I won't touch you, I swear, Niuniu. I just want to see you, to take you for dinner, to talk to you," Ti said, his damp eyes downcast. He paused a moment, then continued, "Niuniu, I apologize for my crude behavior today."

He had jettisoned all his former stiffness of manner.

A fly buzzing around in circles by the bedroom window made it seem like the glass in the window was undulating and my bed beneath the window was swaying unsteadily. From that moment on, it seemed, the entire room would never feel safe and secure again.

Ti's eyes turned toward the big bed, its flax-colored sheets like some spotless, forbidden zone denying him the fulfillment of his desire. The last rays of the setting sun cast a pink glow on the center of the bed like the warm color of flower petals staining a milk-white skin, or the still-warm blood flower of a just-taken virgin.

Unable to stand steadily and gasping for breath, he collapsed on the bed.

The bed gave out a forlorn and bitter cry.

He made the events of their past die quickly in her body.
Working like a bolt of lightning, he frightened her, hurt
her, made her aware that her body had another mouth she
didn't know about that also breathed and moaned. Slowly
developed commitments were his enemy; the quick heat
of friction was his friend. Penetrating the void within her,
terminating her deep, obscuring sleep, he conquered time,
driving it deep into the channel of her being. . . .
    Friction let him see the light of the sun. Friction made
her smell the odor of death.

With some experiences, it is only afterward that I become aware of the extent of their effect upon me.

On that occasion, however, all that I could think of
was getting out of this city, getting away from the chaos
of my feelings. . . .

The day after Ti's unexpected appearance, I hurriedly
packed some things to go away.

I hardly slept at all the night before I left. The pressure of Ti's body against my skin and in my thoughts
was with me constantly. I was enmeshed in a contradic-
tion of denied desire and rejected yearning and at a loss
to explain my needs or my actions.

By early morning, I had decided that I would get rid
of my confusion by thoroughly distancing myself from
its source.

Making use of the then current notion of "getting back to nature" (nothing more than an excuse), I told my mother that for the past several years I had been almost suffocating under the weight of books, living like a lifeless wooden puppet absurdly manipulated on the sticks of the university entrance exams and my future. Living in a city far away from nature had left me exhausted beyond measure. I needed to go somewhere to unwind, to clear my head.

When out of the blue I mentioned that I was going on a trip, Mother, quite taken aback, said, "You want to closet yourself away in some country village?"

"I'm going with Yi Qiu and some of our classmates. It's just for a few days, for a change of scenery," I lied.

Exceedingly anxious, and dubious about my travel plans, Mother trotted out something from her reading to dissuade me.

She said, "Those people who see nature find it wherever they are; those who cannot see it can never find it, no matter where they might be. Even if genuine nature were all around you, it doesn't necessarily mean that you would enjoy it. Your surroundings are not the source of your problem."

"But all I want to do is get some fresh air and sun," I said. Not about to let anything dissuade me, as I was speaking, I stubbornly continued stuffing my clothes into a canvas backpack.

Looking at my pale face and the dark circles under my eyes with an aching heart, my mother heaved a sigh and gave up trying to stop me.

I wasn't at all interested in looking at scenery or in having company. I liked traveling by myself because being with someone else or with a group interfered with my private thoughts.

Sitting by the window on the bus, looking at the hazy green mountains in the distance, the loess hills, the low-lying scattered villages, the quiet streams in the brown mountains, and the bare valleys, I began to feel an unexpected tranquility.

I took a room in a small, out-of-the-way inn outside the city. It was dim, gloomy, and simply appointed, but clean and quiet. A long path through lush grass and bright wildflowers connected it with the bus station. A few mournful steam whistles echoing melodiously in the evening mist provided a musical backdrop, and the evening breeze brushing my shoulders induced in me an expansive, relaxed happiness. The air carried a rich scent of lavender; and roses, strawberries, and a variety of flowering shrubs enclosed this otherwise rather bleak country inn in a confusion of color.

Several low green hedges willy-nilly formed an enclosure for a tiny park. I sat down on a secluded stone bench, a jacket around my shoulders, looking as if I were waiting for someone. In truth, there was no one for me to be waiting for, but I didn't feel the least bit lonely, because I was enjoying a moment of happiness that I myself had created.

Sitting there, I for some reason felt an urge to write someone a letter.

So I went back to the inn, where I sat cross-legged on the clean enough bed, placing the writing pad I had brought with me on my knees, with a book underneath for support.

But who was I going to write to? The first person to come to mind was Ho. Since we had never written to each other before, I thought that it would be perfect to write to her now that we were separated, using my imagination to draw a scene for her. She would no doubt find the most beautiful and the warmest landscapes of my spirit in the letter. I imagined her propped up in her big bed, her slender, delicate figure draped casually on it, like a piece of lustrous, soft silk. When she got my letter she would be surprised and overjoyed. She would touch every word as carefully as if she were touching my eyes.

I realized at that moment that I missed her very much.

After that, I wrote a letter to Ti, fiercely denouncing him for all the ways he had mistreated me over the years, telling him how much I hated him, how I couldn't stand living under the same sky, that I didn't want to see him again, that I never wanted to see him again, ever! But in the close of the letter I contradicted myself, saying that should the opportunity arise, perhaps I might see him again. But I knew that I would see him only to make him suffer out of his desire for my body. I would take great delight in seeing his torment.

Writing letters gives me extreme pleasure. There is no more effective way of experiencing the pleasure of getting away from people and living by yourself. All those faraway moments of sorrow and joy are so close you can reach out and touch them, while when you are actually among the people you know, such feelings can often elude you.

My letters written, I heaved a sigh of relief, as if the sole purpose of my journey had been to write them.

The next day, after I had dropped them off at the local post office, I found myself in a vacant mood. After a few days idly enjoying some of the scenic spots, I found myself thinking of going home.

In the morning, just as I was thinking of packing up to leave and paying my bill, there was a knock on the door.

I knew that it wasn't the chambermaid, because the knock seemed somehow hesitant, exploratory, and eager. It sounded like a familiar heartbeat. Though separated from it by the door, I knew that it was the same heartbeat that had lingered against my breast a few days earlier.

I rushed over to the door and swung it open.

And, sure enough, there was Ti, looking absolutely forlorn.

I don't know why, but seeing him there didn't surprise me in the least. It seemed as if I had been expecting him, even though this made no sense, since nobody knew where I was. Yet I had no idea how he had been able to find me.

When he saw me, he stared at my face, and after a few moments of hesitation, he heaved a sigh and came into the room.

He said, "Niuniu, is there anything wrong?"

"I'm fine," I said.

After staring at me again for a while, he shifted his gaze from my face and took in the rest of the room, his brows furrowed slightly.

"Niuniu, going off by yourself like this is dangerous. There are a lot of bad people out there."

The way he spoke made it sound like he was the kind of person there was no need to worry about.

"It's none of your concern," I answered coldly.

Apparently taking no note of what I had said, he continued, "Next time you want to go away for a holiday, I'll go with you. You mustn't go alone."

I continued my cold rejection of his concern. "What I do is none of your business."

"Niuniu, don't be like that. I set out this morning before dawn to look for you. I figured out where you were from the postmark on your letter. This is the second hotel I've come to. Do you have any idea how worried I've been?"

I made no answer, leaving him to do the talking. But his appearance and his sincerity were slowly weakening my resistance.

He was silent for a while, then said, "Niuniu, I miss you."

Feigning total indifference, I looked away from him, still not saying anything.

Standing there without having moved, without any encouragement, he continued, "I long for you every hour, every minute of the day. I don't know what to do . . ."

His words came slowly and heavily, as if they were great stones blocking the space between us, impeding him; not his usual crafted sentences.

"Niuniu, I don't want to hurt you in any way. I'm out of control. All I want to do is see you, be with you."

I noticed that he had picked up again on the key issue of our last conversation, which I had cut short. I also noticed that when he uttered my name, his voice shook.

The room fell silent as death.

He didn't come over and touch me. Some nameless force seemed to hold his feet frozen to the floor. I still didn't look at him directly, but I could glimpse his face and figure at the edge of my field of vision. He looked totally despondent. The gloom in his heart had completely sucked away the former brightness of his face. Even in the stillness and stifling heat of midday his cheeks looked as colorless and hopeless as a frozen wasteland. He was wearing a pair of military shorts, and his long, brown legs looked as powerful as those of a straining workhorse. Those silent legs had a strange power that drew my eyes.

I forced myself to turn my head away.

Then I turned my back on him and fixed my gaze on a huge spider-web on the wall. Like a delicate wing, the silk web trembled in a slight draft. Pointlessly, I continued to stare at it, as if it were some fascinating thing.

Then I heard movement behind me. I could hear each step as he drew nearer; I could even hear the sound of his breathing.

But the sounds stopped when he was still about a footstep away from me.

He took a breath and then said, "Niuniu, I want to take you somewhere to eat. You must have been terribly hungry over these last few days." As he spoke, he squeezed my arms. "Look, pretty soon you won't weigh any more than your photograph."

No sooner had he said this than my stomach began to growl with hunger.

And at last, I turned around to face him, and nodded my head in agreement.

Crowing with joy, Ti lifted me off the ground and swung me around with my feet in the air.

He shouldered my pack, paid my bill, called a taxi, and we were on our way.

It was the same road that I had arrived on, but now it seemed totally different. When I came, we bounced along depressingly, the pencil-straight road looming out of and disappearing into the encroaching gloom. The interminable road with its indistinctive background, like my own train of thought weighted down with cares, thought only of pushing onward.

But now the road was altogether different. Bordered with a rose haze, under the midday sun it glittered like undulating black silk. The depth and richness of the dark green of growing crops, the black of freshly turned loam, the mottled brown-and-white cows, the trailing shadows of sinuous trees captured the eyes. The roadside stone walls, the granaries, and the lush wild grasses embroidered the borders of this otherwise uninteresting road.

After a drive of two hours or so, we were back in the city center.

Ti said, "I'm going to take you to a new-style grotto restaurant for dinner. It's operated by a friend of mine from my army days. It has a style all its own."

Our taxi pulled up in front of a restaurant called Banpo Village on a main downtown street.

After we had wound our way downstairs and entered the reception room, I gave the place a cursory survey. The lighting was muted, and each of the grottoes had its own natural setting, with winding paths leading to sequestered nooks. Each one was thoughtfully decorated to fit a particular theme, with every detail accounted for, so that they were independent of one another, each with its own distinct flavor. It goes without saying that the place had its own special charm and appeal.

The owner came out to welcome us. After a spirited exchange of greetings with his old army buddy, Ti turned to me and said, "This is the village head, Mr. Zhao."

"Village head?" I queried.

Mr. Zhao said, "We've taken our ideas from the archaeological remains of the Banpo tribal village, and used Banpo culture as the theme of our restaurant. That's why we call it a village. So I'm the present village head, and you, my dear, are now one of our citizens."

Mr. Zhao then gave us a guided tour of the restaurant's six separate grottoes. We went into the bar first. A group of Qin dynasty terra-cotta warriors stood guard in one corner, and a number of niches for the display of a variety of bottled liquors had been cut into the walls. The bar itself was decorated with lengths of ancient, crude hempen rope, and in the cupboards behind it was a display of pottery bowls with the "face-and-fish" motifs, well buckets, colored ceramic jars, and records kept on knotted strings and wooden slips used by the original citizens of Banpo.

Zhao said, "We'll show you around first, and then you can decide where you'd like to eat."

We looked at the "Tribal Chieftain's Grotto" first. Ti said he was sure that the drawings on the walls depicted the story of Hou Yi, the monarch of the Xia dynasty state of Youqiong, shooting the sun with his bow, and agricultural and hunting scenes of the people of Banpo. There were already a number of diners enjoying a noisy meal there, so we looked into the "Fish Room." The walls were covered with ancient pictographic inscriptions. This "fish and worm" writing bespoke the incomparable satisfaction that goes with sipping fine wine as one softly hums a beautiful tune. Next, we went into the "Han Room," which was richly decorated with black dragon and white tiger designs taken from the ends of eaves tiles. A sculpture of a Han dynasty raconteur sat commandingly in the center of the grotto as if he were still telling tales of past and present glories.

Then, the "village head" solemnly recommended the "Yinyang Grotto" to us. When Ti and I entered the room, we were immediately struck by its muted, candlelit ambience and the walls covered with paintings of Han dancing beauties and a series of romantic images of lovemaking.

Ti immediately said, "Here—we'll eat here."

. . . . . .

And now there were only two people in the Yinyang Grotto—Mr. Ti and his student, an initiate in the world of love.

Deliriously happy, he filled the entire table with dishes and wine for her. She had never before sampled such a feast of flavors. Along with a bottle of the finest Madeira, there was bitter vegetable, fiddlehead ferns, whole scorpions in a bed of chrysanthemum petals, spiced golden cicadas, garland chrysanthemum, monkey legs, five-colored shredded squid, scallops in their own shells, gold and silver venison, lotus-flower longans in chilled soup. . . .

When everything had been served, the waitresses withdrew, and the door to the grotto closed with a discreet click.

Their glasses filled, they toasted each other and began sampling delicacies seemingly created for the lips of the gods. Ti's eyes glowed in the soft light, and his powerful body showed a gentleness reminiscent of a stallion with his mare. All the anxiety and despair had been taken from his face, and the distress in his eyes had vanished like clouds. Without cease he told her of his love for her and his desire for her. He begged her that she never again bring up the old business of their life in school. He swore that everything he had done in those days had run against his real feelings, that it had happened because of his helplessness in the face of her total lack of response, but that now he was a single man who adored her youthful beauty and romanticism and could express his love to her because she was no longer his student.

By this time, he had moved around to sit beside her, and she listened to him with gentle and trusting attentiveness. Her sleepy eyes glittering and her usual defensiveness shed, she began to lean slowly toward him.

His breath began to quicken as he placed a hand upon her shoulder.

Her resistence melted away, and all her old feelings of hostility toward him vanished in an instant.

Her eyes closed in seeming invitation, as if awaiting the moment when his fingers would touch her, and her body felt like it was covered with mouths panting with longing.

She could hear his heavy breathing close behind her as his hands slipped around her to touch her breasts and the hot breath from his lips mingled with her hair.

"Niuniu, Niuniu," he called out softly.

Suddenly possessed by wild desire, she turned eagerly toward him, and wrapping her slender arms and legs around his body as if to become one with him, she pressed her bosom against the mysterious beating of his heart.

His arms enclosed her in a tight embrace.

They drank some more, and encouraged by the heat of the wine, he began exploring her body with his hands. He cupped her breasts in his hands like prizes won in battle. Like ripe fruits under her thin dress, sticking up perkily, their nipples erect, they pleased him far beyond her accomplishments in school. Her body seemed to melt in his hands. Pouting her wet, glistening lips as if she were going to whistle, she laid her head on his shoulder and began kissing his ear.

Turning her so that she was looking at the scenes of lovemaking on the wall, he told her that there was nothing in life more beautiful than this. He drew her to him again, her legs spread apart sitting on his lap, and again she felt the marvelous heat of that "third hand," which was working feverishly between her legs as if trying to bury itself.

Eventually he could no longer curb his lust, and begged her to let him take her there in the Yinyang Grotto. Overcome with fear and passion, she half refused, half accepted him. Without saying yes or no, she closed her eyes and waited in shame for him to undo their clothing and let their sexes come together to complete that most shining moment in a virgin's life.

The moment he had hoped and thirsted for for so many years had arrived. His dream come true, he moaned with uncontrollable ecstasy, his eyes filled with a love that glowed with the soft sheen of silk. But she was caught in a conflict of feelings. When she looked at the man before her, held in the agony of his love, her passion welled up within her, and this momentary passion made her former animosity slip away through her fingers like passing time. But she was not gripped by any feeling of love for him. All she felt was the lust that had been aroused in her body and the urge to use his body to reach that deep ecstasy she had never totally experienced before. What she delighted in was this sensual ecstasy, not this man before her. She was twined in his arms only for this feeling of close sexual intimacy. Now, her sexual desire was much more fierce than any lingering trace of her previous abhorrence of it. She was totally unprepared for her descent into this realm. Her mind and her body had distanced themselves from each other. She had become another person, controlled totally by her body's need for sexual gratification.

As she surrendered to the pleasure of her natural feelings, she felt a sudden, tearing pain.

Like a bolt of lightning, this lucid pain cast a bright glow on the skin of her entire body and throughout her innermost being. She could not help but cover her face with her hands. . . .

This man and woman thus met each other. Their pleasure had no "past," and for this female student the hurt of her first "meeting" turned it into their "last supper."

My memories of that day are very sharp. It was like a new birth. This new world was a vast impure ocean that, without sound, called to me, and I threw myself in so deeply that when it genuinely called to me later I did not hear.

It is like someone once said—the significance of any relationship can only be understood through another relationship.

This led me to see that this world controls us through our sexual passions, and it is only after we have traveled a very long way and have already paid the price that we come to understand this.

In the end, a spirit that has suffered wrong finds its way back to punish its tormentors. Sometimes it assumes the shape of a cloud and returns to the world of the living as rain. The dead make use of its special form to continue their fight against their living enemies.

A stranger from another place, or should I say, a man in the guise of a stranger from another place, brushed past me in the stairwell. To be more precise, the first thing I noticed was a shadow abruptly appearing next to my own.

It was late at night, on the way back to my own apartment from Widow Ho's. The gloomy corridors were dead quiet, and the feeble glow from the inadequate lights, like the empty echo of a voiceless sigh, was absorbed, not reflected, by the walls.

Summer was just over, and it seemed like the fresh fall air was step by step climbing the stairs and entering our apartments.

In Ho's apartment, before I bumped into this stranger, or apparent stranger, we had dined together. The dishes she prepared were simple but delicious.

There were stewed peanuts, chili cucumber sticks, fresh fried mushrooms in an oil dressing, minced dried beancurd, pickled duck stomachs, tendons marinated in oil, and a bottle of my favorite sweetened wine.

The fragrant odors wafted enticingly around our mouths, and the lamp enclosed the table in a soft rose glow. The faded floral-print cover on her sofa and her unique curios from the Qianlong period, such as twisted-neck vases, fans, and her gold clock with its book-shaped case, gave the room an ancient feel, a secluded charm. In the light from the lamp her clear skin and long, slender legs shone as her bare feet carried her back and forth across the carpet. The ceaselessly changing aspect of her exquisite figure, and her face turned always solicitously toward me, were also contained within this circle of light. The damp weather and the noise of the city outside could not possibly have interrupted the atmosphere in that room.

When Ho was among other people, she was wrapped in a persistent air of haughtiness, but when she was alone with me, she assumed an intense motherly air that made me love her beyond all reason.

Through all the years when I was growing up, I seldom saw such an intense appreciation of the small beauties of life in my own home. My father and mother were both perpetually wrapped up in their own work, with no interest at all in the little events of everyday life. As far as I can remember, my father almost never involved himself in such things, while my mother was always constrained by the pressures of time. I know that she loved me very much, loved me intensely, but it was an abstract, general kind of love, not the significantly more common maternal kind of love of a hen for the eggs she has laid herself. Many of the things around the home that had to be done, she was unwilling to do but nonetheless did, out of her love for me. But such acts on her part made me feel so uncomfortable that I never wanted her to get more involved in our daily domestic life. I have always thought that having ambitious, work-driven parents is not by any means a fortunate thing for a child. Quite the contrary: ordinary parents can bring their children much more of the gentle essence and devotion of a family.

Ho and my mother possessed a similar graceful beauty, but they were very different in personality. Ho always exuded an air of leisurely easiness. Unlike my parents, she was never pressed for time. Her passion for living came from the core of her being. All through my growing years, every woolen sweater and every pair of woolen drawers that I wore, she had knitted. She said that the woolens you could buy were never warm enough, and that fashion was repetitive. She wanted me to be different from the crowd in everything, to be special. Most of my clothes, and those of everyone else in my family for that matter, had been chosen for us by Ho with assiduous care. In addition to having the same refined feminine understanding as my mother, she also had this charming maternal appeal.

That evening, seeing the unalloyed enjoyment with which she prepared all these dishes truly touched my heart.

She said that really, it wasn't just anyone who got to enjoy this "lover's" treatment; that she felt especially close to me; that if it were anyone else just sitting there lending lots of words but never a hand, then the person would be out of luck for dinner.

Hearing this delighted me. I picked up the copy of *Interpretations of The Book of Changes* lying on the sofa and started thumbing through it, reading all the parts that she had underlined in pencil.

From childhood I had been aware of her love of reading. But our shared enthusiasm for it was something that came later, after I had grown up and done a lot of reading myself. Now, the more we talked, the more we began to realize how much we had in common.

She said that she had been reading *The Book of Changes* lately, and that it was like smoking marijuana.

I said that she should read something a bit lighter, that the ancients had said, "As you sit by your little window reading *The Changes of Zhou*, spring has long since slipped by unnoticed," and that life holds for us only a limited number of such "springs."

She said she was reading some lighter things too, like Zhang Jie's *The Ark* and Yi Lei's poetry.

The end of the '80s was one of those times of great artistic ferment and experimentation in China. Whenever Ho and I were together, we spent hours discussing literature and life. We talked about some of the male writers, but because of our own feminine view of life, it was the contingent of outstanding female writers that got most of our attention. We also discussed the work of such foreign authors as Borges,

Joyce, Kafka, Poe, and Faulkner. The kind of enthusiasm and rapture that infused our discussions of literature in those days is gone now, a thing of the past. And I am afraid that we shall never again see a time as rich in artistic energy.

That day, as Ho spoke on unhurriedly, her eyes began to shine with an intense fervor.

Every time we raised our glasses to drink, she used a line from *The Ark*: "Here's to the ladies—down the hatch!"

I laughed.

There was always a special minty fragrance about Ho's apartment. It was the unsullied smell that you find in the bedrooms of women who live by themselves, not spoiled by the usual mix of male and female hormones. This odor was like the warmth of a perfectly adjusted rich blue flame playing delicately above the surface of my skin, penetrating to its most sensitive nerve endings to make my blood surge with eagerness, yet without any threatening explosiveness.

I could not take my eyes off her as she flitted about before me, behind me, like a restless shaft of silvery moonlight, in a pastel dress trimmed in gorgeously striking purple.

She had had quite a bit of wine that evening and was unusually animated, telling me in endless detail the things she had thought and felt as she read *The Ark*, while I kept nodding in agreement and appreciation.

The sound turned all the way down, the TV was nothing more than a background stage prop to the subtle air of intensity in the room created by the two of us.

She started reciting stanza after stanza of Yi Lei's poetry for me:

Graft me everywhere into your skin
So we shall bloom together in profusion.
Let my lips become the petals of your flowers
Let your leaves become my waving hair.
Your earthen hues become my breath,
And I shall be seen in all things.

Her luminous voice flashed in the room's half-light, words falling from her lips like sparkling liquid spheres upon my upturned face.

I told her that I too was very fond of Yi Lei's poetry.

That I shared her pleasure made her even more passionate, and without another thought she picked up the copy of Yi Lei's poems that was there beside her and started to read "A Single Woman's Bedroom," which was causing a great sensation at that time:

> Do you know who I know?
> She is one, she is many.
> She appears suddenly from any direction
> And as quickly disappears,
> She stares straight ahead
> With no scars of happiness,
> She speaks to herself, silently.
> She is beautiful, without vitality,
> She is three-dimensional, she is two-dimensional.
> What she wants to give you, you cannot take,
> She cannot belong to anyone.
> . . . She is the I in the mirror.
> Divide the whole world by two
> And you are left with one,
> A self-motivated independent entity
> An entity endowed with creative energy.
> . . . She is the I in the mirror.
> My wood-framed mirror is at the head of my bed
> Where it works its magic 100 times a day.
> You cannot come to live with me. . . .

Because my mind was preoccupied that evening, I wasn't giving Ho my full attention. Although I was touched by her excitement, something else was grinding away in the back of my mind.

I really wanted to talk to her about what had happened with Ti. I wanted to tell her about this affair with a man I didn't love. But what would she think? Would she think I was a bad girl, unchaste? Would she stop liking me?

After I'd thought about it for several days, it had become clear to me that I was not in love with Ti. I was attracted to him only because he had aroused in me some nameless desire, but this desire, like a leaf caught carelessly in the surge and suck of a flowing river, had been buoyed and battered out of confusion toward clarity. It was a process both painful and saturated with wet fantasy and desire.

I desperately wanted to talk to Ho, who was older and whom I trusted and was deeply attached to, so that I might make use of her incisive thinking and experience in resolving my own chaotic confusion. This made me realize just how much I needed her.

I wanted to tell her that over the years she had always been the one I truly loved, that I cherished my memories of the way she loved me and looked after me when I was little, that I thought always of her intimacy and tenderness, and that as the months and years fell away, these unexpressed feelings grew stronger day by day. I didn't need anyone else to enter my life or my body. I didn't know what it was that had led me into this unfortunate mess. What was I to do? My desires had pushed me to the edge of a precipice. One more step and I would be lost.

My sexual secrets and everything that I had discovered had become nothing, a blank, empty space in my mind. I felt that all that he had done was lead me through the entrance to another phase of life, nothing more. He was desire made flesh, and I had boldly confronted his probing. He was like a tourist. He had simply visited a young female student's body. We had shared a part of our bodies with each other, a few organs, just like sharing labor in the fields. The itinerary of his journey meant nothing to me. And beyond this, I could see that where he had traveled, that place I had given to him, was in reality no more than an empty space, a kind of illusion.

But Ho was a house made of mirrors that belonged to my innermost being. In it, no matter where I was, I could always see myself. All its blank spaces were my silences, all her joys were smiles reflected on my face. As she watched over me day by day growing up, her fine fingers tightly gripping the barbed railings of life, my own hands felt her pain, and drops of fresh red blood seeped between my fingers. The way she would stand just outside her door, with one hand raised to shield her eyes from the piercing sun, the other resting feebly on her hip, watching me as if I were some kind of big bird leaving the nest to begin my lonely quest for food, made me feel like she was my mother, but she was definitely not my mother. From when I was very small, she had stood there helpless and alone, waiting for me, waiting for me to become a woman, the air around her filled with anxious concern and longing. The way she treated me left me dumb. I would try to say something, but I could never find the right words. Only my body itself could tell her.

But on that evening, this woman who had always been so thoughtful and attentive seemed to have lost control of herself. She ignored my responses, ignored my silences. She indulged herself in her intoxication with the ideas and feelings expressed in these poems by other people. Her cheeks were flushed the color of the wine, and her excitement buried my words and wishes.

I was on the verge of interrupting her a number of times, to talk about me, to talk about the two of us, but the wished-for words wouldn't come.

Finally, at a break in the TV program, I got up. I said I was tired, that I had to get up early for school and was going home to get some rest.

Only then did she seem to become aware of something, and her eager loquacity halted abruptly.

Coming over to me, she looked closely at my face; then, feeling my forehead, she said, "Do you feel ill?"

I said, "No, I'm tired, that's all."

When she saw how distressed I looked, she continued with concern, "There's nothing wrong, is there?"

I answered, "No. We can chat another day. There's something I want to talk to you about, but another day—okay?"

She said, "Well, okay. So you go home and have a good sleep."

At the door, she kissed me on the forehead and said, "Good night, my sweet."

When I left her apartment, I started slowly up the stairs. The corridors were deserted and quiet, and the wavering, stealthy shadows as obscure as code. Digging in my pocket for my key, I was totally wrapped in my own thoughts.

It was at that precise moment that I encountered the man I didn't recognize.

As he slipped quickly past me, I caught an odor of rotting soil or befouled water. Famished and filthy and looking utterly exhausted, he had the appearance of a man hounded incessantly by death. It seemed as if he had been ensnared by some ghostly force that had driven him from known roads, to flee endlessly from place to place to place.

I noticed that his hair was as thick and unkempt as wild grass. His cavernous eye sockets were set deeply into his dark face, the light emitted from them more like a feeble reflection flickering through a fissure in the earth than the glint of eyes. When we met unexpectedly in the corridor and brushed shoulders briefly as we passed, I felt his body sway imperceptibly as if it had been touched by some invisible force and suddenly become tensely alert. And he immediately shifted the bag he was carrying to the shoulder away from me.

His wariness aroused my wariness.

After he had slipped past me, I turned back to watch him.

I felt like I had seen this stranger before, a long time ago. But just how long ago, and who he was, escaped me.

When I got to my own apartment, I stood in front of the open window trying very hard to recall some clue of my past connection with this man. The light from the moon was glaringly bright and a restless wind sighed in the eaves of the building across the street. Some eerie birds flashed past the window, their cries echoing through the sleepy air.

Tired and sleepy, I curled up on my sofa, my eyes lightly closed.

I saw a number of past years and months rising up out of the dust, and, borne on wings, group after group of people I had once known flew past the window, the earth and mold they shook off their bodies smashing as it fell. I picked my way carefully through the morass of memories, with garbage, foul odors, and unfamiliar grasses and toadstools growing rampant everywhere. A forest of chestnut trees in the distance with a small path leading to it was the only inviting thing to be seen, but halfway there the path was cut off and it was impossible for me to continue.

I stared into the depths of my memory, but there wasn't a single trace of anyone.

But just then, a name was lifted from the silence as if by the evening wind. Uttered by many lips, it floated from the streets to my window. Beyond my grasp, it trembled and flickered with blood-red light against the black backdrop of the night. Vaguely, I saw a corpse standing up slowly. When I looked closely, I saw that it looked very much like the Ge woman, except that her face was somehow swollen and a deep scar on her neck had pulled the corner of her mouth to one side. Her protruding lips were like twisted flower petals covered with blood. I saw her remonstrating angrily among the ranks of innocent ghosts, but her desolate cries in the emptiness came back only as the faintest of echoes.

Dreadfully frightened, I listened intently.

Eventually, that faint echo was drowned out by the roar of a huge truck going by outside.

Opening my eyes, I stood up and went over to the window. I closed one side, thought for a while, and then closed the other. But locked up within my feelings, I still couldn't sort out my connection to the unexpected stranger on the stairs.

Finally, I let it go.

After taking a shower, I got into bed and turned out the light.

By this time it had started to rain, and the huge drops clattering on the street below sounded like the hooves of countless horses or beasts galloping by.

. . . The noise outside seemed to have pulled me into a huge party. A woman spinning in one corner of the dance floor glided over and looked at me with burning desire, her warm hand persistently seeking mine. Only when she at last took my hand in hers did I realize that it was Ho.

She asked me to dance.

I said that the two of us couldn't dance together.

She said, Why can't we? Listen. It's the latest music, males and females dance the same steps. The magnetic music pulled us onto the dance floor, and, holding my hand, she guided me out among the dancers. Our feet moved forward, back, in the crowded space, but we didn't bump into anyone, and so we danced our androgynous dance.

Under the bewildering changes of the constantly flashing colored lights, the faces around me kept changing shape. Ho and I held each other closely, afraid that the other might turn into someone else in a moment of inattention. Like the sound of the little drum in an opera orchestra, her heart beat wildly against my breast. Her body emitted an intangible heat as she pressed herself tightly against me. She held my young buttocks firmly in her hands, so exciting me that I began to gasp for breath.

With her bright eyes she coaxed me as we danced lightly down a sinuous, narrow, sloping corridor to a railing. Beyond it, I saw, was a deserted garden. We stopped. Then, in the dim light, I followed her into the garden without question, thinking of nothing but her.

When she started undoing my blouse, the sound of my wildly beating heart so unsettled her that her fingers began to fumble with the buttons. I said nothing, letting her do with me as she wished. When she had undone my blouse, she didn't take it off; she simply spread it open and ran her fingers through my hair, pushing it back from my forehead to reveal my entire face. Then she stepped back several paces so that we were not too close together, yet not too far apart; that is, we were not so close together that she could not appreciate my features, nor so far apart that the dim light obscured them.

Then she began undoing her own blouse and stood facing me in the same attitude in which I faced her, so that we could enjoy each other. A vague anxiety was unsettling me. I longed feverishly for her to reveal her beauty to me totally. Her every movement and gesture overcame me with its perfect beauty, and filled me with desire.

She was my mirror.

We gazed intently at each other for a long time, her eyes looking vaguely dejected and at the same time inquisitive. I had never before seen such a suggestive look in such an intelligent and passionate female face. Her short, neat, glossy hair and the serious lines at the corners of her mouth perfectly embodied her calm profundity and her rich life experience.

It is quite safe to say that at that moment I saw her far more clearly than she saw me.

A giddy feeling of joy began to rise up from the soles of my feet.

When she came over to me and kissed my cheek, it was just as it had been many years earlier—her glowing skin lightly touching mine; the familiar, delicate fragrance of her sinuous figure; from the center of my being, her voice softly calling my name. Just as it had been in those earlier times, my pulse quickened and I began to tremble, until at last I listened to her with my heart, held her within my heart of hearts. At the same time I felt ashamed of my liaison with Ti, my "fall," ashamed because I had betrayed her, hurt her.

Suddenly, I felt weak and helpless and struggled desperately to breathe. Inexplicably, out of nowhere that familiar "third hand" was reaching out toward my body, and ignoring all else, I eagerly received it. As we turned in dance, I was bathed in a shuddering consummation. Everything around me seemed to be melting, and my skin tingled with tense, numbing excitement.

As our passion subsided, we drooped with exhaustion and stood apart as our breathing returned to normal.

Then all at once my dance partner's formerly slim, graceful legs caught my attention. In an instant they had become as strong and thick as tree trunks. My eyes slowly traveled up those legs, as sturdy as those of a work horse, to discover that my dance partner had changed into someone else, a male. Taken aback, I said, What's happening?

He laughed slyly.

I said, I don't need you.

He said, Your lust needs me.

My face flushed red, and I said, In my heart I do not need you.

He said, You don't know yourself. Your real inner need is, in fact, me.

Feeling like I was the object of some joke, I looked anxiously everywhere for Ho.

I backed farther away from the man and shouted, I don't need you, I don't need you at all. . . .

. . . . . .

A deafening explosion jerked me awake. Blotting out the sound of the continuous rain, it jarred all the residents of the building out of their dreams.

The explosion was followed by an eerie silence, then the corridors rang with a piercing female scream, "Someone, please! Help! Help!"

Again, there was a dead silence.

Soon the corridors were filled with the clanging of burglar-proof doors opening and the scattered scuffle of slippered feet. The noise and confusion got louder and louder.

It had taken me this long to fully awaken. Now, I shot out of bed and rushed to the door. Someone was already pounding on it.

I swung it open to see Ho standing there, frightened beyond measure. She said, "Are you all right?"

Without a word, I grabbed her and we rushed to my mother's apartment.

The hallway was already jammed with people asking each other about the explosion. Without stopping to talk to anyone, I raced to my mother's door and started pounding on it violently.

There was no answer.

I knew that Mother was a light sleeper, and when she didn't respond, the strength went out of my legs.

I began to shout and bang the door with my fists.

Ho said, "Quick. Go and get your key."

When we finally got the door open, we rushed into Mother's bedroom and shook her awake, to find to our surprise that nothing had happened, that she was safe and sound.

A great stone of fear was lifted from my heart.

Mother explained that she hadn't been feeling well for the past few days and because she couldn't sleep, she had taken an extra-strong dose of sleeping pills.

The lights were out in the corridors, and in the inky darkness Ho and I groped our way upstairs with some neighbors who had heard where the accident was.

There was already a crowd of people outside the door of the Ge girl's apartment. Pale as a ghost, she stood stricken outside the open door, trembling uncontrollably, muttering repeatedly, "Please help my papa! The kitchen . . . the pressure cooker . . . ," while her husband stood jouncing their wailing son in his arms.

Suddenly I put things together: the familiar-looking "stranger" I had bumped into in the stairwell must have been Mr. Ge. After hiding for so many years, he had finally resurfaced, come home.

Nervously, I followed several of our neighbors into the apartment, looking for the kitchen, but what I saw there made me sick with fear.

The "stranger" was indeed Mr. Ge. He was stretched out on the dull red tile floor. A red and white mess the consistency of paste was splattered all around his head. The twisted, empty pressure cooker was beside his left shoulder, the bean porridge it had contained spewed everywhere, the lid nowhere to be seen. There was a round hole in his skull just behind his left ear, from which the grayish curd of his brain and syrupy thick blood still oozed. It was disgusting.

A middle-aged male doctor who lived in the building came in, and crouching down beside the motionless body, he reached out to feel for a pulse in Mr. Ge's neck. After a moment he stood up and said, "He's gone. With injuries like that, death is a matter of seconds."

I turned away and fled.

With his eyebrows and his fingers, he attacked me.
He was the house I built out of my fantasies.

Third year university was a very hectic time for me. It is reasonable to say that all the major changes in my life had their roots in that tragic period.

First, my mother was stricken with a fatal illness that year; then what could have been the first love of my life was aborted; after that, a serious fire took the life of my most beloved friend; and finally, I became an innocent victim in a serious incident. . . .

On my way home on that particular day, for no discernible reason at all, I was struck by a stray bullet from somewhere. Luckily, the bullet had passed through the flesh of my left calf, and I was able to convalesce at home after only two days in the hospital.

I have never taken the time to describe my years at the university, since I always seek to avoid that aspect of my life because it so wearies me. You could say that for the longest time I have harbored a hostile, antagonistic attitude toward school, with a special hatred for compulsory examination questions of all types that do not allow me the right to answer, "I have nothing to say on that subject." However, because those years involved the occasional presence of a boy named Yin Nan in my life and his very real departure from it, I have no choice but to touch upon them.

The faculty that I was in formed a poetry club called "Frowners." My involvement with Yin Nan was connected with its name.

At that time there were a number of impetuous young male students and teachers in the faculty who had proposed the creation of a poetry society. They started by drafting a charter setting out their principles and naming the club "Subversives," and school authorities responded by banning it. So they watered down their principles considerably and renamed the club "Opportunists." The revised charter was approved, but the name was again shot down. It was just when the club was experiencing these bothersome birth pangs that Yin Nan, one of its members, caught my attention in the cafeteria one day at lunchtime.

He had delicate good looks, with a long, thin, pale face; a straight nose; big, dark, gentle eyes; and flashing white teeth. He was tall and impeccably dressed, and bore a fleeting resemblance to the Chinese-American movie star John Lone.

Carrying my lunchbox that day, without any hesitation at all, I took the empty seat next to him. To be quite honest, I struck up a conversation with him only because of his attractive appearance.

It seemed that when I left Ti, he had removed something beautiful and personal from my life, but that now, with this young man in front of me, this special feeling had reemerged, pristine and pure.

Before meeting Yin Nan I had always had a stubbornly warped view of good-looking boys, thinking that their depth and their accomplishments most often ran in inverse proportion to their good looks. During my adolescence there was only one man of whom I thought otherwise—the former American president Richard Nixon. My adolescent infatuation with this handsome, profound, and also highly successful man came about because, with his big nose, wide shoulders, and amiable manner, he accorded very closely with my conception of the ideal father. Judging my men by how they measured up against the ample intelligence and capability of my idealized father image has probably been the most destructive flaw in my life.

My infatuation with Nixon definitely had nothing to do with politics. In fact, I have no interest at all in getting involved in any kind of political activity. I hate things political because they are so often far removed from the idea of "honesty," which I have held so dear my entire life. In all my years as a student, my grades on political exams were always disastrous. On one occasion, in a second-year survey examination, I think, in answer to the question, "Would you say that you deeply love politics?" my response was, "Only if it is permissible to lie," which netted me a long talking to by the school authorities. The instability and sudden changes in politics make it impossible for me to distinguish what is genuine from what is false. In my mind, political events remain a heap of overblown, amorphous memories. They are very much like huge waves that meet over great depths. You have to wait until the opposing currents are finally absorbed into each other, until the frothing peaks finally subside, before you can again discern the depths. Much as it is with love, political instability can encourage the pursuit of blind passions, but as it is with love, I have a right to choose when I want to be involved and when I want to break it off.

My youthful fascination with Nixon was a very naive fantasy that stayed with me until his death in February 1995. I was flying to a city in the Asian tropics on a South China Airlines flight when I saw his photograph and the headline announcing his death, in that day's overseas edition of *The People's Daily*. I very seriously placed a kiss on that forehead that had borne the brunt of so many of the vicissitudes of life; then I stared out of the plane's window for a while, imagining that Nixon's soul had already risen from the earth and was floating in the air outside my window. He looked in at me as we waved a farewell to each other, and I said, "Good-bye, Mr. Nixon." Then I put the newspaper aside, discarding along with it all those childhood illusions that had involved him.

Many years after my infatuation with Nixon, when as a mature young woman I attended an art symposium, a Chinese artist struck a similar emotional chord in me. Because he was actually physically present, his impact on me was much stronger. Once, during a banquet, the gods finally arranged that I sit beside him, but because of my innate reserve and my social awkwardness, I managed nothing in the way of real conversation. It wasn't so much that I didn't like to "converse," it was just that I didn't have much faith in "conversation." Conversation was fruitless. All I managed was the usual kind of toast to express my esteem. I was already quite aware that an easygoing, unaffected attitude was the best approach to life, a stance of indifference, but this could only be achieved through the exercise of extreme self-restraint.

On another occasion I saw him in a hotel lobby, holding a fluent conversation in English with a foreigner cinematographer. As he turned around, he caught sight of me and waved me over with a smile. I was amazed that someone of his age and prominence was able to converse so well in English. I stood beside him wanting very much to take his calm, confident hand, to bask in the security and comfort that his age made me feel. But my mind seemed to have stopped working and I had lost all ability to respond. I was slipping slowly into a state of bliss where I seemed to float unanchored in the sumptuous lobby, now steeped in sentimental tints of rose. When we said good-bye, as timid as an inexperienced little girl, I stuffed a letter that I had previously written into his hand. All my intelligence seemed to have drained from my head, leaving it an empty hole, and any remnants of my sensibility had retreated into my ice-cold fingertips. After I had given him the letter, I fled.

Regrettably, rather than being a letter expressing my affection for him, it was a request for his support in overcoming some difficulty, because he was the only person whose help I would accept. But as soon as I had left the hotel, I regretted what I had done. I was terribly afraid that he would see me as someone seeking his friendship because of his name. In fact, with my coolness and stubbornness bordering on arrogance, it would be rather difficult for me to show respect for someone just because of their fame.

Later on, he phoned me, and when I heard his voice, I felt as if I were talking to God.

I know myself. I wanted a man who was like a father to pour my love upon, a man whose views on humanity accorded with my own, of whom I would be a female extension, my thinking taking up where his male thinking stopped. I don't know if this qualifies as a question for the ethics of human relationships.

Actually, if you want to be modern, then all questions are both real and empty. One of the significant things about civilization, without doubt, is that it has given classifying names to the fantastic variety of human and natural phenomena. But this is simply one possible system of names.

At lunchtime that day, I sat beside Yin Nan.

Here was a person of a type totally different from the father figure that always won my affection. We struck up a casual, relaxed conversation. After we exchanged a few questions and answers, such as which department and grade we were in, he started talking about the poetry society.

I noted that he spoke very softly, with the easy grace that comes with a good education. When he talked about the name for the club being twice rejected, his brow furrowed slightly and he became very serious, not at all like those young men who are full of promises but empty on results. All you have to do is get them later on the telephone and you'll discover their insincerity.

I fixed my eyes on him, drinking in his brilliance.

Of everything about Yin Nan, it was his eyebrows that first moved me.

When I think about it, this was very strange, because the first things that I usually took note of in a person were the cheeks, the eyes, the lips, the body, and so forth—the big or conspicuous things. But now the things my attention gravitates to are the little or easily overlooked things such as the eyebrows, the nose, the teeth, or the hands or feet.

Yin Nan's eyebrows glistened like flowing strokes of black lacquer below his cleanly chiseled forehead. His slightly furrowed brow made me think of the phrase "worry lines." I have a rather special feeling about people's hair. With women, if they do their hair in a fuzzy bouffant style, I assume that their minds are equally fuzzy. Only after that do I consider the woman herself behind the hairdo. But with men, the first thing that captures my attention is their eyebrows. Only after I've checked their eyebrows do I consider their hair, beard, and the various areas of body hair that signal their level of physical maturity. I carry this so far as to judge their life and their spirit through their hair.

Yin Nan's eyebrows were long and very beautiful, severe yet soft, pliant yet unyielding. On that day his eyebrows gave him away in an instant, revealing his physical nature and his mentality.

Looking at his slightly furrowed, handsome brow, without giving it any further thought, I said, "Why don't you call your poetry club 'Frowners'? It's close in meaning to your original name, but it softens the violent tone. Really, they both convey the idea of negation, but mine does it in much more subtle way."

Yin Nan thought about it for a moment, the long, slim fingers of his scrawny right hand gripping his spoon; then he waved it excitedly as he exclaimed, "Perfect! That's perfect!"

Beginning to see me in quite a different light, Yin Nan very solemnly shook my hand.

His hands were the second thing about him that attracted me.

It was as if his hand emitted a current of air that penetrated the palm of my own, or a unique sound, perhaps the secret sound of the blood hidden in his fingertips, flowing in smooth yet distinct pulsations. It was the kind of hand that the moment you touched it, made you think of phrases that reflect the special ways we use our hands, such as "breathing through one's fingers" or "tears following one's palm lines to slowly fall," to try to mask or hide whatever it is we are feeling; that made you think of the smoothness and weight of skin touching skin. It was impossible to treat it as just a hand. It was a mouth sucking the heat from your skin. It was an eager, attentive ear pressed to the walls of your veins to pick up the pulsations of your blood. It was a hungry nose fiercely seeking the unlimited hard or soft secrets it could gain from the hand it was touching. It was a kind of light, a voice, a rumination. . . .

It seemed as if I had known that hand long ago, before I had ever seen Yin Nan. Long before his face ever entered my field of vision, I knew that hand.

His hand revealed him.

It was at that point that he earnestly invited me to join the poetry society.

I said, "I've never had any interest in joining any kind of group. I'm an 'individualist.' Right from when I was small, no matter what kind of group I became part of, I always numbered among the outside minority, because whenever the majority chorused 'Yes,' I couldn't help but counter with a tactless 'No.' I think that boldly standing up and saying no to the world is a powerful expression of personal responsibility."

Yin Nan said, "Our poetry society makes a point of saying no."

I said, "The unfortunate thing is when you give a chorus of no's, I'm afraid that I'll be inclined to say yes."

"Why? Just for the sake of being different? Not running with the crowd?" he asked.

"Of course not," I answered.

That same year I had begun reading Kierkegaard, so I trotted out his discussion of majority and minority groups. I said, "Members of a minority, or individuals, sometimes have more power than people in the majority, because the views embraced by members of minorities, or individuals, are genuinely their own, while the power of people in the majority is often spurious, because the group is made up of people of diverse views. When a minority or an individual produces a compelling point of view, then members of the majority take it as their own, but the diversity of their readings of the view reduces it to a confused welter of opinions, and the minority group or individual who first supported the view subsequently abandons it."

Yin Nan gave me a startled look, his limpid eyes unable to suppress a look of agitation and perplexity. His long, feminine eyelashes fluttered with excitement.

Then he nodded his head as if lost in thought as he muttered to himself, "I must introduce you to my friends." But after a moment he went on, "Right. I can't introduce you to them." His voice was almost inaudible.

I said, "What did you say?"

He said, "Nothing. I didn't say anything."

He seemed even handsomer than ever, radiating an uncommon inner clarity and authority. I realized right at that moment that in addition to my infatuation with father figures like Nixon, I also had an infatuation with young men like Yin Nan.

For at least an hour after we parted, for the first time in my life I was lost in a reverie over a young man, and his being real and within reach left my heart and my mind in a total mess. It was as if a cage had been stuffed into my breast, filled with birds gaily chattering and pecking away inside. I was pleasantly surprised, but perplexed and uneasy.

My first thought was to go and see Widow Ho immediately, as if I had come upon some kind of rare and wonderful treasure and wanted to share the pleasure with her. I had discovered that whenever anything happened, if I could face it together with her, whatever agitation or unpleasantness there might have been would dissipate like smoke. In my mind, we were lifelong fellow conspirators who understood each other without the need for words. For the past few weeks I had been unsettled because I hadn't had a chance to discuss Mr. Ti with her. But now I had no interest in discussing him at all. I wanted only to talk about Yin Nan. Just having his name flutter across my lips gave me a special feeling.

We were in the middle of icy January with its short days and long nights. On campus that afternoon my thoughts were elsewhere, and just before four o'clock I hurried away.

I wanted to sort out all the things that were on my mind. I find that the best thing to do at such times is to wander wherever my feet may carry me along some street where nobody knows me, with the brisk air in my face and the colors of twilight slowly descending. I enjoy wandering the streets as a stranger, and to make myself feel more the stranger or outsider, I often pretend that I am in a place far away from where I live, preferably in the street market of some isolated village. It has always pleased me, even when I was a child, to think that the people around me don't know me and that I don't know them.

Spring festival was just around the corner and the crowded, noisy streets and brilliantly lit shops put me in a carefree, relaxed mood.

For a long time, scenes of city life have always generated in me a feeling of isolation. I have never felt that they belonged to me, and as time passes, my attachment to them becomes weaker and weaker. For some reason I can't fathom, although I am physically still very young, I frequently lose myself in quiet reflection like an old person. I feel like my life no longer has any real purpose.

But on that day I had a change of mood. I no longer felt that life was cold and hopeless, and an unbroken feeling of joy welled up from the soles of my feet, jarring me out of my moroseness. Once again I pretended that the streets beneath my feet were streets I did not know. I wanted to leave behind the world I knew, to submerge my mind in an exciting new experience. To live through loneliness and inner torment for so long, and surprisingly come out of it alive and still able to encounter such wonders, seemed inconceivable. So at that moment, without being aware of it, I had expanded by a hundredfold the importance of my knowing Yin Nan.

At the side of the road, I saw an old lady sitting on a straw mat, staring blankly as she begged. A male child with an enormous head was suckling at her wizened breast. He had no hands, and the two stumps of his arms had been rubbed so smooth that they shone. An icy shaft shot through my heart, and my beautiful dream was abruptly broken.

Averting my eyes, I dug a coin out of my pocket, dropped it at the old lady's feet, and left.

When I got home, I went to see my mother.

The moment I opened her door, I could hear her labored breathing. It sounded like the hiss of the impure liquified natural gas when we lit the burner to boil water every day.

I was astonished to see that the window was wide open so that it was as cold in the room as it was outside. She was at the window, leaning against the radiator, in a thick, padded cotton coat, struggling to breathe.

I said, "Mama, it's so cold today. How come you've got the window wide open?" As I was speaking, I closed it.

Mother said that she had been feeling uncomfortable for the past several days, as if there wasn't enough oxygen in the room, no air circulation.

I looked closely at her face for a while, and sure enough, her color wasn't very good—pale with a greenish tinge. There was a look of distraction in her eyes, and dark circles of exhaustion around them.

I suggested she lie down and get more rest and sleep.

Mother said that sitting was better than lying down, standing was better than sitting, and she didn't know why, but the room seemed to be so terribly stuffy that she found it difficult to breathe.

While she was talking, I quickly ran over any unusual things she had done or said recently.

She had said to me on several occasions that she didn't know what the problem was, but she often woke up unable to breathe and had to sit up straight for a while to get her breathing back to normal, and that she always slept badly because of her wheezing. Lately, it had been especially serious. Often in the middle of the night she had to prop up the upper half of her body or she wouldn't be able to breathe properly or get a decent sleep. And in the daytime she was always worn out and listless, and would often break out in a sweat for no reason at all. She wondered in frustration if her menopause would ever pause.

All this led me to think of the female leads in the Bergman films *Cries and Whispers* and *Silence*. They were always lying face up on their beds with their heads canted back, a tremendous wheezing noise like the sound of a pipe organ threatening to split their bosoms asunder. Their emaciated, gnarled hands stretching upward in supplication as they struggled to breathe, it seemed as if their empty, ruined internal organs were about to collapse, as if they were about to be swallowed up by the dark, suffocating air. . . . They were locked forever in a cage, where they saw their isolation and individuality as something sacred. They were gathered together to lament their personal isolation, but not only did they not listen to each other, they were suffocating each other without knowing it. They stared into each other's eyes but denied each other's existence. . . .

Like the approaching darkness of night, these scenes enveloped me completely, filling me with a fear and confusion that shot through my entire body.

But, stuffing my hands in my pockets, I forced myself to remain calm, and said with strained casualness, "I'll take you to the hospital tomorrow. I think maybe you're sick."

Mother said, "Let's wait a bit. Maybe it's something to do with my menopause, something that comes and goes, like the trouble I had with fever and perspiring a while ago."

But my instinct told me that this time Mother was really sick.

From the day that Mother moved into her apartment, I had had a vague premonition that something was not right. Just after we had moved into this building, I heard that construction had been started on an inauspicious day, offending Tai Sui, one of the figures from traditional Chinese folklore. Tai Sui holds a rather special position in our folk mythology. He has something to do with the worship of celestial bodies but doesn't represent any particular one of them. Nor is he a symbol for some heavenly phenomenon. Some people say that Tai Sui is associated with the "Year Star," or Jupiter, one of God's year deities. He resides underground and is the counterforce to the Year Star in heaven. If you disturb the soil over Tai Sui's head, you may dig into some moving flesh, which is one of Tai Sui's transformations. Afterward, as long as the people who move into the building are vigorous and thriving, nothing much will happen, but if they are in ill health and their star is on the wane, they may encounter some fatal misfortune. I had long before heard the expression "to dare to disturb the soil over Tai Sui's head," but I had always believed it was nonsense, that Tai Sui was imaginary, invented by people to fulfill a need, nothing more than an esoteric term used in geomancy but sneered at by modern science. So I had never given it any credence.

But now, when I saw how my mother looked, it did seem as if she had been touched by some intangible thing.

I walked everywhere in her apartment, searching for whatever it was that was amiss. Then I said without much conviction, "Mama, I think the orientation of your apartment is bad."

Mother said, "Don't be stupid."

I continued to think about it but said no more.

I pulled her over to the bed and made her sit down. It seemed like the worst was over. Her breathing was back to normal and the color was returning to her face. Moving her hands over the bedstead and the mattress, she sighed. "It was such a struggle to change our lives, and now—such a nice apartment, such a nice bed—and now only the two of us, and we don't have to put up with anybody's angry outbursts. But . . . ai . . ." The way she spoke, it sounded as if all of this was going to be lost forever.

An unaccountable sadness flooded over me.

To take her mind off her difficulty with breathing, I told her about Yin Nan, the boy I had met in the cafeteria.

Mother was an educated woman with a lifetime of reading behind her and had certainly had her share of hardships as well, but she had never lost her romantic, innocent nature. Her mind could be diverted as easily as a little girl's. Now, when for the first time from my lips she heard news of a handsome young boy, there was an abrupt about turn in her focus of attention. At the same time she was asking me questions about his circumstances, she was blindly immersing herself in fantasies of the future.

I didn't tell Mother about my fears over her physical condition, because I had realized that it would be unfortunate if she had the same fears. My mind was a blank, without a single trace of the noon-hour events in the school cafeteria. I stood motionless in the center of the room, staring at the shadow cast on the bare wall by the white hanging lamp.

Eventually I left her apartment, to have my feet carry me directly to Widow Ho's.

She was reading, the smoke from her pipe twining upward like embryonic galaxies.

There was something wrong with her refrigerator, and as soon as I entered the room I heard its noisy whir. This sound and the swirling wisps of smoke made the room look like a laboratory scene from a science fiction movie, or an obscure, miniaturized universe.

Once inside, I stood there rooted to the floor. As if in a dream, one after another, all the things that had happened that day swept past my eyes, filling my head, but I stood there blankly, not knowing what to say.

"What's wrong?" Ho asked.

I didn't respond. There was so much packed into my head that even the whirring of her refrigerator bothered my ears and my nerves. It was as if it too wanted to invade my brain. Trying to resist the sound, I said, "Your refrigerator's broken."

"I know." She asked me again, "What's wrong?"

Again I said, "Your refrigerator's broken."

"I know. Surely you didn't come over just to tell me about my refrigerator."

Again, I didn't respond.

I tried to ignore the whirring noise and spill out, like garbage, all the things that were on my mind. But, strangely, the noise curled around my ears like smoke and dominated my thoughts, even clinging to the skin of my entire body, trying insistently to bore into my brain. Standing there rigidly, I felt dizzy for a moment, and helplessly alone and unable to utter a word.

Putting out her pipe, Ho came over and took me in her arms. At last, I relaxed against her shoulder.

She said gently, "We'll have supper together, then we can have a nice chat."

I knew this shoulder very well. I had been enchanted by its fragrance ever since I was a tiny girl. It seemed as if these soft but strong shoulders had always been the keepers of my body, giving me support as I grew toward maturity. I clasped my arms tightly around her neck, afraid that my inner turmoil might turn them into a pair of flapping wings to carry me away from her, out of her embrace.

"I can't . . ." I said, "live without you."

"I know, I know."

After a pause, I added, "But I can't have dinner with you tonight. Mama's sick. I have to take care of her."

"Well then, you'll have to go." She patted me lightly on the back. "Don't forget, whatever happens, I'll always be here to help you. There's no need to worry. Okay?"

I felt my anxiety slipping away.

We embraced each other again, then I left her apartment.

In the end, Mother went to the hospital by herself, as she wished. Even though I told her my classes were not a problem, that I could graduate with my eyes closed, she insisted that she didn't want me to go with her.

When she came back from the hospital, she was quite casual about the whole thing. She said that the doctors had given her a general examination, x-rays and the like; that the preliminary diagnosis was heart strain; it wasn't very serious yet, but if it wasn't looked after, it could develop into a leaky aortic or mitral valve, which could lead to an increase in diastolic pressure in the left ventricle, leading to a malfunction of the left heart chamber. The doctor gave her a prescription for a cardiac stimulant and a diuretic to decrease the pressure, and urged her to come to the hospital to be put on oxygen whenever she felt it was necessary.

After that, Mother stayed home to rest and took her medicine every day. As her condition began to visibly improve, my concern for her began to ease as well.

After getting to know Yin Nan, I often bumped into him in the cafeteria at noon, and we would sit and have lunch together. But gradually, our relationship began to change in a rather subtle way.

When I first met him, it was mostly his handsome face and engaging manner that captivated me. Seeing him gave me a thrill that quickly overwhelmed me, filling my heart and dominating my thoughts. But this visual stimulation gradually settled down into a stable and lasting affection. He still aroused my passion, but I would think of him in this way only when it was getting close to lunchtime.

It was Yin Nan himself who underwent the subtle change.

Every time I met him he was always sitting in the same place, bent over his food, ignoring me. He never looked up when I approached, until I said, "How's lunch?" or "Here I am," at which point he would suddenly lift his head, pretending he hadn't noticed me, and say, "Hi!"

I say "pretending" because I have plenty of proof that he was adopting a stance to hide his real feelings. It was his fingers that gave him away.

He was always reading some paper or other as he was eating. When I approached, even though his eyes would be focused on his paper, the fingers of one of his hands would be drumming anxiously on the table in a way that had nothing to do with his food or his reading. The closer I got, the faster his fingers drummed. Only when the shadow of my head fell on his paper did those fingers suddenly stop, and curl into a tense, bony half-fist, the fingers trembling nervously. But he refused to look up, waiting instead for me to say something, when he would offhandedly suddenly "discover" I was there.

But his hand quietly and unmistakably revealed his uneasy anticipation. His tense fingers and the studied nonchalance on his face were perfect foils for each other.

I didn't say anything to him about his behavior. These little quirks endeared him to me. I knew that he wanted to see me just as much as I wanted to see him, that he waited every day for my "How's lunch?" I knew that the sound of my voice was all that was needed to make him forget about eating.

After meeting by chance in the cafeteria for a while, Yin Nan and I gradually became close friends, and he was able to relax a bit.

Eventually, he asked me to go on an outing with him one weekend, and I ecstatically agreed.

He wanted to meet me up in my apartment, then go out together, but I thought it precipitous to invite him home like that, and besides, it wouldn't be good with Mother still not feeling well. So I arranged a time to wait for him downstairs.

That winter was unusually mild, and the weekend was gorgeously warm and sunny. At ten o'clock sharp, wearing a cashmere cardigan and carrying a down jacket under my arm, I went downstairs.

Before leaving the apartment I had stood in front of the mirror carefully assessing how I looked. I tried on, took off, tried on, took off a string of things, finally settling on the silver-gray cardigan.

I noticed that my body, which was once as thin as a sheet of paper, and my arms and legs, the Misses Do and Don't of my childhood, once skinny as sticks, had filled out, and that my breasts had been swelling quietly to fullness beneath my blouse. As I looked closely at this young but very beautiful girl in the mirror, I saw her suddenly turn away, and when she turned back again she had taken off all her clothes, or, I should say, they had simply disappeared. Her naked figure was flagrantly bared in the mirror, her deep red nipples glowing as if bathed in sunlight, her smooth white breasts following my eyes like a pair of plump sunflowers following the sun.

I was quite aware of my own narcissistic tendencies, but what followed caught me completely off guard, even shocked me.

I saw my body, frail as a feather, floating lightly toward me from a fog-enshrouded horizon. Whimpering helplessly with tears streaming down my face, I was in the arms of someone who looked exactly like Yin Nan. He was gently caressing my cheeks and my forehead in an attempt to soothe me. The touch of his breast ignited in me an overwhelming desire to be his prisoner. I had never before been embraced by anyone so young, nor had I ever before felt the desire to lose myself like this. I nestled in the mysterious greenish-blue aura of light that seemed to issue from his arms, in the overbrimming vitality of his youth. Yet his youthfulness made me feel uneasy.

Then I heard a voice that sounded exactly like Yin Nan's saying, "You're not at all like the others."

I said, "You've found out?"

The voice said, "You captivate me. You're pure and noble."

I said, "I'm not the least bit pure. You have no idea what kind of person I am."

The voice said, "I understand you."

I said, "You don't understand me. You have no idea how shameless I have been in the face of desire."

The voice said, "I like your shameless innocence."

I said, "You can't understand me. You're too young. And I am already old beyond my years."

The voice said, "I understand you. I've known you for a long time, and I've never stopped watching you."

I said, "Watching what?"

The voice said, "Your cheeks, your eyes, your lips, your breasts. . . ."

Then I felt his gentle, cool fingertips lightly touching and caressing my face and my breasts. . . .

A feeling of faintness overcame me, and I struggled to open my eyes.

I saw my own hands caressing the naked body of the young girl in the mirror. . . .

At exactly ten o'clock I went downstairs. Yin Nan was already waiting for me at the entrance to the stairwell.

I went a few steps closer and said, "Have you been waiting long?"

He didn't say anything, just gave a secretive little chuckle.

He led me over to an inky black Imperial sedan and, opening the right front door, said, "Jump in."

I was rather surprised, because I couldn't see a driver anywhere, and there was no taxi sign. Feeling a bit puzzled, I climbed into the car and sat down.

By this time Yin Nan had already gone around to the other side, slid into the driver's seat, closed the door, and started the engine.

Watching in total astonishment, I asked him, "The car—did you drive it here? Can you drive?"

Cocky and secretly pleased with himself, he ignored my questions.

Following the sun-mottled streets, the car left our neighborhood behind and moved quickly out onto the multiple-laned Third Ring Road, where it quickly accelerated. We flashed past the roadside shops, trees, and scattered residential buildings. When I saw that the speedometer had already hit 140 kilometers per hour, I began to feel a bit uneasy.

I said, "Don't go so fast. We could have an accident."

Saying nothing, not even turning his head, Yin Nan kept his eyes on the road as we raced along.

I was starting to feel afraid.

I knew that he had carefully planned everything that day to show off his driving skills and impress me with his speed.

So I said, "Okay. You've already scared me stiff."

But only when we were turning off onto a side street did he finally slow down.

It was a small and very quiet road that connected with the city's eastern suburbs. The sun was shining directly into my face, so I cupped one hand over my eyes to block the piercing light.

Then I noticed that he had moved over as close as possible to the edge of the road to get us into the shade. His thoughtfulness touched me.

Dropping my hand, I said, "You needn't worry. It's just that the sun's a bit bright."

He said, "We better stay in the shade as much as possible. With your hand forever hoisted up like that, you look like you're saluting a military review."

I started to laugh. This was the first time I had seen his sense of humor.

We continued to drive. Gradually the city's variety of sights and noisy flow of people fell away, and on either side we began to see fields lying fallow, storage sheds, and run-down cottages that looked a bit like old-fashioned thatched huts.

We conversed very little along the way. I didn't feel like showing my curiosity about such things as his driving or whose car it was. I was totally engrossed in watching his every action as he drove, afraid that I might miss something—so much so that I began to feel faint from eyestrain and had to close my eyes and lean back against the seat and rest for a while before I began to recover. I was as serious as if I were a driving school student studying for my test.

When I closed my eyes to relax a bit, I felt Yin Nan pull the car over to the edge of the road, stop, shut off the engine, then turn to me.

"Do you feel sick?" he asked solicitously.

I said, "No. It's just that my eyes are a bit blurry."

"Then we'll rest for a while," he said, turning on the radio. As coincidence would have it, they were playing a song I loved very much— "The End of the World."

> Why does the sun go on shining?
> Why does the sea rush to shore?
> Don't they know it's the end of the world?
> . . .
> Why does my heart go on beating?
> Why do these eyes of mine cry?
> Don't they know it's the end of the world?
> It ended when you said good-bye.

This kind of soft-edged sentimentality could no longer stir me to tears. I simply listened quietly, feeling a bit sad.

I opened my eyes and looked out the car window at the golden sunlight streaming after the withered leaves as they raced across the ground. The bright light and the brilliant yellows pierced my eyes like hot flames. My eyes smarted, filling with tears, and I wiped them away with my fingers.

Noticing this, Yin Nan turned his head inquisitively to look at me. After a moment he said, "You're not crying, are you?"

I said, "Don't be stupid. There's something bothering my eyes."

Then we fell silent, listening quietly to the song.

As we listened, there must have been something that somehow touched me, for I was struck with an inexplicable grief that reduced me to tears, real tears whose flow I could not stem, and the more I cried, the more intense this grief became.

Even today, I still have no idea what was behind those tears. But I do know that they had little, if anything, to do with Yin Nan and me.

For a moment, feeling absolutely dreadful, I turned away from him.

As I did so, Yin Nan very softly put his arm around my shoulder, so softly that it seemed weightless, independent of his body, as if it had no connection with him. It was as if the arm had feelings of its own. But that exploratory action aroused a strong reaction in my body. I was helpless before a subtle force, like an irresistible drowsiness, that kept pulling me.

Slowly I let myself go and leaned against his shoulder.

When his hand felt my response, its strength returned and it grasped my arm, its fingers squeezing me. Then his other hand encircled me. But his movements were extraordinarily gentle. There was no unrestrained lust, but there was an impassioned and uneasy curiosity. Perhaps it was because he lacked experience, perhaps he felt awkward, but for a long time he was content simply caressing my arms, my neck, and my cheeks, his actions all highly restrained. I noticed that he was struggling to keep his breathing normal. He didn't want me to see him suddenly lose his self-control.

We continued like this for a long time, until finally he slipped his hand down over my breasts and began undoing my buttons.

He did this very slowly, like a general who was all confidence leisurely leading his troops to retake territory that had been momentarily lost, with none of the impetuosity of a young man blind with passion. His shy dignity stirred me, deeply filling me with a tender warmth as I helped him undo the last few buttons. I felt a breath of cool air touch my breasts. Glancing up into the rearview mirror, I saw one of my ripe, young breasts bob into view, joggling in the sunlight, like a plump, firm apple bursting with juice. I watched as one of Yin Nan's hands moved to touch it ever so lightly, then quickly covered it with my sweater as if he were afraid that someone else might be furtively watching. Then the hand fastened every single one of the buttons on my sweater, ceasing its movement only after it had pulled my collar closed as well. But it didn't move away from my breasts. It was as if it was only resting for a moment, as if it couldn't bear to have such a good show end too quickly.

I say this because the subsequent scene bore it out.

After pausing for a while, the hand began undoing my buttons afresh. When the "apple" bobbed into sight in the rearview mirror again, the hand touched it tentatively, then covered it with my sweater again. It seemed as if he were intoxicated with this kind of fleeting but deeply prized visual and tactile gratification, as if he didn't want to let unbridled desire ruin the feeling of aesthetic appreciation that I had stirred in him.

When I recalled this scene after I had gone home, it still moved me deeply. It seems to me that the feelings involved in this kind of innocent behavior run much deeper than those generated by undisciplined self-indulgence, whether you look at it from the physical or psychological point of view. I found myself irresistibly drawn back to that scene again and again, with every detail played out in slow motion out of fear that I might at some point forget something. For a long time, I steeped myself in naive, romantic reveries, longing for my life to unfold.

That day, we stayed there in the car for about an hour. Finally Yin Nan, with an unexpected, almost reverential seriousness, placed a very light but very long kiss on my left earlobe, then pulled away from me, and sitting there behind the wheel as primly and sweetly as a little boy, he started the car.

We drove along the bare winter road between the fields. In front of us, patterns of sunlight danced on the black pavement, beckoning us onward. Holding the hand Yin Nan had put in my lap, I immersed myself totally in the pastoral scenery around us.

As we drove he repeatedly turned to look at me, his eyes lingering affectionately on my face and my body. He would stare at me a while, give a little laugh, then focus his attention on the road again. But after a moment he would turn to look at me again, the desire in his eyes like fingertips exploring my body.

I was afraid that we might have an accident if he continued like that, and finally, unable to contain myself, I said, "You mustn't look at me all the time. You'd better watch the road."

He didn't say anything, but he gave a little laugh, then didn't look at me anymore. But his hand again slid from the steering wheel into my lap and cupped itself around mine.

We were silent again for a long time, the only sound the faint noise of the car as it moved along the uneven road, like a boat on an undulating sea.

The rural scenery swept past my eyes. The piles of gold-colored straw, the withered, bare trees, the farming villages dotting the vast landscape, and the waving fields of winter wheat all had a wonderful appeal quite unlike anything the city could offer.

At last, unable to contain myself, I said, "I love the countryside."

Yin Nan said, "You mean the scenery?"

I said, "It's not just a matter of enjoying it from afar. I would love to live in the countryside."

"Living in such a place would be peaceful, all right. Nobody'd know who you were," he said.

"I don't want anyone to know who I am," I said.

Yin Nan hesitated for a moment, then said, "You're saying you'd like to be a hermit? Whatever for? We're young—the world is calling us."

I said, "It's too exhausting to live among people, and too dangerous. Living in China is like being dropped into a monstrous labyrinth. To get through it, it isn't knowledge, talent, or intelligence that you need; it's something else. I can't handle it."

"You're right on. If we want to achieve anything of significance in life, aside from accumulated knowledge, to survive we have to learn to recognize opportunities and to ignore what other people think. I've just been reading up on this. They say that in Japan the final training for anyone who wants to do something significant in life, whether in business or politics, is standing on the street and shouting, 'I'm a scumbag! A bastard!' Think about it. What can you do to a person like that?"

"So it's like you're saying that ultimately it's the person who has no sense of honor, who turns his back on friends and family, who gets ahead. But do you know how much that person has to bear in his heart?"

"That's exactly why I say we have to learn this lesson."

"But why exhaust yourself like this? It's far better just to hide."

"Oh, is that so? Well, it's different for a man. You can hide yourself away out here, but I can't hide. I have to get involved."

In all the time we had known each other, this was the first time I had seen the determination that lurked beneath his shyness.

A bit surprised, I watched him for a while, then said, "Of course. Of course I understand that."

He turned to me, and as if he were trying to get away from some unpleasant line of thinking, he abruptly switched the thread of our conversation. "All that stuff is so boring. Why waste our time talking about it? Mmm, do you know . . ." He turned away from me again to watch the road.

"Do I know what?"

He didn't answer me directly. He stared at the road ahead, increasing our speed.

"Do I know what?" I repeated.

He said softly, "I . . . like you."

I didn't quite know what to say, so I didn't say anything.

"Like you . . . an awful lot. Don't you know?" he added.

"Of course . . . I know."

I don't like it when two people always want to talk about their relationship. I think a relationship is a natural thing, not something you talk into being.

So I shifted the direction of our discussion. "How come you never told me you knew how to drive a car?"

"There's lots of things I haven't told you," he said, as he took his driver's license from his shirt pocket. "Look, I passed my driver's test last summer during the holidays. It's my big brother's car. He doesn't know I took it today. He's got lots of money. It's just that he doesn't have any real goal in life. So he's pinning his hopes on me."

I said, "That's a heavy weight to carry. I get the feeling that you want to do something big with your life."

He didn't say anything. He just turned to me with the shy little smile that I had come to love so much.

"You're a bit of an enigma," I added.

It was already quite late, and feeling a bit hungry, I began checking out the restaurants we were passing.

Yin Nan said, "When we get into town, we'll look for a nice place to eat."

"With your brother's money, too?" I asked.

"If he wants to support me, why shouldn't I take it? I've got lots of ideas. Maybe you'd call them dreams, but even if they are, what's so bad about that?"

"What dreams?"

He gave a little laugh. "Lots of them. You—you're one of my dreams. I don't know how you feel about it, but as far as I'm concerned, I'm not just one person anymore—you're part of me."

We were already in the city, and the car slowed down as we threaded our way along the street jammed with people celebrating Spring Festival Eve.

I lingered on his words, "you're part of me." It was as if I was unaware of what was happening on the street outside. They were like flames, a numbing drug that intoxicated me. I felt a new kind of strength welling up inside me.

We found a place to park, but before we got out of the car, Yin Nan, as if suddenly emboldened, grasped my shoulder eagerly, and pressing his cheek against mine, said in almost a whisper, "Would you like to be with me always?"

Although it was a question, it was obvious that he didn't want an answer, because he immediately enclosed me in his arms and placed that firm, sweet mouth squarely upon my own, preventing any reply. Like a big, lovable frog, he sucked in my fragrance, his breathing hoarse and desperate with excitement.

I could feel the sharp metallic beat of his heart penetrating into mine through the interstices between his ribs, which were pressing into my breasts like so many powerful fingers. That huge and ardent chest opening itself outward was like a large country bent on expansion, eager to annex, or more precisely, to welcome or accept a small country.

He mumbled incoherently as he ran his trembling hands over my back. I felt his fingers and gradually his entire body begin to tremble, and the tighter he embraced me, the more awkward and tense he became. I knew that only genuine love could stir that kind of awkwardness, excitement, that kind of restraint and tentativeness.

We embraced so long I felt faint.

At last, we got out of the car.

The strains of some strange kind of flute music drifted toward us, mingled with the rustle of the barren tree in front of us. Beneath it, a blind man with sunken eyes, his whiskers ceaselessly flapping, was lost in his playing. Expressionless, his bones grinding, he swayed to the tuneless music that floated upward through the branches and power lines into the yellow evening light to be carried away by the wind. That music, like piercing light, left you feeling lost and uncertain.

Facing the sun, he played the flute wildly, then shouted in a hoarse, dry voice, "I have come from a faraway place—far, far away. I have seen, I have seen the clouds of war drifting upon us . . . many people sticking out their young tongues . . . their eyes as bright as dazzling stars that have fallen to earth. . . ."

He tore his shirt to shreds and threw the pieces on the ground to be blown away by the wind. "Look! Many, many young tongues have been scattered on the ground like this, on the ground where they continued their song . . . their eyes rolled away and were crushed like grapes. . . ."

As we passed him, he suddenly "caught sight" of us, and he seized Yin Nan's hand. A strange light shot from his eyes. "You've only got half a head. . . ."

Then he turned to me, "You've only got one leg . . . run! Run. . . ."

"He's mad." Frightened, I pulled Yin Nan along with me as I fled.

Behind us, his cries grew more and more desolate and terrifying.

I want to share your bed in heaven. The dead best understand the dead.

Even today, there is still no clear reason why that fire had to start. It was simply the will of heaven. When I look back on it now, it still seems totally unreal, like a dream within a dream that leaves you lost and uncertain. What this fire that shocked the whole neighborhood took away from me, or, I should say, the grief that it brought to me, left me unable for days to shed the tears that were choking me.

I usually go to bed very late, because I find the noise and confusion of the daytime very taxing. The days seem interminable, they exhaust me so; but from the moment supper is finished until late into the night I am filled with a carefree contentment. I often sit quietly by myself not doing anything, with countless images of people and events passing endlessly through my mind like scenes from a movie. I relax, viewing whatever scenes happen to suit my fancy. During this time I also have dreams, dreams that are exceedingly real. I don't as a rule turn on the light, imagining instead that I am in a cave or in some huge stone crevice, talking to a person very much like myself. She sits just in front of me, breathing and talking, but I can't see her face or even her outline, because I am enveloped in a thick, obscuring darkness. I immerse myself in it, a secret and safe world, where time and space no longer exist. I sit on my sofa or pace the carpet as quiet as a cat, very careful in my movements and my words, as if I were afraid of breaking something.

I see a great many people in my dreams; for example, I once saw Mrs. Ge among a group of ghosts. She was shouting herself hoarse, holding up a small flag bearing the word REVENGE. Although I couldn't hear what she was shouting, I could see her words on her lips, which were twisted with anger. Her lips were a flame the color of fresh blood, which took the shape of a pictograph as it leaped upward. It was through this pictograph that I could read what she was saying. On another occasion, I saw a huge open-air market. It had just rained, and I had muddied my trousers. The vegetables in the hawkers' stalls were so gorgeously colored they looked like beautiful still-life paintings. The place was crowded with familiar faces from my childhood. When the confusion and noise subsided, through the darkness I noticed a single eye sticking very closely behind me. I tried to get a better look at the person's face or body, but aside from the eye, I couldn't see anything. That is to say, the only thing left of this person was an eye, and it was following me.

At first I was afraid, but I very quickly realized that it was my nanny's eye. When I went to buy vegetables the hawkers would always cheat me, but this time the eye beside me would let out an ear-piercing shriek that sounded like it came from hell. The hawkers looked around in alarm for the source, but they could see that it wasn't coming from my lips. Then they looked at the eye beside me as if it were some weird and terrifying thing, and nervously weighed out my purchases in full measure. Pleased as punch, I swaggered about from stall to stall, buying all kinds of things.

At last, I addressed the darkness. "Nanny, let's go home."

The eye said, "I am already intertwined with the moonlight. Never again will a man be able to crush this eye of mine as if it were a flower petal. I live on the roof of the mortal world. I am the adversary of darkness. Never again will I allow women's eyes to be violently snuffed out one by one, like so many candles."

Her words were borne by the wind from some unknown season. Eventually her quiet voice and her footsteps drifted off toward the sounds of vicious struggle in the darkness. Amid this many-voiced, or, should I say, polyphonic "chorus," her voice became a strong and powerful solo. . . .

In the past the people and events that I encountered in these real yet unreal visions were all old people and events from my own past. But on this particular evening, to my complete surprise, it was Widow Ho that I saw through the darkness.

She was poking her head around the door, a book in her hand, smiling at me. Like rings of ripples on a pond, her beautiful smile spread slowly across her face. What was strange was that she didn't have a stitch of clothing on. She stepped out of the room absolutely naked, her smooth skin flashing like a red fish under a dazzlingly rich red glow of light. But she didn't appear the least bit shy or hesitant as she casually passed people in the corridor. I watched her from a distance, and although her face looked a bit drawn and had that sleepy look of someone who has just been suddenly awakened, those big eyes of hers, glazed with sleep but as lovely as ever, were fixed confidently in front of her, showing absolutely no awareness that she was stark naked. Astonished, I anxiously waved my hand to get her attention, to get her to leave, because evil spirits often haunted this place. I shouted her name, only to discover that the sound of my voice faded into nothingness. It was no use, no matter how hard I tried. I wanted to go and push her away, but before I could reach her, she pulled back to be swallowed up in the shadows, and I lost sight of her.

Indistinct shadows kept shifting all around me, and with a dim and distant hope that I had been mistaken, I continued looking for her along that endless, silent, tortuous corridor where every face was masked in sorcery. It was very dark, and to find my way I closed my eyes. I went

back and forth along the long, narrow corridor not daring to look behind me, for I had heard that in the countryside they say you should
never look back when you are walking in the dark, because on your
shoulders you have little flames—"shoulder flames"—that keep away
ghosts and evil spirits when they are lit; if you look back in fear, the
turning of your head and your heavy, fearful breathing may extinguish
your shoulder flames and let the evil spirits ensnare you.

Then all around me, not very far away, I heard a voice that was more
like a moan calling out softly. Because I was so desperate to find Ho, I
was convinced that it was her.

The corridor suddenly became so hot that I had to take my jacket
off. There was a door in front of me that I immediately recognized—it
was the door to Ho's apartment. I pushed it open and went in. The
faint moaning sounded closer and a fierce wave of heat slammed into
me. On the edge of collapse, drenched in sweat and gasping for breath,
I desperately called her name.

The moaning was getting louder. I followed it till I came to a door I
knew very well—the door to her bedroom. I knocked wildly, but there
was no answer. I pushed with all my strength. The heat hurt my hands.
It was so intense that it had twisted the door frame so the door could-
n't be opened. I could hear very clearly that the moaning was coming
from inside that inner room.

Peering through the keyhole, I saw the completely transparent
corpse of a woman curled up on the bed, her legs strangely contorted,
both arms clasped rigidly across her chest. She was lying motionless on
her side, her hair and eyebrows totally burned away. Countless bright
red tongues were darting up like flames beside her body. It was these
fiery red tongues that had licked away all the hair on her body. I struggled to see her more clearly. It seemed like it wasn't Ho, it was somebody else, but when I listened to the moaning, there was no doubt that
it was the magnetic sound of Ho's voice.

My heart thumped.

I shuddered as I returned to my senses.

I felt a bit frightened, aware that I had stayed too long in that dark
world of my own making. I was afraid that I had sunk into some secret,

irrational territory. Whether other people ever got to that place, I had no way of knowing. But when I think back on it, from when I was very small, that place had always been a constant companion in my thoughts. Like the wind, it followed my every footstep. Whether I was in the rain, on the streets, in a deserted square, or in a crowd, it would always appear in some form or other, some situation or other. It was a bottomless pit; if I didn't make an effort to control my thinking, it would lead me on endlessly.

Thoroughly frightened, I hurriedly jerked myself out of my thoughts. Then I turned on the light.

It was already late. I stared dumbly at the clock on the wall for a while; then I got up and wandered around the room, my mind at odds. I felt strangely unsettled but had no idea why.

I decided to go and visit my mother, then later on come back, have a bath, and relax a bit before going to bed.

Mother was in the middle of writing something when I entered her apartment.

I said, "Mama, what are you writing when it's so late?"

She hesitated a moment; then, smiling very awkwardly, she said, "Oh, I don't want to hide anything from you. I want . . . " She stopped again, uncertain.

"Tell me," I said, a bit impatiently.

"I want to find you a . . . father," she said; then she turned her eyes to me uncertainly as she waited for my response.

I was totally floored by this.

Then I started snorting. "Really? Good. That's good." When I stopped laughing I added, "But it has nothing to do with me. It's for yourself that you're looking for a man."

Mother said, "What do you mean it has nothing to do with you? I'm not going to be around that much longer. Whether I have a man or not really doesn't matter, but I have to find a father for you. One of these days will see the end of me. I can't just leave you as an orphan. We've got a house; what we need is someone to live in it."

I said, "Mama, you're really a laugh. I'm not a child anymore; and besides, what's this about your 'not being around that much longer'? Our best times together have only just started."

Mother said, "I read a story in the paper today about a terminally ill doctoral candidate who was looking for a wife. He was an only child, thirty-one years old and quite good-looking, but had never found a suitable match. This had become the chief worry in his parents' life, never affording them a moment's ease. It was about a month before this that he had found out he was terminally ill. The doctors had told him that he had two years at the most. This was truly a bolt out of the blue. His first thought was suicide, but when he got home and saw his aged parents, frail with worry, he felt that giving up like that would be tantamount to abandoning them. He turned it over in his mind for a long time and finally gave up the idea of killing himself, determining instead to fulfill his parents' chief wish and concern, and provide them with a descendant. Because he didn't want to bring worry to his family, he never told them about his illness. Secretly, he put an ad in the paper looking for a wife, including the details of his condition and his hopes. Many women wrote to him, and in the end he set his heart on a doctor, and she devoted her life to him totally. Not long after they were married they had a baby daughter. Although he couldn't in the end escape his dark fortune, he lived a fulfilling life, and left a daughter for posterity."

"But . . . but what about the woman?" I said. "Do you really want to praise that kind of deed? Only here in China does that kind of thing draw great choruses of praise."

"The woman did it because she wanted to. Forget about ethical judgment. All I'm saying is that stories like that are uplifting."

I said, "Well. If that's the way you feel, I guess you'll be submitting an uplifting ad for a husband."

She paused for a moment, then responded, "Well, anyway, we've just been chitchatting."

At this point, perhaps because she'd overstrained herself talking, her breathing became labored and she began struggling obviously for air.

Her exaggerated breathing seemed to influence me, because I too had unconsciously begun gasping for breath.

Then I noticed a burned smell in the air.

It is really very difficult to recall the events of that evening, because my instincts unremittingly block them out. They have become so distant and indistinct that they seem like a fabrication immersed beneath all the other disasters of that year.

In that year of death, it was only the power of my reason that kept the memory of those flames from being extinguished. For the longest time I have been looking for a way to lay aside the memories of that year, but it seems like the wind carries secret orders. One old house after another, the curtains tightly closed, the bars on the windows covered with rust, or dense forests of gnarled, old trees seem vaguely, like some kind of screen, to impede my way. It was as if I were pinioned in a crevice, with no way to get out into an open space, into some city square, no way to get rid of this crushing weight. There was no way out—all I could do was get by from day to day trying to stick to safe, familiar routine, my mind burdened with those killing memories. Through the silence, I purposely weighted my footfalls so that they might bother people, thinking that sooner or later there would have to be an echo that would come back to me.

The evil mists that enveloped that year were more than enough to distort many of its realities. But nature seemed to think they were not enough, and on that winter evening the choking black smoke obliterated my life. Like the prelude to a tragedy, this opened the curtain onto a more and more savage plot that within several months had engulfed the entire country.

That night, the clouds of smoke that filled the room brought Mother's and my conversation to a sudden end.

The first thing I noticed was Mother's face going fuzzy like an out-of-focus photograph, her features seemingly no longer where they had been originally. Her nose, eyes, and mouth looked like they had moved to a different place. I rubbed my eyes and stared hard at her. Her face was blurry, as if I were looking at her in a bathhouse through thick clouds of steam. In fact, she was still sitting in the easy chair in front of the desk. She hadn't moved at all. Now she was back where she had been sitting originally, but I still couldn't see her clearly, because she looked as if she were behind a mosquito net or a gauze curtain.

This frightened me, because all sorts of odd scenes had been appearing in my head around that time, filling me with a strange, unreal terror, so at first I was uncertain whether what I was seeing was real or not.

Then Mother asked, "I wonder what's making the smoke?"

As the smell of something burning grew stronger, Mother and I had at almost the same moment become aware that smoke was filling the room.

We looked at the door and saw smoke funneling in through the cracks.

I said, "Mama, is somebody lighting a barbecue in the corridor?" As I spoke, I went over and opened the door.

Thick, dense smoke rolled in around my legs, and I saw that it had completely blotted out the dim light in the hallway. It was obviously eating away at the oxygen as well, for I started to choke and cough. Immediately I shut the door.

In the hallway you could hear, over the clatter and clamor of people fleeing, a chorus of confused voices.

"Hurry up, run . . ."

Mother and I exchanged a quick glance. There was a fire in our building.

"Mama, we've got to get out of here." Because I was so scared, my voice sounded different, as if it were coming from someone else's throat.

Mother put her hands on her breast as she struggled to breathe. "Where can we go? The elevator's shut down. There's nothing but smoke out there. It'll be impossible to breathe." Gasping for breath, she said, "If the fire's downstairs, wouldn't we just be jumping into it? Smoke and flames always go up, so there's no way the problem is above us. For sure it's somewhere below us," she gasped.

My mother is not a woman to panic in a crisis. In such situations she remains calm and collected.

"But listen"—I wasn't thinking clearly—"everybody's running downstairs."

Now the racket and confusion of fleeing feet and the sounds of household goods and suitcases being kicked and dragged along in the hallway was even worse, and there was the sound of things being smashed.

Because she couldn't breathe, Mother shot over to the window and opened it.

I shot over behind her saying, "Mama, you can't open the window."
I remembered reading about that in the newspaper.

As I listened to the wind outside, all of a sudden I heard her coarse,
rasping cry blot out the clamor in the building. "The only way out is to
jump."

Ignoring my mother's plea, I closed the window and pulled her out
the door.

We were immediately swallowed up in the thick, rolling smoke,
which stung my eyes until the tears flowed. I clung to my mother's
hand like death. We were right next to each other, but I couldn't see
her. All around me through the turbid air, I could hear the sound of
fleeing feet and people bumping heavily into things blocking their way.
Unable to see them clearly, all we could do was grope our way down-
ward with them.

There was very little air to breathe and the smoky hallways were
filled with the sound of coughing and frightened shouts. I felt like a vise
was clamped on my throat, choking me so that it was impossible to
speak. Afraid that Mother might collapse from asphyxiation, I gripped
her arm tightly as we fled.

I say "fled," but in actuality we could do no more than fumble our
way along slowly.

I could feel that the heat and smoke were spreading upward from
downstairs. The thick, endless smoke seemed to foil us with the
tremendous buoyant force of sea water. The faster we tried to go down,
the more our feet were buoyed back, making it difficult for us to press
forward. But we had no choice but to force our way down—the only
route to life lay below us. The feeling was exactly like many other absurd contradictions we encounter in life.

Mother's arm began to weigh heavier in my hand, and I was afraid
she was going to collapse.

"Jump . . . jump . . ." she blurted out with difficulty.

I knew right away what she meant, because we had just groped our
way to a landing in the stairwell, where the moonlight was shining in
through the window closed tightly against the winter winds. Normally, the moon was like a round, silver eye glittering against the indigo

curtain of night. But now it was like the faded eye of a dying man, casting only a thin thread of light in the narrow landing.

I knew what Mother was thinking: if there was no other way, we could jump from the stairwell window. Obviously she wasn't thinking clearly. We lived on the eleventh floor. We'd only come down a floor and a half, so we were between the ninth and tenth floors. Jumping would be suicide.

Paying no attention to what she said, I desperately tugged her along behind me. We groped our way down, one foot after the other. My slippers long since lost, I moved along slowly in my bare feet with only one thought in my mind—getting out of there.

What was odd was that at this particular moment, for no apparent reason, I recalled an incident from my past.

Again, it was when I was in middle school. There was a period of time when I could see no point in living—all I could think of was ending my life. I was not at all like most people contemplating suicide, who go around talking about how they "want to die." I kept it to myself until eventually I decided the time was ripe.

When I got home that day, I very seriously said to my mother, "I've thought about it a lot. Life is stupid. I don't want to live anymore."

Mother gave me a very surprised look. She looked at me for the longest time, but she didn't seem to be in a hurry to answer me.

So I said it again, much more emphatically. "I really have thought about it a lot. It's pointless to continue living."

There was a long silence, then finally Mother said, "Really? So you've made up your mind?"

I nodded my head decisively and said, "Yes!" as great big tears tumbled from my eyes.

My mother was very well read and not your ordinary woman at all. When I said these things, she didn't get alarmed or flustered and try to dissuade or urge me in any way, or stop me, as most mothers do with difficult children. She was wise enough to know how to handle a "problem child." Again, she considered this for a while; then, with a look of having thought it through and made a decision that was a counterpart to my own, she said, "Mama loves you very much. You know that. But if you've decided you want to die, then nobody can stop you. China's such a big place, and we can't put a lid on the Yangtze River and the Yellow River. But Mama would miss you terribly."

It was my turn to be surprised. Mother's words completely stymied me. How right she was. There was no need to mention the Yangtze or the Yellow River, even the little canal outside our front door had no lid. Death was as easy as that. I didn't say a word.

I never mentioned it to Mother again.

By this time, with me hanging on to Mother and pulling for dear life, afraid that she would collapse at any moment, we had made our way down one more floor.

I quickly saw that the smoke was already thinner and the heat no longer so intense. The farther down we got, the easier it was to breathe.

All of a sudden it came to me: we had passed the floor where the fire was. As if we had just been rescued, I exclaimed to Mother joyfully, "We're safe, we're going to make it. We're almost out of it."

Naturally, when we went down another floor, the air gradually cleared, and the stairwell's feeble lights flickered and gleamed. At last Mother stopped and took several deep breaths. Then she spoke.

"The ninth floor," she said, "or maybe the eighth."

My guess was the same, it was probably the eighth or ninth floor.

Finally, we were out of the building, and standing there in the rushing wind on that late winter night, I saw that there was already a dark press of people gathered around. Some who had fled from their beds with no time to dress were standing there shivering, wrapped in their quilts. Whole families huddled together, their teeth chattering. Because we always went to bed very late, Mother and I both had sweaters on, but each gust of wind left us feeling like we were wrapped in nothing but a thin sheet of paper. Like countless icy worms, the cold penetrated deeper and deeper into our bones.

I started looking for Ho in the crowd. One after another the frightened, unsettled dark faces passed across my field of vision. This crowd of people that had fled from the thick smoke of death now stood numbly looking up at our building, trying to see where the fire was.

When I couldn't find Ho, I started to get anxious, realizing that the fire might well have started on her floor. When I thought of her lying on her bed in those plain green pajamas, my mind erupted suddenly into flame.

Then, the wavering bleat of their sirens adding new confusion to the scene, the fire engines raced up. The crowd, the trees, and the building were now all bathed in a brilliant orange glow. The sky flashed with the uncommon blue of diamonds, like the eyes of so many corpses floating in the darkness of heaven, their cold lips caressing the earth.

We were immediately ordered to move back 200 meters to an empty place on the side of the street away from our building. I was in the middle of a group of men who wanted to go back into the building to look for family members, or particular things that they had left behind. They struggled to get to the building, but they were kept firmly back. We were so crowded together that we couldn't move.

I looked up, praying fervently, Let her be safe, let her be safe, all the while shaking uncontrollably.

By this time, two firemen were climbing up the wall with the aid of ropes to rescue whoever might be in the apartment where the fire had started. I focused all my attention on them. I watched those two small, flamelike, greenish shapes dart up the wall like a pair of salamanders. In no time at all, they were at the ninth floor. At last, at the place I was most afraid they might stop—Ho's balcony—half suspended in space, using metal hooks to secure themselves, they flipped over the railing into her apartment.

My heart contracted violently, as if I had suffered a blow from some sharp weapon, and the blood in my veins congealed into silence.

There was no denying it. The fire was in Ho's apartment.

I stood there transfixed, until an uncontrollable wailing burst from me.

Just as the valves on the fire hoses were opened, I gave way to a flood of tears.

Eventually, they got the fire under control. Water from the upper floors poured down the stairwell and flooded out of the main entrance. Then two firemen bearing a stretcher emerged.

That naked pink corpse, or better to say that vaguely human-shaped lump of flesh, moved slowly toward us.

The crowd stirred.

A fireman shouted, "Is there anyone here from apartment 905?"

Ho's apartment.

My head and feet felt distorted, my eyes burned, my hands were like ice. I kept trying to bring myself back to my senses. I was hallucinating. None of this was real. But Mother was with me, holding me, her hands gripped tight around my shoulders.

All of it, everything before me, was real. I knew it.

When the stretcher moved across the street toward us, a great roaring filled my head and then began to die away, as the people around me, the street lamps, and our building began to sway.

Things started to blur; the noise around me faded. Then the world went black as I collapsed on the street.

The roar of the demented wind screaming Ho's name blotted out the clamor of that scene. The crowd of people had fled the roar; only Ho was there, floating in a dazzling circle of light. . . .

Much later, long after that disastrous fire, I heard a silly but upsetting rumor that it was caused by Ho's faulty refrigerator. . . .

Even until today, we still use silence to avoid our past.

These have been days that I do not wish to remember. Everything has been changing too quickly. With every day, I become more substantial; with every day, this world is less so.

I am at a doorway. If I pass through, perhaps I can be young again—yet I know I can never be young again. . . .

How that stray bullet came to find me, penetrating my left calf and exiting without my feeling it at all, remains an unsolved riddle.

It was late one evening in early summer. I was on my way to see my mother, who had been confined to the hospital because of a partial malfunction of the left chamber of her heart.

It was strange that this shady, cool street directly behind Tian'anmen Square, which for many days had been part of a boiling ferment of debate, was now suddenly deserted and quiet. I was rather puzzled. How could that tangle of traffic and press of crowds simply vanish into thin air?

My senses sharpened. I could hear in the distance a strange, clanking sound, the rumble of wheels, and what sounded like exploding firecrackers. At the corner two or three hundred meters in front of me, lying there like the carcass of a huge dead horse, was what appeared to be an overturned object blocking the road. All around it, I thought I could make out the wavering shapes of people, but I couldn't be sure. Farther away, a corner of the descending night sky suddenly darkened as if it were preoccupied with plotting some secret.

Then I heard an angry sound like the snort of a wild boar hang briefly in the evening air at the same moment that I felt something hard strike the calf of my left leg. It felt hot, numb. I struggled to keep standing. It seemed as if suddenly my leg had been wrenched away from me, was no longer mine. Feeling no pain at all, I looked down curiously. A thick red liquid was running down the left leg of my trousers onto the street.

Jerking up, I looked all around me. The dying echoes of that angry sound were followed by a dead silence. As the blue of twilight gradually thickened, the dying light clung like a tight mesh around my body. I stood there frightened and afraid to move. I couldn't see anything unusual, nor had any idea what had struck my leg.

As I looked around in fear, I kept thinking that these were unusual times, everything was distorted, changed. Evil intentions lurked everywhere and anything could cause them to erupt.

The muffled clanking sound in the distance became clearer and clearer, turning into a rumbling thunder. As I strained to listen, I heard once more that angry sound, like the snort of a wild boar, this time protracted and unbroken.

I turned fearfully in its direction.

What transpired was a miracle. Beyond the street corner in the distance, a wavering mirage suddenly appeared and began to rumble slowly toward me, cutting through everything within my field of vision. . . .

I was dumbstruck.

Dropping to my knees, I scrambled to the side of the road, and grabbing hold of a spindly tree, hid there like a thief, holding my breath, pressed behind a huge block of stone. Only then did the pain in my leg start rising upward, to engulf me. The wound was like a dark red cave, the mouth of a living spring. Around the opening, the flesh, like the split cardboard casing of an exploded firecracker, was curling outward. . . .

Only after being taken by the people on the street to the nearby hospital where my mother was, not as a visitor but as a patient, did I finally find out that the hard object that had struck my leg was a wayward bullet. It had passed between the two bones in my calf and out the other side before it even registered that something had hit me.

When Mother, all upset, came to the emergency room to see me, the whole thing struck me as totally absurd.

. . . . . .

The turmoil in Tian'anmen Square that summer, which was causing a sensation around the world, had become fanatical and violent, stirring the hungry winds of discontent into a fierce storm that left the city shedding silent tears. The fledgling trees and the grass along the roadway may be beaten and bent by the blazing sun or the slashing rain, but before too long they begin to sway, then slowly straighten up again.

We had been keeping to the house for a number of days, but could still hear an unbroken chorus of fierce and rabid shouting coming from the streets. There was a forest of green uniforms rooted like trees in every street and alleyway. Like the leaden gray sky overhead, these stiff uniforms had been around from ancient times. Present in every age, every region, they penetrate all time and space. Perhaps this is the nature of things. Every time it rains, every time the wind blows, the slightest movement is passed from one point to another until it is everywhere and every tree, every blade of grass becomes a soldier.

I could sense that something was astir.

The afternoon of the day prior to my being struck by that pointless bullet, I still wasn't aware how serious the situation had become. Standing looking out my window, I saw that the light of the sun that summer had changed, and now cast everywhere an air of destruction. Under that sun, down on the street, I saw a group of leather-booted young soldiers shouldering rifles, their belts cinched tight around their thin waists. Moving through the crowds like a neat little troupe of children, swinging their arms with drunken fanaticism, they were part of a chaotic scene that one couldn't, but had to, believe. . . .

I was both enveloped in this atmosphere and apart from it.

That night of flames had not yet released me.

Ho's death had left me feeling empty and almost paralyzed these past several months. I simply couldn't believe that a close and intimate friend could be taken from me without a word. I was immobilized by some kind of mental block or breakdown. It was as if I had walked into a distorted mirror where time ran backward. . . .

I kept seeing Ho's crimson body lying on that big bed, looking like a huge dissolvable colored medicine capsule. An empty rocking chair beside the bed creaked back and forth imploringly, as if longing for a trusted old friend to come and sit, still its vexation, and make life normal again. Ho was earnestly beckoning me to come and sit beside her, one hand covering her seared brow, the other extended toward me. Standing apart from her, my breath quickened with fear, I couldn't bring myself to go over to her. I looked down to see that my watch, its strap, and its case had all disappeared, but the hands were still going around. I said, "Ho, you're dead, dead. It isn't you that I see. What do you want from me? Please don't frighten me, I can't come to you." But when I stopped talking and looked up at her again, her face had already shrunk to a third of its normal size. Coughing up pink-colored spittle, she continued to shrink until all that was left of her was a little heap of her thoughts and a single arm still extended toward me. As I cried out a silent No, no, I found myself back in the world of reality.

Sometimes she would suddenly appear from some totally unexpected direction, the front of her skirt dancing in defiance against the summer wind. She would come into view from around a distant corner or emerge from a subway station, threading her way through the crowd. I would follow her with my eyes to where she stopped and stood on the opposite side of the street in the shade of a ghostly looking scholar tree, watching me. She would be holding a bouquet of shimmering fresh flowers that sparkled with the dew of her tears. They would be so beautiful that the lawns, the chestnut trees, and the wedding-cake houses in the background would fade into obscurity. Such an enchanting bouquet of fresh flowers of grief, such an enchanting young widow! Were they perhaps for her own grave?

Ho would be about to work her way over to me across the traffic-thronged street, but the endless flow of vehicles would block her way and also block my line of sight. I could do nothing but wait as they crept by like a line of snails. When at last there would be a break in traffic, I would not be able to see her. I would stand there, dumb as a wooden chicken in the middle of a cacophony of car horns and bicycle bells, blocking the traffic, Ho's image having vanished completely. . . .

On that stifling afternoon, I was standing there looking out the window because I knew that Yin Nan was out there somewhere in those seething crowds in Tian'anmen Square, although we hadn't seen each other for over a month and I didn't know exactly what he had been doing. Now he was my only friend and comfort, and I was worried about him.

On top of this, my mother was now in a different hospital suffering ongoing respiratory problems because of her heart condition. All these things coming in concert left me crushed with a deep anxiety.

Yin Nan had just called me from a public telephone booth, to say that something extremely urgent had come up and he had to see me. From the tone of his voice and the fact that I was to meet him in an abandoned warehouse we had chanced upon one night after seeing the movie *The Unrequited Love of a Man and a Spirit*, I knew that this was to be an unusual and secret meeting.

Over the telephone, I could hear the clamor in the background and the wail of an ambulance as it went past.

As soon as I put down the telephone, I rushed to the abandoned warehouse.

Half an hour later, I was standing in front of its rust-encrusted, half-open door. Through it I could see straw, iron plate, used lumber, empty paint cans, and scraps of plastic, and everywhere everything was coated in dust. There were no windows, and the darkened interior opened before me like the gaping mouth of some huge monster about to devour me.

I felt my way in warily. I shuddered as the dank air brushed my skin, imagining a sea of rats and insects overrunning my feet. But I couldn't see a thing. The biting odor of oxidizing metal invaded my nostrils, and I took out my handkerchief and covered my mouth and nose.

My eyes eventually adjusted to the darkness, and I could see where I was going. I groped my way toward a long wooden bench sitting on top of a heap of straw at the far end of the warehouse. It was there that Yin Nan and I had kissed each other passionately.

At last I heard something shuffle.

I stopped and called softly, "Yin Nan, Yin Nan?"

Out of the shadows, I caught the fleeting glint of a row of snow-white teeth, like a flash of lightning on a rainy night.

I knew those two rows of lovely, regular teeth, as neat and stirring as an impeccable, white-uniformed guard of honor.

If you took a group of men and women and covered them completely, leaving only their teeth showing, I would be able to pick out Yin Nan immediately.

Those teeth suddenly flashed again, this time from out of a different shadow, in a different place.

I said, "Yin Nan, it's me, it's me."

It was silent again, then a dark form shot forward and I was caught in his embrace.

I still couldn't see his face clearly, but I could hear the familiar pulse of his urgent, rough breathing at my ear and feel the warm fragrance of his country-fresh breath on my cheek. He was thin as a starved horse, every bone in his body thrumming with tension, like overtightened lute strings.

I said, "Yin Nan, you're so thin. What's happened?"

He didn't answer. His entire body was shaking as if he was out of breath from running in place. In fact, he hadn't moved a muscle and was still clinging to me desperately. Maybe it was his mind and his blood that were racing.

I said, "What have you been doing lately? Why haven't you come to see me?"

When at last he spoke, there were tears in his voice, tears I had never heard from him before. "Niuniu, I haven't been able to tell you . . ."

"Tell me what?"

"You've just had that fire in your building, your mother's back in the hospital again—it's enough. I'm afraid you can't take any more, that you'll worry. . . . I've been down in the square. . . ."

"Involved . . . ?"

He didn't answer me.

Finally, he said, "Niuniu, I'm going to . . . go away."

"Where?"

"I have to . . . go . . ."

"No! No!" My voice was raised. He pressed his lips on mine, kissing me to still my words. I bent my head backward to escape his face, saying quietly, "You can't leave me, you can't say you're leaving and then just go."

"Niuniu, I . . . love you, love you beyond all measure . . . but there's no other way, I have to leave." His tears fell on my cheeks, my lips—salty—sour.

In all the time that we had known each other, this was the first time that Yin Nan had ever used the word "love."

For the past several months, I had been feeling almost choked to death by the pressure of events in my home and outside. Now, hearing him manage to get this word out at last, I could no longer contain my feelings. The sluice gates were opened and a tumbling flood of tears gushed forth. I clung to him saying nothing, afraid that in the midst of my sorrow over losing Ho, I was losing Yin Nan, the only close friend I had left, as well.

He eased away from me slightly, and as his own tears fell, his lips and tongue brushed my cheeks, kissing away one by one my huge tears, as if he wished to drink down my sorrow.

"I love your . . . tears," he whispered.

We cried a long time, but our tears eventually subsided.

Yin Nan said, "I have to leave in half an hour."

I said, "Do you really have to go? Is there no other way?"

He shook his head. "I can't wait any longer. I've got to get out of here."

Again, we locked in a tight embrace. His heart was pounding like a war drum against my breast.

Clinging to his shoulder, I said, "But—where will you go? When?"

"Late tonight. Lufthansa, flight 721. Ten hours to Frankfurt, then a connecting flight, 2410, to Berlin."

There was some kind of skylight or opening in the roof of the warehouse through which a desolate, eerie thread of sunlight angled its way. Up near the ceiling it was a turbid yellow in color, but as it penetrated into the darkened warehouse, it slowly deepened in tinge, to brush obliquely across Yin Nan's face, lending his cheeks the color of rice straw.

In the half-darkness, the black lacquer glitter of his big eyes, filled with a heart-wrenching hopelessness, never left my face for a moment. I raised my hand to gently touch the lids of those eyes that made me think of the faint fragrance of ink-dark flower buds. He was leaning lightly against my shoulder, his head bent over me, so that I could feel the heat of his breath on my back, as if it were being gently massaged with warm milk. My arms were wrapped around his shoulders. I could feel his weight and his warmth as he pressed against me, his chest flattening my breasts. In the gloom, I could feel the heat of his groin tight against my thighs. I could see the shadow of his head inclining slowly toward my bosom.

I said, "Yin Nan, I want you . . . to remember me."

He said, "I'll always remember you."

I said, "I want your body . . . to remember me."

I felt his body tremble slightly, and a tremor in the pit of his stomach seemed to answer a silent call from deep within my body.

I took him by the hand and led him to the battered old wooden bench on the heap of straw.

Yin Nan seemed suddenly like an obedient little sick boy who had to have everything done for him. I motioned to him to sit down. I slowly undid my jacket, then took off my clothes and spread them on the bench. I took his head in my hands and made him slowly lie back. I pushed down his knees, straightening out his legs. He seemed almost awkward under my hands, but he offered no resistance to my will. His breathing became agitated and his long, delicate hands hung down helplessly on either side of the bench.

I touched his face lightly, his eyebrows, his ears. Slowly, lingeringly, my hands moved behind his ears, around his neck. I slid them under the neck of his undershirt to explore every inch of his back.

I felt a tremulous shiver run down his spine as he moaned my name.

I bent over him as I gently undid his clothes and his belt. He was like a willing, eager prisoner, letting me do with him whatever I wished. His eyes were half closed, his head turned to one side, his soft hair hanging down.

At last, he lay there hot and naked before me. This was the first time I had actually looked at the naked body of a man, and caressed him like this. His rib cage arched upward splendidly. In the gloom, his pale skin glowed like clear crystal.

I don't know if other women remember their first loves like this. But I cannot forget how in that abandoned warehouse the soft, white radiance of his body emerging from under his rather dirty clothes actually left me feeling faint.

I squeezed a space to sit on the bench beside him and, twisting over him, I let my fingers flow like water, unceasingly, over every curve and hollow of his tense frame.

His body, stretched out in the murky shadows like a reef submerged at one moment in passion, at the next in anxiety, could do nothing but wait helplessly as those hands rolled ceaselessly over him like waves, touching his hard hips, his thighs, his groin, and that fatal private place.

At last, I bent my body over his head, and cradling it in my hands, I lifted him gently until my breasts were touching his lips. I bumped them back and forth against his mouth like two sweet, ripe pears. A strained and aching moan escaped him as he opened his mouth to accept them. His arms jerked upward around me as he pulled my body and those sweet, pendulous pears down against him. His entire body was trembling violently as he desperately, blindly sought the way.

I took hold of him, and gently guided that lost and hungry lamb into the sweet pasture of its yearning. . . .

Ah, his love! So young, so vital!

Our half hour was too soon over, and it was time to bid each other good-bye.

As we separated from our last burning embrace, I felt the unaccountable rush of a winter chill sweep over me. The open pores of my hot skin shrank shut at its touch.

With the approach of our last moment, I began to tremble uncontrollably.

Yin Nan had his hand on my shoulder as we made our way out of the warehouse. As I moved toward the door, I kept thinking that in another hour that hand would be reaching out in the blue empyrean, making its way westward to Europe, to that city of profound speculation and philosophy, Berlin. Never again would I be able to touch him. The heat I could feel at that moment from the hand on my shoulder would have dissipated within less than a minute, perhaps, of his last good-bye.

I very clearly remember the weather that day. It was as gray and listless as the exhausted faces of people on the street, who had endured more than a month of tortuous summer temperatures. To pull up my spirits, I began hoping that Yin Nan would suddenly change his mind or that something unexpected would occur, making it impossible for him to leave me so soon. Even just a day would be good.

Only at the very last moment, when his back finally disappeared at the end of the street, did I give up this hope.

By the time we parted, the light had already started to fade, so I set off toward the hospital where Mother was convalescing.

Again my silent tears began to flow. But I didn't know whom I was shedding them for, because I was quite aware that our relationship had not been so long or deep-rooted that it was to be cut forever into my soul. But after Ho's death, this young man with whom I had shared such intimacies was the only close friend I had left. Having departed, he was to become a memory that I would cling to desperately, a lifeless cloak that I was to invest with vitality. This "cloak," which from the moment of Yin Nan's last good-bye would never again be real, enclosed an image of him that was to become ever more perfect. All those intimacies obscured in shadow because they were too private were wrapped up, locked within that perfect, shining, inviolate outer "cloak." It took on an eternal radiance that had a more lasting allure than the actual person. This sudden, unexpected termination of our love gave it an enduring beauty, like the eternal beauty of the living flow arrested in marble.

Of all the ways that human relationships can end, this is the most moving.

It was for this that I shed my tears.

At last, I lifted my head to look in the direction of the airport, and sure enough, I could make out a silver-gray object that looked like a huge kite floating against a blue backdrop, dancing at the end of an immensely long cotton string that I held in my hand. Little by little, I pulled it in until it was directly above where I stood.

As it came slowly toward me, its shape became clearer and clearer.

Eventually I could see that it apparently was not an airplane, but not until it was very near did I realize that it was a person. And what was strange was that it was not Yin Nan. The person soaring up there like some huge bird was myself.

There on the ground was the real me holding a kite string, controlling another self-same me up there in the blue. . . .

One summer many years later, to my total surprise, I once again encountered this fleeting illusion, which had been very much like a scene from a film.

In the hottest part of the summer of 1993, when I quite by chance saw the Italian movie 8½, it seemed like the gods had arranged this meeting with Federico Fellini, the film's eccentric director, who had created the same illusion.

Again, in the summer of 1994, I embraced the work of Ingmar Bergman, another male who was to infatuate me, when I saw in multi-track sound his films *Wild Strawberries* and *The Seventh Seal*.

But all of this happened later.

They and I lived in different, mad ages, but for a fleeting moment our minds had shared the same visions.

Wild Strawberries:

. . . I think it was also on a bright summer day. An old man dreamed that he was walking on a quiet, deserted street in a strangely desolate city. His shadow was outlined by the sunlight, but he felt very cold nonetheless. As he strolled down the broad, tree-lined street, the sound of his footsteps echoed uneasily from the surrounding buildings.

He felt strange, but he had no idea why.

While he was passing an optometrist's shop, he noticed that there were no hands or numbers on the big clock on the store's sign. He took his watch out of his breast pocket and checked the time. But the hands of his very accurate old gold timepiece had also disappeared. His time had run out; those hands would never again indicate time for him. He held the watch next to his ear to check that it was still ticking, but all he heard was the beating of his own racing heart.

Putting his watch back in his breast pocket, he looked up at the optometrist's sign, only to see that the big pair of eyes on it had almost totally rotted away. Frightened out of his wits, he turned around and started walking in the direction of his home.

At a street corner, he at last saw another person standing with his back to him. He rushed over and bodily spun him around, only to discover that under the floppy brim of his hat there was no face, and as his body turned it collapsed as if it were nothing more than a heap of dust or wood shavings, leaving an empty suit of clothes crumpled on the ground.

Only then did he discover that everyone along that tree-lined street that connected with the city square had died. There was not a living soul. . . . A hearse clanked by, its wheels rumbling loudly as it lurched along the rough street. Just as it reached him, the coffin fell off as three of its metal wheels rolled over, and clattered down beside him. As he was looking at the coffin, its lid sprang open. There was not a sound or a breath coming from it. Curious, he ventured slowly over to it. As he did so, an arm suddenly shot out from those splintered planks and clung to him desperately. Then the corpse slowly arose. He stared at it transfixed. The corpse standing there in the coffin in a swallowtailed coat was himself.

Death was calling. . . .

The Seventh Seal:

Overhead, the dull gray sky was dead as the vaulted ceiling of a tomb.

A black cloud stood motionless on the horizon as the curtain of night began to fall. A strange bird hung aloft, severing the air with its unsettling cries.

The knight Antonius was seeking the road back home through fields littered with corpses in a pestilence-ridden land.

He surveyed the scene around him.

There was a man standing behind him all dressed in black, his face an unusual ashen gray, his hands hidden in the deep folds of his cloak.

Turning to him, the knight asked, "Who are you?"

The man in black with the ashen face said, "I am Death."

The knight: "Have you come looking for me?"

Death: "I have been watching you for a very long time."

The Knight: "I have known this—it is your way."

Death: "This is my territory. Are you ready to 'set off' with me now?"

The knight: "My flesh is a bit frightened, but I myself don't give it much note."

Death spread open his black cloak to enclose the knight.

The knight: "Wait a moment."

Death: "I cannot delay your time."

The knight: "You like to play chess, don't you?"

Death: "How did you find that out?"

The knight: "I have seen it in paintings, heard it in people's songs."

Death: "You are right, of course. I am an excellent chess player."

The knight: "But you're not necessarily better than me."

As he spoke, the knight carefully laid out a chessboard on the ground and started setting up the pieces. Then he said, "The condition is this—as long as I am in the game you must let me live."

The knight extended two closed fists to Death.

Death let out a burst of wild laughter as he held up the black pawn in his hand.

The knight: "So, you will play the black?"

Death: "Is it not most appropriate for me to do so?"

The knight and Death sat down rigidly, facing each other across the chessboard. Antonius hesitated for a moment, then moved a pawn. Death countermoved.

An intense heat surrounded this desolate field, which was immersed in strange mists. In the distance, crowds of people were dancing their dance with Death, and Death was dancing his fatal steps with each of them.

Death concentrated on his game with Antonius, determined to take him away. Eventually, Antonius lost, and Death carried him off. . . .

But there is a chronological discrepancy involved in all of this. On that oppressive early summer evening when this unbroken string of strange scenes flashed through my mind, I had not yet seen these films.

That evening, as these anticipated scenes were unfolding in my mind, I was walking along that tree-lined street behind the square. It wasn't very far from the hospital where my mother was convalescing.

At that point, an ill-omened wind from above seemed to press down upon the street with an anxious disquietude. The depressing sound of my footsteps on the street, now trapped in twilight gloom, seemed to mark the respite that precedes the onslaught of a storm's main force. Their sound brought me back from the unreality of those illusionary scenes that had held my mind.

The overturned object at the corner of the street looked like a dead mare, her belly swollen with foal. Its smoldering fragments gave off a stench of burning rubber that filled that tree-lined, peaceful street with the nauseating smell of war and floated upward to clog the translucent twilight sky above the city.

The smoke floated up like curling wisps of incense above an altar toward a silent, unanswering heaven.

It was at just that moment that the stray bullet, with complete disinterest, came out of nowhere to pierce my left calf on one side and exit from the other.

*A person's ability to act in accord with her own con-
science depends upon the degree to which she can go
beyond the limits imposed by the society in which
she lives, to become a citizen of the world. The most
important quality she must possess in this is the
courage to say no, the courage to refuse to obey the
dictates of the powerful, to refuse to submit to the
dictates of public opinion.*

In the early autumn of 1990, my mother's heart condition brought on a serious heart attack, and one night,
sometime after a last wrenching bout of pain, she "died"
quietly in the midst of her dreams.

I put quotation marks around "died" because that
was what the doctors and the others around her said.

But that was not the way I saw it.

Lying there in her sleep, Mother looked wonderfully serene, as if she were having a beautiful dream. Perhaps she was dreaming that she was strolling down one
of Beijing's broad, paved avenues. I knew that after she
got sick and had difficulty breathing, she especially
liked open spaces with lots of green trees and lush
grass, and the grand streets of Beijing were a perfect
match for the ideal streets of her dreams. I imagined
that in her dream that night, she was surveying that

city where she had lived for more than fifty years through those eyes that would never know youth again, ardently looking at every old tree along the streets, every old-fashioned doorway, and even the stray stones along the roadside worn smooth with time. She looked intently at every wall she passed along her way, as if searching for the secret dreams of her youth hidden in the patterns etched there by the rain and grit-laden winds. Like a pair of loving hands, her eyes caressed the passing scenes along the streets. Time seemed to be flowing backward, and from the deep sockets of her eyes there issued a cloudless radiance.

She so looked like she was sleeping that final night, that I could not believe she had died.

And from that time I have also harbored a quiet secret in my heart: my mother, in actuality, had not left me. Because she couldn't breathe properly, her organs slowly atrophied, perhaps very much in the way that things left in badly ventilated places go wormy, so she got rid of her body and became invisible. She was playing a joke on the living.

But the doctors and the people around me had no sense of humor. They insisted that she was dead, period. Even the stupid professors in my school believed this, and they said I was losing my mind and sent me to the hospital for treatment. (That was where I met Qi Luo, the psychiatrist I mentioned at the very beginning.) The school also used this as an excuse to make me discontinue my studies.

In my heart, I have gone over the factors involved in my case many times, and I know the source of the problem. The key thing is the fact that I still don't know whether the bullet that pierced my calf was red or black. The two different colors for bullets indicate two different things. This has a bearing on all my other problems.

But I never found the bullet. It was total chance that I got caught in the line of fire. There was nothing I could do.

I remember that at the time, when in confidence I told Doctor Qi about my conjecture, I saw him write in my case history: "block in logical thinking; excessive fragmentation in symbolic thought association."

I regarded him as a friend, but I found out that he was not on my side.

So after a while I didn't talk openly with him anymore, though he still wanted to help me. I lied to him all the time and didn't let him know what I was really thinking, but this didn't stop him from wanting to be my friend. He was always loaning me psychology books to read. I really learned a lot from those books, which helped me to eventually understand myself and straighten myself out.

In the beginning, I insisted on telling the people around me, "My mother hasn't really died; she's just playing a joke on us."

But when I talked like this, all of them (except Doctor Qi) felt uneasy about me and then started to avoid me, as if they were afraid.

Eventually I smartened up and didn't talk that way anymore. But in my heart I knew that what they saw as reality was false.

I went home and looked in the mirror to find out what it was about me that made them avoid me. There was nothing about my appearance that was frightening; even my eyes weren't swollen, because I hadn't cried at all.

Why should I have cried? I didn't in the least believe that my mother had died, as they all said.

After Mother's body was gone, all the sounds in her apartment, such as the ticking of her wall clock and the gurgling in the water pipes, seemed to die away.

But her clothes were still alive, I'm absolutely certain of that.

Often, I would knock on her door, then, opening it with my key, I'd go in, saying, "Mama, are you sleeping?" After that, I would talk with her clothes for a long, long time. They were definitely alive, because I clearly heard them talking to me.

One evening when I was out for a walk, I saw a girl who looked a lot like my friend Ho. She was standing under a scholar tree watching the dancing shadows of the leaves beneath the street lamps. For a long time I stood watching her as she watched the shadows moving like dark clouds.

At last, my curiosity got the best of me. I went over and asked, "What are you looking at?"

Of course, I really didn't care what she was looking at, I just wanted to get a closer look at her face.

Pointing to the mottled shadows that the leaves under the street lamps cast on the pavement, she said, "Look at the way the leaves are shaking. There must be an earthquake."

I said, "That's impossible. If there was, you'd feel the shaking too. It's just the wind."

The girl said, "But look, the tree's trunk is shaking too."

I stepped back out of the tree's shadow and looked up at its trunk and main branches, and they were indeed moving—quietly, almost imperceptibly. Extending my arm, I touched the tree to see if this was really so. Like great heads of flowing hair, the shadows of the trees were dancing in the lightly moving air, their roots like giant buttons fastening them to the earth.

I wasn't quite sure what to make of this.

But whether or not it was an earthquake didn't interest me in the least. An earthquake was nothing compared to the upheavals my heart had been going through.

I said, "How can you stare so long at the shadows of the trees under the street lamps? It must be terribly boring."

The girl said, "What else is there that's interesting?"

I said, "I don't know."

After Mother was gone, in the evenings I would spend a long time sitting in my room watching how the sunlight slowly shrank away from the walls. I also followed the tracks of a mouse as he moved about secretly over the course of a day, and I measured how the footfalls of winter first found the tips of my fingers, then slowly covered my whole body. This habit of watching was something that came to me only after all my dearest friends had left me.

So I totally understood this girl.

The wavering shadows of the trees suddenly made me feel that there was a separation between my own body and the insubstantial things around me. It was as if there were a crevice between me and the rest of the world, or a great glass screen, and anything that passed through it lost all substance.

My mind suddenly changed, it was no longer my own mind. The person standing there was no longer me, it was someone called "Miss Nothing."

This peculiar feeling lasted for only a few minutes, then it was gone. After that, the lineaments of the girl's face gradually became clearer to me. She did not really look that much like Ho, it was only her outline in the distance that seemed a bit similar.

I turned to leave.

"Good-bye," I said.

That evening in my mother's apartment, I opened her closet and told her clothes about this encounter.

Mother's clothes said, "The girl must be very lonely."

It was amazing, it was just as if my mother had been speaking.

Once, on another evening, when I was walking aimlessly down some street, the pale pink light of the setting sun fell through the gradually thinning leaves of the trees onto the faces of the bustling crowds below, and the sweet fragrance of autumn floated on the air. All the shops were closed and the broad street seemed filled with casually wandering souls. Cars flashed past me, weaving their way to and fro.

I was seized by a sudden impulse to throw myself under the wheels of the speeding cars, unable to resist the feeling that it would be a kind of reincarnation, that I would be reborn.

Just then, a handsome young man came up to me, breaking my train of thought.

He said, "I want to give you a pair of tickets."

I was a bit nonplussed, but eventually said, "Tickets—to what?"

"To a disco dance," he said.

I said, "Why do you want to give them to me?"

He laughed, said nothing, and swung around and left.

How strange!

That evening I heard the sound of my mother's voice in the air in her apartment. "Don't go to the disco dance. Maybe it's a dark plot, or maybe it's an open plot."

I was frightened. Why would anyone want to hurt me?

In the end, they sold my mother's apartment to stop me talking to her clothes—"abnormal behavior"—and to give me something to live on.

That's the money I use to cover my living expenses.

But this didn't stop us from talking to each other. And anyway, I could still keep listening to my own silent thoughts. There was always the sound of conversations going on in my head. They were filled with the things I thought about but hadn't yet spoken.

One afternoon, I was sitting on my sofa just about to open a book when I noticed a spider on the ceiling. I watched him for a while, but I couldn't figure out what he was doing tucked up there the whole day. A misty drizzle was blowing against the screen on my window. I watched the threads of rain as they slowly trickled down to congeal into large drops, like little damp birds clinging to my window screen.

I heard a voice that seemed to come from an invisible tongue somewhere in the air saying, "Read, read!" So I bent my head and started to read.

I remember the book was Kafka's *Metamorphosis*. It was a novel I had read before, about a man who turned into a huge cockroach. But for some reason the work had not struck the passionate chord in me that it did that day. I was wildly excited and agitated.

I read and read. I don't know whether it was something in the book that had infected me or something else, but suddenly I felt something inside me tugging, or tearing, or flowing, or walking, or crawling, something I could neither place nor identify. I was highly agitated. Finally, I thought that maybe it was masses of little black words scrambling back and forth in my veins like so many insects.

With that, I went to get a pen and some paper so I could copy down all those insectlike words crowding through my veins.

It was from that moment that my life of ceaseless writing began. And once that life began, it could not be stopped.

I wrote a story at that time that was different from Kafka's: *How a Person Turned Into a Book.*

I took evolution as my starting point:

They say that mankind evolved from animals; therefore, human beings should not eat pork, beef, or mutton. Furthermore, animals evolved from plants; therefore, human beings should also not eat vegetables. And since vegetables grow up out of the earth, mankind should not tread upon it. . . .

If we were to accept this theory of evolution, we would have to forever keep our feet on our shoulders, and it would be impossible for
mankind to continue. So I think the theory is fallacious.

I think that our endless journey down the road ahead of us is what
gives shape to human evolution. For every ten thousand kilometers we
walk, we evolve one step. For every time we walk through the life span
of a clock, human history evolves one more level.

Later, I drew a schematic picture of the molecular structure of Earth.

I continued writing:

From the moment we entered the stage of civilization, humanity has
been swallowed up in an endless sea of written symbols and signs that
seep down into the core of our breathing, crawling all over us like ants,
in and out between our bones. Just how these "ants" have the ability to
gnaw away a person's bones and turn her into a book is another long
and complicated evolutionary process. . . .

A confused mass of totally disjointed thoughts kept crowding their
way into my head, from every direction and of every ilk. Anything
might come suddenly into my head, and just as suddenly turn into
something else equally unexpected.

Before I knew it, the paper was covered with strings of words.

What's your name? My name's Ni; I look like I'm one person, but actually I'm several. Familiar place. One foot running off in different directions. An ear in a flower garden listening, a knocking sound. My one
true love. Psychosomatic amnesia. Everywhere. Nice guy, okay. Look be-

fore you leap. Machine gun. Have some more. Ahh, yes, rumble, rumble . . . crackle . . .

I must have been pressing too hard. My fingers were so stiff and sore that I had to stop writing and flex my wrists for a while.

When I looked over what I had written, I found that not a word of it made any sense to me.

After writing for a while, I began to feel tired. At the edge of my field of vision, a glass sitting on my desk caught my eye. From it, the fragrance of fresh red wild strawberries was slowly spreading. I felt an immense thirst, so I got up and made a cup of tea. When I came back and sat down on the sofa again, I felt like there was someone sitting across from me, staring at me.

Just as I was about to sip my tea, I heard a voice whisper in my ear, "Drink, go ahead, drink."

How strange.

It started to rain, and when I jumped up from the sofa to close the window, I saw a thick silver-gray mist gathering everywhere, crushed down by the countless feet of the thickly falling rain, the entire city like a deserted ruin. Gradually, my thinking was steeped with the darkening color of the evening sky. It lurked behind every raindrop. Staring at those thoughts colliding with the approaching shade was like staring into my past. I jerked the curtains shut, refusing to face memories.

I hurried into the bathroom to go to the toilet. When I pulled the chain, there was a strange voice mingled with the rush of water: "thusspakezarathustra! thusspakezarathustra!"

Frightened stiff, I ran out of the bathroom.

But again, I heard a voice mingled with the thump of my feet, crying, "Endure, endure!" Chasing my feet, it beat them into the living room, where it circled and burst with a sound like a brick being dropped on the floor, leaving me totally helpless.

I couldn't take it anymore. Frightened out of my wits, I collapsed on the sofa.

In the ensuing days of confusion, to evade those overpowering fears, I started frantically putting down on paper any and everything that came into my head. I didn't eat, I didn't drink, I just kept madly scribbling—more and more and more:

Stray Lambs

The Bible says that God is a "shepherd" and that human beings are "lambs that have gone astray" and can't find their way home. This is seen as the essence of the human tragedy. I think that it is ridiculously naive for people to yearn to sit and talk as equals at God's table. Because they are not his equals, exchanges between them are impossible. If this is not so, then why don't we human beings have exchanges with extraterrestials? And why don't we have exchanges with ants? Because we exist on different levels. In relationships involving superiors and subordinates, exchanges are two-way in form, but the messages of the two sides are in essence totally different. The "shepherd's" concern for his "lambs" and the "lambs'" expectations of the "shepherd" are totally different. The main questions of concern for the "shepherd" are the quality of his mutton and wool, the fertility of his flock, how long it takes to fatten them for market, and the natural environment; while the "lambs" hope they will be well fed, that their keep will protect them from the cold, and that they will not feel the sting of the whip. If the "lambs" raised by the "shepherd" do not stay obediently in their fold or shed, but take it upon themselves to go into the "shepherd's" sumptuous home to exchange ideas, then of course they will have violated the ordinances of heaven and will be dealt with accordingly. . . .

Concerning Miss Nothing

Put simply, there is no me. I should clarify what I mean by "there is no me." A cold wind blew into my brain through my forehead, dividing my hair into three crystalline, glittering brocade segments falling straight over my shoulders. These three segments represent the three sections of my mind. The part on the left is my unwillingness, which goes against my wishes; in the middle sits my equivocation—yes but no; and on the right, my desire. I stood in front of the mirror and looked at the black wings moving on top of my head. Those black wings, the color of June, suddenly snapped, but the bird on my head flew away, leaving only a thick heap of feathers. Each day was darker and more cheerless than the day before, as if the world were rotting away.

I wake up to discover that my skull is empty. An uneasy silence on the edge of words pervades my body. I am afraid, terribly afraid. I want to go home, back to that old familiar place. The door to the glass-enclosed, abandoned garden is tightly closed. She is not to be seen. She has been put into an oval wooden box. Her legs grow unsteadily out of the box. She is the expressionless face of death. This coffin walks toward me. I don't know what to do. A secret is hidden in its wreath of fake flowers.

Strangers keep coming over to shake my hand and flash some kind of secret and important hint to me about the existence of a "germ factory." I hear the sizzling of an atomic pile. Something keeps circling around me for some reason. Looking everywhere, I discover that this city is not my home; the square has disappeared. Even the rusty frames around the windows are gone. The sloping, narrow alley that used to kiss my feet is overgrown with weeds and moss. It is silent.

All the people that I knew masquerade in make-up, they are not real. . . .

I no longer exist . . . I have disappeared. . . .

I am Miss Nothing.

The New Emperor's New Clothes in Cartoon Captions

Q: "Hello. How come this cartoon is just a blank sheet of paper?"

A: "You mean to tell me you can't see it?"

Q: "Where are the new clothes?"

A: "The emperor is wearing them."

Q: "Then where is the emperor?"

A: "He left after he put on the new clothes."

Q: "Oh. So that's it. How stupid of me."

A: "So, you see, I'm a fantastic cartoonist."

One Way of Being a Master Teacher

You're a girl, stunning double-X chromosomes, so young and sexy you make a man's head spin. You see on the desk that XY-chromosome male chop, carved in relief, and the man sitting stiff and buttoned up behind it—the strategist, the maker of plans, the masturbator (sorry, master teacher—an inadvertent error), his big red fists the symbol of authority. You ring the rusty doorbell, but there is no response. He purposely busies himself with boring trivialities, his hands filled with countless numbers. Every number that falls on the paper has XY chromosomes. To him double-X chromosomes are germs, evil spirits. His clandestine yearning for double-X chromosomes cannot be openly, honestly put to paper. He shuns them for fear they can't be shunned. You step into the room and move toward him. He quickly backs away

and huddles up in the corner, fearfully gripping his hat, hat in a hat. . . .
My hat, he shouts. As if your approach must make his hat fly away.

The Origin of Money

He constantly has to go for a piss—off to the washroom once every minute, back and forth, taking a drink and getting rid of it. Every visit is a solemn moment of hope and struggle. If the piss won't come, he strains with all his might, even for just one drop, while the thin liquid in his veins flows unconcernedly. He imagines his sperm are swimming freely in his bladder, frolicking like little minnows. If he keeps going to piss, he'll fill the bowl with flashing crystals of sperm. His sperm are his gold . . . so he can't stop pissing.

Artificial "Interpersonal Relationships" in the Garden of Mankind

I'll be "nice to you" if you'll be "nice to me."—This is not at all what "I" want in an "interpersonal relationship." Admittedly, one person's circumstances in life are very frequently influenced by the circumstances of someone else. "I" am not in complete charge of my own life. "My" happiness is very often a gift that "you" have given me. "I" exist only through "you." Nonetheless, I insist that it is only when "you" and "I" strip away our private agendas that we can have a genuine relationship. Our multifaceted world has obliterated the pure "you" and "me." "You" and "I" have already lost control of our destinies. Let me tell you a secret: "I" am not I, and "you" are not you. We don't know who we are. "You" are in make-up and "I" am a pretense. The masquerade ball in the garden of mankind is in full swing. . . .

. . . . .

I must have peace and quiet unto my second death.

The things that followed have distorted my memory, or perhaps I should say that my memory has distorted the things that followed.

At any rate, those days were a confused labyrinth of tangled knots, mirrors within mirrors, paintings within paintings, through which time wove its way.

This terrible time left me feeling like everything was upside down, backward. It was as if I had gone to see a film, but instead of me sitting among the audience in the darkened theater watching a fictitious story unfolding on the screen, the fictitious characters on the screen were malevolently watching me, sitting down there in the audience. Unceasingly, enviously, they ferreted their way into my innermost being, leaving me feeling totally exposed though I sat in darkness, completely shattering the old structured patterns of my thinking. . . .

I was placed in a hospital.

I lay awake all night in my room staring at the ceiling, pursuing the shadows of the past in a desperate effort to remember . . . something. What? Even to have been able to grasp a few traces here and there would have been all right, but it was like trying to look into the impossibly distant future, as if nothing had ever happened—a blank.

. . . . . .

It was only in the spring of 1992, when I returned home from Qi Luo's hospital with my mind straightened out, that I was at last able to face the truth: my mother and my friend Ho, whom I loved dearly, were both dead. And my friend Yin Nan had left me forever.

The apartment was dark and silent, dust everywhere, lifeless.

My once so familiar home no longer recognized me. It was as if a new tenant had arrived. Even though I tried to behave like a familiar old friend, it remained silent and uneasy.

I could tell that from the moment I left, time had stopped in these rooms.

As I stepped softly inside, I said to myself, "I've come home! I feel terrible—just when everyone else left you, I left you too. But I had no choice, they took me away."

I looked out the window. The sun was bright, beautiful. The trees with their soft green branches, unable to restrain themselves, waved softly, solicitously, back and forth. The window curtains in the ranks of apartments opposite were fluttering slowly like colored photographs come to life, blocking out all the grief outside. Beyond the buildings, the cold, impersonal highway stretched its hungry hand toward the distant spring mountains and the limitless blue sky. On the mountains the hazy firs, proud poplars, and brightly blossoming clove trees waved their pastel wings in the gentle wind, an embroidery of spring colors set against the gray clouds and lovingly delicate mists. The languid spring sun inclined its sleepy head upon the warm pillow of young leaves.

It was truly the beginning of spring.

I turned to look at the empty room. I didn't want to believe that so many years had actually passed away. It was like awakening from an immense dream, unable to remember any of it.

From a neighbor's window, the faint, unsteady strains of a woman softly singing floated on the air. It was a song that Ho used to sing:

My sobs well wanton,
As I open the window, gray.
Oh, take me, take me away,
Or bury me. Open this door,
This door I beat with my tears.
All time has passed away
And left me here alone.

I closed the window. I couldn't bear listening to that song. I wanted to get rid of it, along with all the numberless white and pink and blue pills dissolved into my system in the hospital, along with all the grief and despair in my heart and the marrow of my bones that I had already jettisoned.

I spent the following days assessing this new, erupting world of dreams.

I call it a dream world because I did, in fact, essentially spend those days in a dream state. Like a little baby, I needed endless hours of sleep. Most people would likely regard such a constant need for sleep as simple physical fatigue. That's just a biological explanation.

But seen from an outside, objective point of view, this excessive desire to sleep was the product of the need to suppress or alleviate my fears, my sense of hopelessness, and my suffering. It's rather like the sexual drive of a failed man. It is much more likely that a person who has experienced failure in life will have some sort of overpowering need that must be satisfied to bring him peace of mind than that a person who has achieved great success and a good reputation in life will, because the former must prove his ability and his worth to himself, and his importance to others. He will use his sexual prowess to overwhelm others, to place himself in a dominant position.

After thinking about it for a long time, I began to recognize the many questions I needed answers to, and to find some of the answers.

But I still wasn't ready to reveal this to anyone.

All I can say is that this new understanding had not come to me abruptly, but rather had taken shape gradually, in the way that the arrival of night is not the sudden dropping of an impenetrable black curtain but a slow and gradual deepening of shade.

At the same time I had also come to realize that if a person lives within a fragmented world, unless she can find harmony and completeness within herself, she will walk the same road to perdition as the world around her. Every outward nervous symptom is the product of a fierce conflict between a person's inner needs and the realities of the world around them. It's the same as symptoms of a physical illness. They are manifestations of the struggle within a healthy body against influences harmful to it.

I leafed through the pages of confused notes left on my desk from before I was taken to the hospital. I couldn't clearly understand many of them, but still, I could try to guess.

I had a feeling that these notes could be extremely important because of the time when they were written. This led me to think that I should write down my personal history, that with my individual peculiarities I could take my place as one of the many unique entities that make up the multiplicity of humankind, my uniqueness determined by all those other unique natures with whom I coexist. Though every person is alone, a single isolated entity, with a history that is different from everyone else's, she cannot live without connection to her fellow human beings. She has no choice but to share in the joys and sorrows of the people of her time.

So, although she is a unique entity, she is also a representative facet of what it is to be human. This realization set my resolve to analyze those notes I had scribbled prior to my hospitalization.

One afternoon, I had dozed off, curled up in a blanket on the sofa leafing through some of my notes.

Suddenly the doorbell rang.

Punching my feet into my slippers, I went out to open the door.

It was Qi Luo.

I was delighted.

He said, "I brought you something."

A bit nonplussed, I took the big envelope he handed me, without any notion of what it might contain.

He said, "Aren't you always asking me about how you got sick? Wouldn't you like to go over your own records to trace the development of your illness? As your doctor, I'm not allowed to give them to you. But you're different, not really a patient at all, at least, not one of my usual patients. So I've brought them over for you. They'll help you understand what you've been through, put things together."

I pulled out a stack of paper that smelled of disinfectant and there it was—a complete record of my former condition:

```
NI NIUNIU--MEDICAL RECORD
(1) General Information:
Name: Ni Niuniu
Sex: Female
Marital Status: Single
Nationality: Han
Place of Birth: Beijing, China
Religion: None
Education: University
Present Address: Suite 1105, Bldg. 2, Houguaibang
Street, Beijing
Date of Admission: 15/4/91
Commencement Date of This Record: 16/4/91
Informants: Yu Shui (patient's neighbor), reliable.
Tong Li (university deskmate), reliable.
Ni Wen (patient's father), not reliable.
(2) General Observations:
For several months patient has been impulsively
writing and drawing. Hears and converses with voices.
Suicidal tendency.
(3) Family History:
Patient's uncle, mental breakdown at 40. Wouldn't
leave house. Feared arrest. Afraid to meet people. Pas-
sive. Talked to himself a lot. Hanged himself after
five years. No other mental illness, idiocy, epilepsy,
suicide, alcoholism, unusual behavior, or addictions on
mother's or father's side for three generations.
(4) Personal History:
Mother's pregnancy normal, but she suffered mental
pressure and tension because branded a capitalist road-
er. Pregnancy full term, birth free of complications,
but patient frail in childhood. Development normal,
walked at one year, talked at 18 months (liked talking
to herself, called her arms and legs the "Misses Do"
and the "Misses Don't," conversed with them often).
```

Entered primary school at six, good student, always
near head of class. Continued on through middle school
and university with excellent grades.

Began menstruation at 14. Irregular (4-6 days/28-35
days).

Born to a cadre family, only child. Parents' relationship strained, both involved in work. Home life
lacked warmth. Patient introverted, thinking patterns
unusual, even startling. Behavior often involuntary and
strange. Once cut legs off father's new trousers with
scissors. Doesn't relate well with classmates or teachers, prefers own company, shuns conversation with others. Given to fantasy, relates having seen people on
the street turn into a pack of wolves, which then surrounded her. Sporadic passion for drawing. Quiet and
uncommunicative as a child, dubious intimacy with an
older female neighbor. Grown up, still finds it hard to
mix, couldn't adjust to dormitory life at university,
lived at home. Few close friends. Indecisive, reverses
decisions repeatedly. Likes walking, connects it with
personal evolution, insists her personal action has
overturned Darwin's theory of evolution.

(5) Past Illness:

Contracted measles and double pneumonia at age
three, frail in health since then. No record of epilep-
sy, tuberculosis, external injuries, poisoning, or
other infectious diseases.

(6) Present Illness:

Illness likely induced by loss of a number of relatives and friends. Refuses to face the truth. Before
this, no obvious abnormality. Recently patient has been
unable to sleep, eats little, is inactive and indifferent, ignores people for no reason, and is unable to
attend her classes. Compulsive urge to write and paint,
thinking incoherent and disordered. Claims there are
instruments controlling her, such as atomic piles, and
voices that talk to her; that we are all, herself included, substitutes for our true selves. At night, too
excited to sleep; unable to feed herself.

PE:　Heart, lung, liver, kidneys--normal
Temperature--37

CNS: Patient refused to cooperate

ME:　Mind clear, but patient disoriented

(7) Behavior:

Denied she was ill, hospitalized against will. Pays
no attention to her appearance, thin and weak. No in-

terest in food or drink. Incapable of managing her own
daily life. Unable to sleep at night due to agitation.
Refuses to be examined. Frequently throws away pre-
scribed drugs. Cooperates occasionally with nurses. Has
nothing to do with other patients, refuses to partici-
pate in group activities, staying in room by herself.
Talks to herself, says she is surrounded by enemies.

(8) Cognitive Processes:
Language fragmented when agitated. Disconnected com-
ments such as: "What am I doing in a planetarium?" "I
might as well die, civilization is a fraud." Believes
one of her hands is controlled by outside forces. Asked
which hand, she replied, "Right hand." Also claims she
is held in tight bonds.
Memory fragmented. Says her name is "Miss Nothing."
(9) Intellectual Ability:
Able to explain the apparent contradictions of such
phrases as "opposition through agreement," "the poverty
of golden dreams," "witching for water to quench your
thirst," "rebellion through submission"; can explain
such things as why those born deaf cannot learn to
speak, why the soles of running shoes are always so
uneven, why ice floats on water, and why railway trains
cannot run on highways; recognizes the different conno-
tations of such terms as "modesty" and "self-
abasement," "fantasy" and "ideals," "respect" and
"flattery," "liveliness" and "frivolity"; clearly un-
derstands the different implications of the phrases "a
wolf in sheep's clothing" and "a sheep in wolf's clothing," and illustrated this rather humorously by picking
up a writing brush made of wolf hair with a core of
sheep hair, saying that it was a sheep in wolf's
clothing. But patient's responses to mathematical questions slow and inaccurate. She was unable to count down
from 100 in sevens, and could not figure what the
change on a dollar would be when purchasing three
eight-cent postage stamps.
(10) Emotional Processes:
Largely keeps to her own thoughts, showing no interest in what goes on around her. Pays no attention to
others. Sometimes will not even answer doctor's questions.
(11) Motivation and Behavior:
Generally inactive, spends much time in bed, makes
no effort to communicate with others, doesn't look
after herself well. Once in a while her old energy

returns. On one occasion she suddenly embraced one of
the doctors and said, "Yin Nan, let's get married."
(Yin Nan was name of patient's former boyfriend.) When
her father unexpectedly came to see her, behaved as if
she did not know him, saying, "Leave me alone, leave
me alone"--nothing else.
. . . . . .
Patient's first hospitalization; light care.
Doctor: Qi Luo

I began an intense scrutiny of these records, digging deeply into
every entry and taking copious notes.

One day as I was working away at this, I got all excited as I recalled
Nostradamus's prophecy. I started figuring the time left.

It was already the spring of 1992, with seven years to go until 1999. I
really like the number seven, and nine was my absolute favorite of all
numbers. But that wasn't important. I did a little figuring—seven years
is 2,555 days, only 61,320 hours, and I had to straighten out all these
questions before I died.

Time was pressing, and I didn't know if there were any shortcuts.

Not long after that, I had a perfectly normal dream.

The character in the dream was my then self, but the time was
pushed back to when Mother, Father, and I were all still living together.
It was at the time in my childhood when we lived in the house with the
huge date tree in the courtyard. The wet courtyard was carpeted with
lush green leaves blown down by the wind, the branches of the tree
stretching like great long arms, the longest arms in the world, from the
east wall right across to rest firmly on the west wall of the courtyard, and
the ground was sprinkled with sweet dates as fat and round as little pigs.

That opportunistic cat that I had so hated in my childhood also
put in an appearance, strutting self-importantly back and forth in
front of me.

Everything in the scene was from my childhood.

I dreamed that I was getting ready to go to a palace I had never been
to before, a palace with shining golden walls that everyone else knew
about but I didn't. And I still didn't know how to get there. From the

map I could see that it was a long, long way away. Then that opportunistic cat paraded over in front of me to tell me about a little path. He said it was much shorter and would save me a lot of time and energy. Because I didn't trust him, I phoned the palace to make sure. They said the little path would take me to the palace, but that when I got there it wouldn't be the same palace anymore.

When I woke up, the symbolic message of the dream was obvious.

It let me see that there are no shortcuts in this world, so I started to work furiously on the material on my desk.

How ironic it was that just when I felt that every day might indeed be my last, my story had finally begun.

For an entire year I put everything into my work. I spent the greater part of every day recalling and setting down my personal history, or burying myself deep in thought. Probably because there were so few things in that apartment that had any energy or life in them, the feeling began to affect me. It felt as if my blood were congealing, and even my period was affected, the cycle getting longer and longer, my period coming later and later.

At first I paid no attention to this problem. But after a while, I began thinking that maybe, just as with mental illness, my body was signaling me that it was involved in a struggle against forces harmful to its health. So I decided to go and see Qi Luo.

By this time Qi Luo and I had become genuine friends, not just doctor-patient "friends."

He gave me a little bottle of pills with the medical name "levoro-methylnorethindrone," or, in lay terms, birth-control pills.

"What kind of a joke is this?" I asked. "I spend the whole day locked up in an empty house like a vestal virgin, yet you want me to take birth-control pills?"

He laughed. "You don't understand. Aside from preventing the implantation of eggs in your uterus, they regulate your body's production of endocrinal hormones." That, I could understand.

Before I went to bed that night, I swallowed that little round yellow birth-control pill, and turning to look at my empty, guiltless bed, I couldn't stop laughing. I laughed and laughed. I laughed until tears were streaming down my face.

It seemed like that little pill did not want to do what it was told. It stuck in my throat where it jiggled about, refusing to go down, as if it were enjoying some preposterous joke.

After that, my long, arduous research began in earnest, and my dogged persistence at this endless and draining work left me exhausted.

Life, like grass, needs moisture because our cells cannot survive without it; therefore, life can exist only in mire.

"It's the season of love—everybody, everybody, hug hug hug . . . the lonely are a shameless lot." Since the beginning of the '90s, everybody in Beijing has been singing this song. You hear it everywhere you go, in the shops and on the streets.

Perhaps they have to give their lives some meaning or purpose in order to carry on.

But I have to admit, I'm without doubt one of the "shameless" ones. Rather than keeping up with the beat of the times and throwing open my door to the season of love, I find that I have closed my door even tighter. And I have a love that runs totally counter to the times—in my bathroom. To be precise, my bathtub.

In such a big apartment, such an unexpected place to find love!

It all began one day when I was having my bath. As I lay soaking in the tub, in the water's warm and eager arms, all my loneliness and fatigue melted away.

After my mother and my beloved friends left me, I felt that the bathtub and I were all that remained, but this was the first time I had lain like a lover in its embrace. In that quiet and still apartment, only it could clasp me in its arms and make me forget the past, make me forget my isolation. I leaned against the tub quietly like a thirsting plant nursing its way back to succulent life.

I lingered there for a long time, and, coddled in the languid mists, I fell asleep.

The gurgle of the drain awakened me. I must have dislodged the plug with my foot.

I raised my head and looked around. As the steamy clouds of mist dissipated, the pristine white tiles began to reappear, looking like crisp biscuits that seemed to fill the air with a fresh fragrance. With the leaky faucet, its neck solicitously bowed, drip-drip, drop-dropping like a quietly reiterated "hello, hello, hello," and the grumbly surging of the toilet tank like the hubbub of a noisy street, I could never feel lonely again. Especially with the wooden rack on the wall above the tub with all my favorite cosmetics on the top shelf and a pile of books and magazines on the bottom, so I could read while taking a bath.

What an unusual and marvelous place!

In this apartment, aside from me, it is the only thing that is still alive.

One evening, after soaking in the tub for a very long time, I felt especially fresh and relaxed. Having dried myself, I slipped on my nightgown and settled down on my sofa with a nice hot cup of *Biluochun* green tea.

As I drank my tea looking at the empty room around me, I suddenly felt unaccountably hungry, and I could hear the empty growling of my stomach.

But I knew that I wasn't really the least bit hungry. I had eaten a big dinner, and according to my usual pattern of digestion, I shouldn't have felt hungry again until I got up the next morning.

Nonetheless, I couldn't suppress my hunger pangs.

Through the crack in the curtains I could see all the bright lights of evening. Nightlife in Beijing has been getting more and more varied and lively. People are back into late-night dining, dancing, health clubs, entertainment parlors, and the like. I think they are probably hyper-functioning like this because their digestive systems are out of whack. I don't know.

I had left a long piece of plastic string on the tea table, the white kind that is amazingly strong. I had taken it off a large bundle of books I had picked up at the post office that afternoon.

I had unconsciously picked it up and was idly twisting it around my fingers as something stirred vaguely in my head.

Under the guidance of my subconscious, my fingers divided the string into four equal lengths, shaped them into a strong loop, and knotted the ends together securely. I then stood up and went over to the thick drainpipe that ran from ceiling to floor in the corner between my front hall and my living room. There was a black metal hook on it that looked like a thrust-out empty tongue waiting to be fed. I brought a chair over, and standing on it, I hung the loop I had made on the hook.

This series of actions was executed in a sort of dreamlike state. I really had no idea what I was about, or why.

When I had finished all this and jumped down from the chair, I looked up at what I had just done. Hanging there in front of me, waiting, was a terrible hangman's noose.

Only then did I jerk back wildly in fright.

Fully conscious again, I was appalled by my actions. Palpitating with fear, I sank back into the sofa, my eyes locked on the suicidal noose, my mind racing wildly.

If I were to go over and stand on the chair, it would be as easy as pie to slip that noose around my neck. One little kick of the chair and the whole thing would be over.

As easy as walking through a door—nothing to it.

But then I thought, what if nobody came to see me for a long time? My corpse would be hanging in the house all that time—what a disgusting scene that would be! On the other hand, it would give people a terrible fright should they come and find me. That wouldn't do at all.

I didn't want to think about it anymore.

To dispel these nameless anxieties, I turned on the stereo system. The station it was tuned to was playing that same song, "The Season of Love."

My thoughts picked up on the line, "The lonely are a shameless crowd."

I pondered it from every angle. Just why are they "shameless"? I tried a number of approaches, but I found it impossible to either validate or disprove the statement.

My Postulations

1. Only when we all hug each other are we normal. If you don't behave in this way, you're abnormal, and abnormal people are shameless.

2. Feudalism and conservativism are finished. The age of openness has arrived. Once it was revolution that shook up society, now it's love. If you aren't part of the trend, you're shameless.

3. After so many years of being "fake models of male and female virtue," our bodies need to relax in leisure suits. Our brains also need to don leisure suits. If your brain doesn't take it easy along with us, then you're shameless.

4. "Classical culture" is a thing of the past. The "postmodern revolution" is in pursuit of relaxation and superficiality. If you stupidly insist on being or playing profound, then you're shameless.

5. I hate my loneliness. I want to enjoy myself along with everyone else, but I can't throw off my loneliness. I curse myself as a shameless person in order to escape my loneliness.

6. I have no desire at all to change the loneliness I love so much. Before you try to tell me I'm shameless, let me tell you that I'm shameless because that's the way I want to be.

7. . . . .

Eventually I gave it up.

I said to myself: You're shameless. Totally shameless!

Then I went to bed, turned out the light, and settled down to sleep.

206   The flashing red and green neon lights outside had found their way through the window curtains and were dancing like pink fragments of windblown cloud on the wall of the room. I stared at them for the longest time, unable to go to sleep.

For two full hours I lay there pointlessly, wide awake. Through the stillness, from the neighbor's open window, I could hear again and again the unbroken strains of "The Season of Love."

After a while, I had an idea: why not sleep in the bathtub? Its long, warm, and cozy oval shape made it the perfect place to sleep.

I bounced up, pulled my robe over my shoulders, and headed straight for the bathroom.

After wiping the tub dry, I fetched my bedclothes and pillow from the bedroom and arranged them in the tub as meticulously as a bird building its nest.

Finished, I stopped to catch my breath, pleased as punch with my new "bed."

When everything was just so, I tunneled my way into my feathery bathtub nest. Lying on my side with my knees pulled up and my arms folded over my bosom was like lying on a golden beach with the sun-warmed sand pressing against my skin, its heat seeping into my blood. The sun's golden warmth raced through my body like marijuana, leaving me languid and drowsy.

Across from the bathtub there was a big mirror. In it I could see a young woman lying on her side in a tiny, swaying white boat. I watched her. The lines of her face were beautifully soft and gentle; her skin was fair and delicate. Tumbled loosely around her neck, her fragant hair was like a dark glistening flower floating on a pool of water. The light, sweeping curve of her body was outlined beneath the flowing wave of her soft silk quilt cover.

This was the first time I had seen myself lying down. I never knew how intriguingly beautiful the passive languor of a reclining body could be.

This led me to think of the beauty of deep sleep, the beauty of death.

Right then, I made a decision: when it came time to die, I would die in the bathtub. There couldn't be a more beautiful place.

I stared at myself in the bathroom mirror, as if I were judging some other girl altogether. All the joints beween the white tiles were like a great net stretched out behind my body, a kind of still and indifferent backdrop trapping my inner thoughts.

I turned my head and lightly closed my eyes.

Then I did something to myself.

Something you only have to imagine and it's done.

While I was doing this wondrous thing, the two dearest loves of my life flashed through my mind: beautiful but ill-fated Ho, and brilliant and immaculate Yin Nan.

This marvelous combination and sexual confusion operated on two planes.

When my fingers caressed my round, full breasts, in my mind they had already become Ho's fingers, her exquisitely slender fingers, touching my skin, those two spheres soft as swan's down . . . fingers like pure white feathers floating, dancing, turning . . . the fragrant delight of rose petals . . . rich red cherries swollen till they burst . . . the thick fragrance of maple leaves in autumn brushing your lips, entwining your neck . . . my breath quickened, the blood in my veins caught fire.

Then the hand, like a freight train, sounding its whistle, huff-huffing nearer and nearer along those familiar tracks toward the fragrant dark grass of the "station," slowly pulled in. Just as it reached the deep place covered over with leaves, Yin Nan suddenly stood there rigid, and filled with the spirit of exploration, he plunged deep and solidly into the center of my breathing. . . .

The experience of beauty and the fulfillment of desire brought perfectly together.

. . . . . .

That evening in the bathtub, I sank quickly into dreams.

After not leaving the house for a number of days, I took a very long walk. This walk led me to a much deeper understanding of life and of Beijing.

This is a city completely devoid of any feeling of being shut in. I discovered that the city's broad and long streets in no way separate the people in its different corners, either in terms of space or in their hearts. The streets are filled with modern means of communication so that moving between widely separated places is as fast as making a phone call. In the twinkling of an eye, an uninvited guest who wants to talk to you can be on your doorstep. With the spiderweb network of telephone lines over the city, the noise and clamor of an even more distant world, however you might protest, will force its way into your innocent ears. Like a green wind blowing across the sea of people, postmen whisk everything from far away, the true, the false, before your eyes. You become the news for others; they become the news for you. Endless rounds of information keep bursting like shells all around you. Row upon row of new buildings crowd together cheek by jowl. Windows like endless rows of eyes stare inquisitively into each other from every angle. Walls as thin as insects' wings . . . whether you're at home or on the street, your breathing, your muttering, your deepest inner thoughts are common knowledge among the crowds. . . .

Because of all the noise and clamor, the city's heart is becoming every day emptier as its arms extend everywhere into the surrounding farms, covering the soft-complected fields of wheat and vegetables with hard asphalt roads, making them its own. It is getting harder and harder to find scenes of country life around the outskirts of this city, or smell the rich fragrance of the vegetables that grace our tables growing in the soil that nurtured them. All we can do is retreat to our balconies, where we can symbolically "promote agriculture" to get a little feel of the farmer's life. As this city grows bigger and bigger, it is becoming more and more stupid and obtuse.

I took a long walk along the streets between the Third and Fourth Ring roads. As I looked around at this huge, crowded city, I thought back over the recent years of my life. I realized that I was becoming like an old woman, my old enthusiasm for dreaming about the future all gone. Aside from observing, there was nothing left in my head but memories.

Senility at my age—how ridiculous!

Maybe I really am sick, but certainly not "agoraphobic" or "mentally disordered" or whatever, as diagnosed by the doctors. My mind is as sharp as ever; I know myself. My problem is "premature senility"—simple as that. And I'm convinced that there are a lot of other people suffering from the same thing. More all the time. It's going to be an epidemic by the end of the century.

When I got home, instead of reporting to the hospital where I had convalesced for a checkup, I wrote them a letter:

Dear Doctors:

How are you!

To be accurate, I should really refer to you as my teachers or guides. You clarified my thinking, rectified my attitude, and reformed my overall outlook, rekindling in me the same flame of enthusiasm for living and life that burns in the masses! My intractable obstinacy and extreme pig-headedness must have exhausted you, given you no peace at all, and left you emaciated from the need to give me constant attention. I remember you once saying that it would be easier to deal with an undercover commando or a posse of female American CIA agents than to deal with me. Obviously, I've been a major headache to you, and a thorn in your side. And worst of all, despite your help, I treated you as my enemies. It fills me with shame and distress to think back on how heartless I have been.

Now, at last, I understand, and it is because of this that I am writing to you here to express my sincere thanks, and to give you a full report on my life and work at present.

My mood has changed, and I'm always happy now. Sometimes I have a hankering to feel melancholy, but I just can't bring it off. I often go out for a walk, and I've discovered that every day it's a new sun, and the touch of its golden light makes me smile. All the women that I meet on the street are just like my mama. They ask me if everything is okay, if I'm hungry, or not feeling well. And all the men I meet are just like the model soldier and citizen Lei Feng. If I should carelessly stumble, they fight to be first to rush over and pick me up, and make great efforts to help me brush the dust off my clothes, and they offer me money to go to the hospital to get my cuts bandaged, even if I haven't so much as scraped the skin on my knee. I really don't understand: when I walked on the streets before, why did those empty scenes leave me so cold, so troubled? Why could I not suppress my tears?

Even a vegetable seller in the farmers' market gave me things for free. It was one time when I had gone there to buy some cucumbers. There was a little boy in line right behind me. Actually, there was all kinds of room around us, but he stuck there right behind me anyway. I had seen him around before. He was always in the market, perched on the top of a heap of vegetables in the sunshine, eating an apple or reading some children's book. I guess he was one of the sellers' kids, maybe the lady's in front of me. I thought they looked a bit alike, so I didn't pay him any further notice. The lady selling vegetables was particularly friendly that day, talking nonstop about this and that, asking me where

I bought my dress, and how much money the mayor earned. Picking over the cucumbers, I said, "The mayor serves the people. He just doesn't think about things like that." When I went to pay her, I discovered that my purse had disappeared. I must have carelessly dropped it somewhere. I was so upset I started to cry, but the lady said, "Don't cry. We all have troubles sometimes. Here, the cucumbers are free." I was so deeply moved!

Now my house is always jammed with visitors. I wend my way among the happy crowds, nodding my head in greeting, smiling, clinking glasses, never the least bit lonely. And the telephone is constantly ringing off the hook. I used to have a sign on the front door that said, VISITORS PLEASE SAY "BYE" AFTER TEN MINUTES. There's still a sign on the door, but the message is totally different. Now it reads, MAKE YOURSELF AT HOME—YOU'RE WELCOME ANYTIME. Now in my home, the front room is like a market, the front door always open. When one group leaves, another arrives. My friends go on about my complexion, they say my face is beautiful, my skin delicate and fair. When I say, "I haven't had a chance to wash it yet!" they all laugh. What bothers me is that I can't figure out why all these male and female friends love me so much, or whether or not I should get married. I'm afraid that if I marry one of them, I'll lose too many friends; yet if I marry the lot of them, not only will they wear me to a frazzle, I'll be in trouble with the law as well. It's such a happy time—the days flit by like minutes!

Even if it should happen that none of my friends comes to visit, I am very happy all by myself. With my supper I have a tiny glass of American ginseng whisky (please note: just a tiny glass, not a large one), for health purposes only. With the weather gradually getting colder, and my blood circulation being rather poor, as you know, my hands and feet are always cold, and a little shot of whisky warms up my nerve endings. Although there was one time when I drank just a tad too much and chatted with myself the entire night. Asking this and answering that, I was quite a scene, a veritable symposium all by myself, so much so that the next morning when I bumped into my neighbors in the hall, they asked me, "Just how many guests did you have in your place last night?" But, I promise you, nothing like that will ever happen again.

My present rapid progress is, of course, all the result of your guidance and your treatment!

What is especially pleasing is that no longer do I just sit at home staring at the walls, living off what my mother left me. I have gone out into the world and joined the work of society. Not too far from home, I got a job in a warehouse, keeping track of incoming and outgoing inventory. Because of my extensive educational background, I was very quickly made the manager of my section, but even then people thought the job didn't tap my abilities. But I was very pleased. Even though, counting me, the warehouse had only two workers, being manager of a section was not too far from being deputy head of a department, and after that it's only one more little step to becoming a bona fide cadre.

Of course, a road up is never without its twists and turns, and responsibilities are always arduous. As you all know, I'm not very good at mathematical calculations. Although I am quite aware of the old saying that when there's a tiger on the mountain you should skirt around it, when you choose a job checking inventory you can't avoid dealing with numbers, and even after a tough stretch of trying, I still managed to mix up incoming and outgoing inventory. So I had no choice but to give up my management job. But this didn't dishearten me at all.

Yesterday, a city census officer knocked on my door. Looking through the peephole, I first thought it was a man, but when I looked closely, I saw it was a woman. She was beautiful, very striking; and, quite reassured, I opened the door. With Mother's death, the number of people in the house had changed from the original two to one, and she had come to take care of the change in registration. Right then and there, I decided that I would like to be a census officer. I told her this and asked her to help me. She talked to me for a long time that day. I could see that she really liked me and would surely be able to help me. As soon as I thought that before long I could put on my uniform and go from house to house mixing gloriously with the common people, knowing who was eating rice, who was out of soy sauce, who borrowed an onion from whom, who had a new daughter-in-law, I felt an ineffable joy and completeness. What pleasure all this will bring me!

It is obvious from all this that my "agoraphobia" has been thoroughly rooted out by you. And from this written report you should be able to see how clear, how precise, and how logical my thinking has become. So, since I am now fully recovered, there is no need for any further examinations.

Thank you all once again for your care and attention!

Ni Niuniu

Early winter, 1994, Beijing

After I had mailed the letter to the hospital, I went to the store and bought a blue lampshade, a vibrant yellow artificial sunflower, and a milk-white and lavender porcelain flower vase, which I took home and carefully arranged in my beloved bathroom.

When I was finished, it was just like another world.

Whenever I go into my quiet, simple little bathroom suffused in pale blue-green light, for example, at noon when the sun and the hubbub of the streets are at their height, it makes me feel the hush of nightfall, when everyone is sound asleep and the world is at peace, and I feel totally secure.

On one of the ledges at either end of the snow-white bathtub sits the solitary, green-and-yellow sunflower in the plump lavender vase—the effect, a twilight scene bathed in pale sunlight. On the floor beside the bathtub, a faded yellow straw carpet of dense and intricate pattern adds a touch of old and simple beauty. A soap-scented towel hangs casually over the long chestnut-colored wooden rod across the white tiles behind the tub, and a pair of pitch-black pajamas, the color of sleep. It is as misty as the rainy season.

A three-dimensional modernist painting, a fictitious world.

It doesn't matter what time of day it is, all I have to do is cast a glance into the bathroom and I feel as if I had just come back from a long journey and, tired and short of breath, all I want to do is feel the warm currents of water flow around me as I lie there quietly, naked as an eel in the shush of running water, conscious only of its caressing warmth.

The scene in my bathroom is rich in pattern, order, and certainty, while the scenes in the world outside are brushed in sloppy, incoherent strokes, a constant uproar of changing appearances and structures.

Two worlds, one inside, one outside, and I can't decide which one is nothing more than dreams.

One by one, the days go by. All time has passed away and left me here alone.

On one such day, I noticed that my rubber tree, my tortoiseshell bamboo, and all the green shrubs on my balcony were growing so vigorously that there was no longer enough room for them. My first thought was that perhaps I should move them to the flower beds outside. From the way they were gazing down from the balcony window, I could see that they too had been thinking about this and couldn't make up their minds. If they were to move outside, they could draw nourishment from the rich soil of the broad, deep beds, but they would also have to struggle ceaselessly with all the other plants to survive. And they would be unprotected from the wind and sun. On the other hand, although they could escape nature's ravaging heat and cold on my balcony, they would be deprived of any deeper sustenance.

They are thinking about this. So am I.